LONG
GEORGE
ALLEY

LONG GEORGE ALLEY

A NOVEL BY
RICHARD HALL

WSP

WASHINGTON SQUARE PRESS
New York London Toronto Sydney

Washington Square Press
1230 Avenue of the Americas
New York, NY 10020

ISBN: 0-7434-7899-1

First Washington Square Press trade paperback edition February 2004

10 9 8 7 6 5 4 3 2 1

WASHINGTON SQUARE PRESS and colophon are
registered trademarks of Simon & Schuster, Inc.

Interior design by Davina Mock

Manufactured in the United States of America

For information regarding special discounts for bulk purchases,
please contact Simon & Schuster Special Sales at 1-800-456-6798
or business@simonandschuster.com

For Deborah DuBock
and
my son Richard
and
Eugene V. Faber

EPITAPH

Thou passeth
Mortal man
In one gate and out another:
Yet scarce
Hast thou heard
The first gate's opening
Ere the last gate
Closes
With a clang.

—Hall

BOOK ONE

FRIDAY

 **CAL**

He stood on the freedom house porch, leaning his tall body against the wooden railing. He watched his troops move out of the dusty yard—his freedom soldiers, the young volunteers under his command. Dumb shits, he thought. Tit-sucking summer wonders. Behind each lurked parents, security, a college education. He envied them their advantages. He despised them. Cal spat into the humid incandescent morning. Freedom fighters, he thought. My ass. He remembered his old comrades and their campaigns: Selma, Jackson, Natchez, Bogaloosa, Birmingham. Name it, he could show you something or tell you. He looked at the summer charges again. Freedom fighters, he thought. My ass.

But in spite of himself his eye followed one of them, a tall, slender, gentle-looking white girl wearing sandals and a plain summer dress. It was Parnell that he watched as she and Tom Rice separated from the others and together descended the steep embankment leading to Franklin Street. He looked at her bare legs, at her nice ass, at the straight brown hair roping in a braid down her back. He had wanted her all summer. Yet he had set the rules of conduct—rules intended to keep down friction. But again he admitted he would break the rules for her if she'd give him the slightest encouragement. He smiled, amused. *Fuck rules when it comes to pussy.*

Now he saw Parnell and Rice reach the street level and stop abruptly on the sidewalk. Cal spat again. Tom Rice, he thought. Twenty-eight and still a dumb motherfucker. Worse: a dumb *black* motherfucker. A niggah without cool. Didn't know his ass from a hole. A house niggah full of Up North airs, high talk, and bullshit. Who the hell couldn't rap that intellectual crap if they wanted to? Hadn't he himself finished a term at junior college before quitting to join the Movement? Better fucking believe it. He was not illiterate like those snotnose bastards out there thought him to be. All *they* could do was talk. Talk. Rap, rap, rap. Never anything to enlighten, just vomiting up what they'd memorized. He spat again, angry now. *Doing* was what counted—and he was a doer. At that instant, in the street below, a car pulled up opposite Rice and Parnell and a white man with a movie camera got out. He steadied the camera against the car roof and started shooting pictures. Rice and Parnell averted their faces. Finally the man climbed back in the car and it started away; the driver's head poked out his window; eyes turned toward the freedom house—the face heavy, reddened, somnolent. He cursed up at Cal, the words coming slow, drawled, hanging hot and lazy in the humid air. Cal laughed, standing erect now. Then he saw Rice shove a stiffened middle finger at the driver. Cal laughed again and spat. Rice was sure a dumb sonofabitch. Didn't know his ass from a hole. Cal memorized the license number. He'd wait until he found the car parked in town after dark. Then a knife into all four tires, or fresh paint over the roof and hood. That meant something. The other was bullshit. He laughed again, feeling his stomach squeeze, feeling the scorn and hate well up in him deliciously.

Everyone who knew him said he was soaked bitter with hate, with resentment and contempt; accused him of being *freedom high,* shell-shocked from four years straight in the Movement. Name it, he'd been in it; shot at, head beat, ass kicked, thrown in jails, pulled out at midnight, his ass kicked again, teeth knocked out, and his jaw broke. And no congressional medals. No enemy killed or wounded. Just his comrades falling on those hot, grim asphalt streets or bleeding in the dust and isolation of back-country roads. Guerrilla warfare; better fucking believe it. But a strange war indeed: one side with guns and the other side with little else but dumb black bodies to sacrifice—bodies that would never be altogether right again. His hands clenched suddenly into fists and his eyes burned in the green shade behind his sunglasses. No more nonviolence for him. Finished with it. Not another motherfucker would lay hands on him without a fight. He was too tired now not to fight back. Tired to his black-assed bones. Spent. Weary. *Soul* weary; and barely twenty-two. He swore aloud: "Goddammit!" This was his last summer in the Movement. He was quitting. He felt his fists unclench and his shoulders slump, and he sighed deeply. Hadn't he sworn that before, time and again? The Movement was his life, all he possessed. It had turned him around, made things simple; made a man of him. But four years now seemed like ten, and he felt old. Say good-bye now while there was still some strength left; before the accumulation of hate and bitterness rotted him. But what would he do? Where would he go? Not back home. Christ almighty, not back to the Delta; that dark, imperturbable, flat-chested, unrelenting bitch. No, not back to the three-room shack where his brothers and sisters held him as an idol and his father still sat in mournful silence on that porch: mute, broken, his eyes fixed, staring across the unplowed fields at nothing. No, not again back to thirsting cottonfields hotly stretching into forever; and baths in those stagnant caramel-colored waters of bayous. To return there would be to surrender his last energies, have them sucked from him, consumed, and he himself humbled forever against the unforgiving earth. He turned slowly, sighing again, and opened the screen door and entered the house, moving with a graceful muscular arrogance, his back stiff and defiant, straight as a soldier's. Yes, he would leave the Movement soon. But first . . . Duncan Park. Tomorrow afternoon at two o'clock, Duncan Park. Maybe a bullet for him; maybe this time the one with his name on it—the one he'd been expecting so long. And certainly one more demonstration wouldn't end the war; not *this* damn war. But after Duncan Park, at least then maybe *he* could rest.

 **PEAVINE**

"**T**hem damn freedom riders! Them goddamned troublemakers. . . ." Silas Wakefield says, storming into my barber shop at the beginning of the week—I believe it was Tuesday. "They'll get us *all* kilt!"

"What? Niggah talk straight," somebody says. "What they done now?"

The shop was crowded. It must've been around noon. I was cutting at the first chair. B. Jacks was at the second and Dennis Edwards at the third. Nobody in the shop knew what the hell he was talking about.

Then he says, "They gonna march on Duncan Park. Gonna try to integrate it!"

That made us laugh. Ain't a niggah ever set foot inside Duncan Park for his own pleasure—least not in the forty-three years I've been here since my mother birthed me. So naturally nobody believed him, and we went to laughing and joking—Silas standing there in the middle of the floor puffing and pouring sweat, and his pot belly stretching his white shirt and straining to the very limit the pearl buttons.

"Y'all think I'm lying," he says. "But you gonna laugh out the other side of your damn mouths come this Sat'day. You'll see. They's crazy. They'll try *anything* once. Anything to bring white folks down on us like eagles out the sky. Anything to get on the television."

I was thinking it's a lie or some damn rumor. Ain't nobody that foolish. Not even them. I kept cutting.

"Maybe it's a rumor," somebody says. "Who told you? How do you know?"

"Zenola Pritchard," Silas says. "Zenola was down at the freedom house and heard it."

"Aw hell," the other says. "Zenola ain't got the sense he was born with. Crazy as he can be."

"Crazy or not. He can hear good as you or me," Silas says. "This coming Sat'day. Y'all mark my word."

"I'll believe it when I see it," somebody says. "But I sho ain't taking a man's word for it. Don't care *who* was telling me."

Then I commenced to thinking. My business. My wife and kids. Two loans already at the bank, plus the house mortgage. And next month my eldest boy, James Junior, starts college. I have my burdens. If the white folks at the bank got riled enough at the civil righters, they'd cut off credit to us colored businessmen. I'd be ruint. A lot of us'd be ruint.

"They oughta stick to the little stuff," Silas says. "Lunch counter sit-ins and boycotts. Stuff like that."

I could hear the overhead fan rattle the corrugated tin ceiling, and see the spiral of yellow flypaper below it spinning.

"Look what happened over in Red Lick," Silas says. "Look what the white folks done to young Jimmy Freeman so's he cain't do nothing no more like a man. And him just organizing black voters—not even marching or nothing."

"Coward talk!" B. Jacks says, loud. "Scared, handkerchief-head coward talk. I hope they do march on Duncan Park. It's 'bout time white folks in this town learned some respect for us. Nobody respects a sonofabitch who don't respect himself."

His real name is Bertrum, but he don't like that, so most call him B. Jacks or Jack. I'd guess him thirty, a great tall niggah with wide heavy shoulders and thick arms—and skin so black it looks blue as gunmetal.

"Y'all is scared niggahs," he says, pointing the scissors around. "You know it's always the scared ones that get hurt first. It's time to stop talking and *do* something. Niggahs are always talking. Me, I'm finished. I'm tired of begging for what's overdue. And if them civil righters go to Duncan Park Sat'day, I'll be right there beside 'em."

"Go 'head. Go 'head," somebody shouts. "Talk your shit, man."

"And I'll have my stove on me, too," B. Jacks says, louder. "And it'll be loaded. I ain't taking no shit from *nobody*."

It got quiet then and I could hear the fan again.

"I guess I better be going," Silas says. "My motor's still running." Then he shoved both hands in his pockets and looked over at me. "You ain't opened your damn mouth, Peavine," he says.

"I believe it's a rumor," I says. "Even the freedom rider boys wouldn't lead folks to a slaughter. And that's what it would be."

"They oughta lay low a while," somebody says. "Wait 'til this hot spell passes. Wait 'til things cool off some. Right now everybody's on edge. Touchy. They oughta slow down on this voter registration stuff. Stop all these damn boycotts. Sit down like gentlemen and talk with the white folks. Maybe they'd agree to let us use Duncan Park on some days. And the whites on other days. Why bring all this violence down on us? I mean to say—hell, Rome weren't built in a day."

"I believe it's the heat more'n anything else," somebody says. "If we would just get a little rain it'd cool things off. Ain't had nary a drop in more'n two weeks."

"I gotta be going," Silas says. "If I find out more, I'll stop back by. Good day, gentlemen," he says.

"I hope it's no rumor," B. Jacks says, his hooked nose like a curved piece of rock against the sunlight, his cheekbones high and proud, and the skin black and shiny—pulled taut across the cheeks like over a drumhead. "I'm fuckin' tard of riding by there Sunday afternoons explaining to my little son that it's just for whites. And then not being able to look my wife in the eye," he says.

I looked hard at him then, wondering where the hell he finds time to spend with her—him so busy chasing others.

"My kids don't understand either," Dennis Edwards says—an extra polite fella, slight-built with protruding ears and gold caps on his front teeth. "Just driving by slow," he says. "Looking in through the gates like we's peeking. Watching white folks through the fence, seeing them enjoying theyselves—swimming, playing baseball and golf and tennis. Seeing them sitting out on the clubhouse porch taking their ease, throwing down Kentucky Beau and Mint Julips. Just another Sunday to them. But to us—"

The fan was spinning the flypaper in a wide circle and rattling the ceiling again. We watched Silas walk back outside and get in his taxicab and drive away. That was the first time the word came up the hill. I believe it was Tuesday, though it could have been Wednesday morning. It's slipped my mind. But that don't matter now, 'cause it turns out it wasn't a rumor. Tomorrow they're marching on Duncan Park. And God help 'em. *I* sho ain't going to be there.

 **RICE**

I follow Parnell down the narrow path to Franklin Street. Sun yellows brightly through the tall grass. Behind us, on the freedom house porch, Cal stands watching us, hating us—me more than the rest because of blood. Or because of her. She looks around at me.

"He's up on the porch," I say. "Don't you see him?" Her face is large-boned, gentle; her eyes serious, blue-green and uncertain—full of lake and sky colors.

"Who?" she says, looking up at the porch.

"For Christ's sake, don't stare!"

She looks back down the embankment again toward the street. "Why is he watching *us?*" she says.

"Maybe he's jealous. How the hell should I know?"

"Jealous! Of what?"

"Me. The stud in your life. The nigger in your woodpile."

Parnell laughs, two abrupt eruptions of sound—loud, tomboyish. "Patience, Mr. Rice, is a virtue. If we get through the war, then maybe—"

"If we get through the war, sugar, I'll buy you the best steak in New York City and a bottle of cheap red wine. And we'll fuck all night."

Parnell laughs again, her sandals kicking up the red clay dust. "Will we fuck in a big hotel? I like hotels."

"No. It wouldn't be the same in a big hotel. We'd have to dress up. You'd have to take your hair out of that damn braid and stop bouncing on your toes when you walk. We'll do it in my apartment."

"Jive motherfucker," she says. "I wouldn't even associate with you after the war. You'll probably go back and be a middle-class nigger again. Know what I mean?"

"Yeah. That's probably true. What about you? Back to Boston, married, kids, the town house in Louisburg Square. Telling your crumb-crushers bedtime stories about how you were *down home* pulling niggers up by their bootstraps."

Parnell laughs. "Niggers don't wear boots."

"By our brogan laces then. Our potato heels. Hell, baby, we won't be friends after the war. You wouldn't like my apartment anyway—it's small and dirty and cluttered."

"Like your mind," she says.

At the street we see a car approaching slowly, a big green Buick with a Confederate flag on the front license plate. A whip antenna rides above the rear bumper. Sun flashes off the chrome.

"Trouble," I say. "C'mon, let's try to make it back to the house." We turn and hurry toward the path. It's too late. The car speeds up. Then I hear it idling directly across from us, its tappets ticking like a loud clock. We stop and stand waiting. I wonder if they have guns. We aren't allowed weapons. A strange war.

"Hey, c'mere a minute, black boy," the driver says.

Three white men sit in the car, all on the front seat. They look out at us with bright, swift eyes. The driver is massive-looking with a large sun-flushed face and wears a soiled white ten-gallon hat. "Bring that bitch with you," he says.

I lie on my belly, sighting down through the slanting scope, my cheek flat against the rifle stock. They come toward me through the high grass in a halftrack, its engine loud, whining; three of them, including the driver. I draw in a breath and hold it and squeeze off the first round.

"I said c'mere, boy," the driver says. "Cain't you hear good?"

"Baby, how'd you like to suck my dick this morning?" the one in the middle says, craning his face past the driver's.

"If she put them lips on your pecker, Ed, hit'd turn black as that nigger there," the driver says. They laugh. Then the one on the far side opens his door and steps out.

The muzzle jumps up and through a pale-black puff of smoke I get the driver through the head. The halftrack swerves out of control. The one on the far side tries to jump clear and I squeeze off another round, catching him in midair with his feet apart, flipping him once. The last one dives for the wheel, keeping his head low and out of sight. Both his hands are on the wheel. Two more rounds. They let go.

He is carrying a movie camera and braces it against the roof, then starts taking our picture. We turn away quickly.

"I'll be goddamned," I hear him say. "The nigger's camera shy."

"We ain't got all day," the driver says.

"Shit," the one with the camera says, "I'd know him anywhere. A New York nigger. Look at him."

I hear the car door slam shut and I turn around. The one with the camera is back in. The driver looks up the hill at the freedom house, his huge head half out the window.

"That where you niggers fuck these white girls?" he says, not looking at me, but his eyes fixed up on the porch where Cal stands. He clears his throat and spits into the street, onto the hot asphalt, then guns the engine and drops the car in gear. It starts away. "You black sonsofbitches," he says. "You scum of the goddamned earth." His words come slow, protracted, drawled, and tedious—as though fatigued by their own weight, by their own ineptitude. My stomach squeezes hard and I jerk my finger stupidly up in the air at him as the car moves down Franklin Street.

"C'mon," Parnell says. "Let's get off this street. Go over the alley and up St. Catherine Street to Sloane Hollow. C'mon, Rice."

I stand there staring after them; then it leaves me and I turn and go up the path with her, neither of us talking. The sun is in our faces now and the embankment seems steeper. Near the porch I look for Cal. He's gone. We follow the path around to the rear of the house; then, pausing for breath, we start up Long George Alley through the heat.

I been around this fucking Movement a long time. A summer's long. Two summers is like a year. I've been three summers and three winters, and I'm ready to get the hell out. *Ditty-ditty dum. Ditty-ditty dum. Ditty-ditty dum.* No cooperation from anybody anymore. Things falling apart. Spirits are bad. Equipment's bad. Headquarters people don't give a shit about us out here in the field. Nobody gives a shit anymore. A couple of years ago things were different. There was spirit in the Movement. People were together. None of the hate you feel now from them, the blacks. Hatred against us, the white ones. They want us out. "For blacks only," they're saying. *Ditty-ditty dum. Ditty-ditty dum. Ditty-ditty dum.* It used to be that we all pulled together. Marched together. Went to jail together. Got our asses kicked together. We were friends with a common enemy. We fought against the bad things in this country. We wanted to make it good for *everybody*—blacks, whites, everybody. We fought like soldiers in an army. We were brothers. We had momentum. Goals. No time to think 'bout personal differences. Now that's all but gone. We're like drifters, like refugees. I should have left already. Last spring I seen the handwriting on the wall, but I stayed. It's hard to leave something you've loved. But if that thing's already left you. . . . *Ditty-ditty dum. Ditty-ditty dum. Ditty-ditty dum.*

We climb through the oppressive heat, through the damp late-morning air pasting our clothes against us. We climb up Long George Alley, this narrow scorched clay road between Franklin Street and St. Catherine Street. We see again the rows of tumbledown shacks, bleak and mournful, and lean-ing downhill in a sort of doomed anticipation—wooden tombstones set on a soft red hill. Black folks stare out at us, the men with hands pushed deep into their pockets, the women with arms folded across their breasts. The faces are numb, frozen, cautious. How insane we must seem, Parnell and I, walking together here. They stare out at us and the land is in their faces, in their calloused hands, in the weary slump of shoulders. Old people sit rocking on gray rotting porches. Barefoot children play in the grassless bone-bare yards, or race through the red dust, laugh and frolic in the road. Old people look out at us. Suspicion. Children beg for pennies, nickels, chewing gum. Old people watch the chil-dren, watch us, then stare away again at nothing; or maybe search inward along deep, deep roots for an explanation, for a way of acceptance. . . . *But it's late and heavy and the old guard tires of looking. He closes his eyes and rocks again, hearing rotted porch boards creak faint comfort; his head nodding in half-sleep above muted terror, above Bible-reading stump of self who grew taproots because he was not allowed branches.*

# PEAVINE

The first I laid eyes on him—right at the start of the summer—I knowed he was a wild one and would bring us trouble if he stayed. I was standing at the front window of my shop taking a breather—my other barbers busy. All of a sudden this powder-blue Plymouth came barreling down St. Catherine Street and past my shop—Calvin Drew at the wheel, riding into town like some damn cowboy galloping a stallion; sitting straight up tall in this souped-up Plymouth. Right off I said: *stranger.* No local colored would drive past the speed limit. And something else: his car sported one of them fancy high-riding short-wave radio antennas like the Ku Klux cars. I'd never seen one on a colored man's before.

Well, he went on up St. Catherine Street for a spell, then turned around and came back and pulled up across the street. I figured he was wanting directions. He got out and came in, a tall light-skinned niggah with a good build—wide shoulders, slender through the hips, hard-looking in the eyes. He was wearing a green T-shirt, dungarees, and a pair of low-cut white sneakers with no socks. Right off I noticed his neck needed a cleanup. His hair was natural style, nappy and long, like B. Jacks's.

"Haircut, mister?" I said.

"Trim," he said, right short. "How long a wait?"

"Won't be no wait. Take you right now. Sit down," I said.

"How long for *him?*" he said, pointing at B. Jacks.

" 'Bout a half hour, brother," B. Jacks said, and smiled like he knowed him.

Two of a kind, I thought, watching them. Then this other looked around with them cold eyes of his like stones, pale as slate, narrow and mean. He was sort of good-looking, though, in a arrogant way.

"Cain't wait that long," he said. "I'll be back."

"Try us first thing in the morning," I said. "Open at eight sharp."

"I'll do that," he said, turning them cold gray eyes of his around again, then he started back out the door. "Where can I get a drink of liquor around this dump?"

"Right down the street. The Cozy Inn Café," I told him, the smart-ass son—"or at the White House Café. If you're looking for some good food, too, and respectable company, the White House is better. The Cozy Inn's got good food but the company's fast, if you know what I mean." I winked at him and laughed. He didn't even budge a smile.

"Much obliged," he said.

"If you want some good corn likker and a little sport to boot, just go 'cross the street. Through that empty lot yonder at the head of Long George Alley." I pointed. "First shack on your left," I told him. "Ask for Aurabelle."

"Much obliged," he said again, and walked outside and got back in his car. And right there in the middle of St. Catherine Street—the biggest in our part of town—the fool gunned his engine and let the damn clutch fly and wheeled the Plymouth around in a tight half-circle, tires screeching and smoking. The durn fool. I knew then for sure he'd bring trouble if he stayed. And damned if that ain't exactly what he's done.

His bedroom was spare—a small army cot pushed against one wall, a bureau with a cracked mirror, two battered old suitcases stacked in a corner, and a small worn throw rug on the floor near the bed. Above the cot was a window, its lower pane missing and replaced with a thick square of cardboard. The window looked out toward the rear of the house and the foot of a gently ascending hill. The hill was crowded with run-down wooden shacks, paintless and on the verge of collapse. They stood rotting in the sun, their tin roofs rusted, their stoops and porches sagging exhaustedly downhill. Cal did not like to look up that hill, Long George Alley. But he looked anyway and swore softly into the heat, into the enervating air. He felt the rage and disgust return. And beneath it the pity. The pity shamed him most. His father. His grandfather. Once men of splendid strength, men who would lay a heifer flat with a single blow of the fist. Men of peace, charity, and goodwill. God-fearing men, noble in their simplicity. Bullshit! Fear of *white folks* had kept them muzzled. *The gun and rope; a razor blade and poured turpentine. Hound dogs howling in the last black woods.*

And he himself had not been much different at the very beginning, simply another vessel filling slowly but inexorably with *emptiness;* filling toward that distant day when it would burst within him, the poison overflow and drown him in his own self-hate—paralyzing him as it had his father and his father's father; making of them cattle, incoherent stumbling automatons—walking dead. And it was so that sometimes his anger grew intolerable, and he'd lie down and pound his fists into the dark Delta soil and weep. No, nothing for you, motherfucker. Black-assed motherfucker: overseer of that same and single patch of worthless ground where the others lay buried; where your own black ass will be buried too. Then the Movement came along. How fortunate for him; how well-timed the moment. Precisely right. For the poison was already seeping into his very soul, leaking into his deepest parts. And any day he might have leapt upon some unsuspecting white man and cut his throat. And then. . . . *The gun and rope; a razor blade and poured turpentine. Hound dogs howling in the last black woods.* But the Movement saved him, came rushing like a tidal wave across those fallow acres of his spirit, its waters spilling over the still lip of the decade, rescuing him from the very edge of those unreturning woods.

He quickly straightened the bed, got his car keys off the bureau, and walked back out to the main room. There he saw Cates still fiddling with the short-wave radio. Something's wrong with him, Cal thought. Something serious. He looked at Cates sitting hunched at the desk—a big silent North Carolina farm boy. He felt sorry for him. Cates had been around the Movement a long time, and given plenty. But though he felt affection for him, Cates was still white—and it was time to move them out. Too damn bad about the good ones. Poor bastard. He passed Cates in silence and proceeded outside and into the driveway where his Plymouth was parked. He got in and started the engine and backed out onto the street, then headed for the open highway, driving at precisely the speed limit.

Sitting on his porch, he watched Parnell come up the alley, the wet in his eyes making colors when he squinched the lashes together, and Parnell and Rice walking in the little rainbows. In the front yard his favorite oak tree, and its leaves a green roof over the porch. Sun on the leaves. Sun hot on the porch. When Momma kissed his face she said, "You sit there and watch for the insurance man, Benjie." But Momma always said watch for the insurance man when Daddy Ross came in the daytime. Then Momma and Daddy Ross nap in Momma's bed with the door locked. Momma always sleepy when Daddy Ross came. Sister Ludy said Daddy Ross have a strange power over Momma. The insurance man have another power, Ludy said. "He look after folks when they dead," she said. The insurance man didn't always come when Momma said watch. Benjie despised Daddy Ross. Of a sudden everything went drippy and full of colors, and Parnell and Rice washed away in the bright running.

He looked out at the alley. He knew it since a little boy; every secret hiding place, each ghost. He remembered best the hard rains and the red clay running down the hill like blood; and all the alley children splashing barefoot in the red water—each with his own fast river running past his door; running over ankles and rocks, and floating dead flowers and Popsicle sticks, weeds and white rubber things like balloons. Someone once told him Indian warriors were buried under the hill, and in the hard rains the red water from the clay was really blood mixed with war paint washing off the bodies of the braves. He believed that then, but he was not so smart as now. Still, there was a lot. He was only a kid. Momma and Daddy Ross said it all the time: "You only a kid, Benjie. You s'pose' to be seen, not heard." He could hear them now, he could always hear them. He looked up, Wind in the oak tree. The leaves shivering blue holes of sky. Momma and Daddy Ross. Faces in the spaces. Then, of a sudden, Daddy Ross's ugly face by itself; and Benjie happy grinning, melting it in yellow-butter suns.

Across the road Aurabelle—Miss Mamie Lee's girl. Benjie waved. Aurabelle waved back, smiling. Aurabelle was almost pretty as Ludy. Miss Mamie Lee had a big belly that jobbled when she laughed. Momma said, "Them two is a shame and disgrace to this alley." Aurabelle on her porch now talking to some man, the man wearing blue overalls and a big yellow straw hat. Aurabelle walking in the house with the man. Closing the door. All day long sometimes, grown colored men to see Aurabelle and Miss Mamie Lee. In the night, plenty of times, they went in cars with white men who come far as the head of the alley and wait with the parking lights on. Benjie let out a deep breath. There was a whole lot. "One day," Momma said, "Puddin'-an'-Pie, you'll know the answers to everything. So don't ask those many questions now. You's only a kid. You s'pose' to be seen, not heard." He loved Momma. Loved her soft hands stirring butter into his grits or breaking eggs on the smut-crusty edge of the frying pan she most times called a *spider*. Or cool hands touching nice after the tall lump came beside his weewee—Benjie straining himself climbing the high fig tree in the backyard. Momma marked it with smut from the bottom of the spider—made a cross on it and said, "Don't worry, baby, that'll make it go away." Or hands like butterfly wings, after naps with Daddy Ross. That was the strange power. The horse teeth. Daddy Ross standing on the porch whistling through the horse-teeth gap. Momma on the porch swing humming—the swing wanting oil. Shadows stretching down the hill far, the alley fully of kids and bony-backed dogs and chickens for plucking and eating on Sunday morning with grits and flour gravy.

The lump never went away like Momma say. Shadows stretching down the hill. And wind. Daddy Ross whistling through his teeth between the hole in front past where the horse lips live. . . . Daddy Ross touching Momma deep where it was secret. "Now you stop, Ross. Don't you see Benjie there? Quit it, now. Quit it." "Aw, baby, he just a kid." Or afternoon hands ironing the white folks' sheets—Momma working in the shade; her blue apron with red apples for pockets. Slide the yellow shade up and see Momma and Daddy Ross napping in the white sheets and shadows running down the alley far to the old ghost house where the Indian man lived in his own blood water of fast rivers loud-sounding like baby licking Momma milk and two rubber nipples like white things floating in the red rain. Or tired hands touching Daddy Ross after the sun falls past the oak tree—Benjie searching for ghost tracks with Puddin' Head and Lollypop Johnson in the deserted shack where the Indian man lived before they buried him under the hill to make rain go fast; the ghost shack everybody said was *condemned*—that "Don't have to fight this damn hill no more," Momma said. Daddy Ross was *a big black sonofabitch* Ludy said once after supper— Ludy bathing Benjie on the porch in the tin-zinc tub Momma used for white folks' wash and for regular too. He come walking on the porch, Daddy Ross, and reach down one hard black hand and pinch Benjie's cheek. "You runt," he said. "How you doing?" Then he pinch Ludy's bottom—Benjie so mad he 'most splash bathwater on Daddy Ross's favorite pointy-toed shoes. But Ludy said, "Don't be ugly, Benjie." Then he walk away and Ludy said, "The big black sono-fabitch."

Ludy fifteen and a half, almost tall as Momma. And the prettiest on the alley and the fastest runner. Ludy's hair like Momma's; smelling olive oil and honey. Benjie's last birthday in the winter, Ludy wore him out, gave him one to grow on, nine. Daddy Ross gave him one to grow on and one for good measure, ten. He despised Daddy Ross; even more than Daddy Earl from last summer—or Daddy Floyd. But when he remembered hard, Daddy Clark was the worst of all the daddies. Tall as a raincloud. Black as Shine-o-la shoe polish. "Uglier than homemade sin," Momma said after he went away. Once, drunk, he kicked down the front door and hit Momma in the face—Momma standing by the wood stove in the kitchen with a nosebleed. Benjie felt the colors running again. He drew in another deep breath and let it out slow. There was a lot. He wished he wasn't a kid all the time. Then, across the porch, he saw the yellow shade hiding Momma's room move in the wind. His heart moved. Then, on the roof, the leaves moved—scratching fingernails against the tin. He heard Momma. She went "Oh, oh, oh." Then Momma's bed went like the porch swing when it wants oil, but faster. Then Daddy Ross went "Whew! Whew!" And Momma said "Oh, oh, oh" again. Then no noise came and in the hush he felt scared. He trembled. He had to go to the bathroom. He sat holding it, watching the yellow shade, listening—and the colors running.

Parnell and Rice came on up the hill—Parnell almost at the edge of the porch; Benjie rubbing his eyes harder, Parnell standing in the new rainbows.

"Benjie. Benjie McCloud," Parnell said. "What's a big boy like you sitting there crying for? Let's see that face," she said. "There, there. Tell Parnell what's the matter."

"Nuthin'," he said. "Ain't nuthin'."

"Then blow hard here," Parnell said.

He stuck his face straight into the white cloth.

"Again," she said. "Harder."

"That's better," she said. She wiped his eyes and put the handkerchief away. "Now then, where's your momma? Where's Bertha?"

"Her nap with Daddy Ross," Benjie said.

Parnell stared at the yellow shade. She looked at Rice. Rice smiled at Benjie. Rice was nice. "Tell her I was here,"

Parnell said. "Say I'll be back this afternoon." Parnell patted
his face. Her hand was white and soft. Her hair was pasted to
her head. "We need everybody tomorrow," Parnell said. "For
freedom." Parnell tipped her head out of the sun and kissed
his face. Wind blew the yellow shade. "Bye," Parnell said.
"Bye now." Parnell waved. Just the end of her fingers moved.
Parnell was going away to Rice. They went on away. In the
tree, leaves and wind, fried bacon. The shade moved—Benjie
blinking, but the rainbow spoiling it.

AURABELLE

He push down hard on me with his hammer, driving his nail
deep to where it hurts. It's maybe the Lord's way of making
me suffer, of giving me my burden. But I give this fella good
for his money; this big black motherfucker moaning over me
with his eyes rolled back in his head. He is much to endure
but he won't go long in this heat; him with his hat still on
and his overalls pulled down and the metal strap buttons rak-
ing me hard. Much to endure, the sweat popping outen every
pore full of last night's liquor, and him stinking of the barn
and fields. And the weight of hisself pressing on me is like a
elephant had lay his belly hard on mine and squatted down
to smother out the breath from me and shut off the light
from the onliest window.

We walk along St. Catherine Street. The cafés are already open. Music from the jukeboxes drifts out through the dusty screens. Cars pass in the street, their tires sounding wet against the hot asphalt.

"Let's take the shortcut," I say. "Sloane Hollow's a long way."

"Through the woods?" Parnell says.

"What's wrong with the woods?"

"Well, it wouldn't look too good, now would it? You and I in the woods together. Alone."

A group of church ladies approach, dressed in white; elderly women moving cautiously through the scarlet heat, walking in pairs beneath faded dime-store parasols and talking in hushed, recessed, secret voices. They pass and look at us with bright, denying eyes; their oiled and sanctimonious faces offended.

"Look, Rice, I know what you mean," Parnell says, waiting until they've passed, her eyes darting from them to me. "But you know we've got to be cool. We're not in New York." She stares at me expectantly, her eyes light green like clear sea over sand shoals.

I say nothing. We have stopped walking.

"All right," she says finally, her voice sliding away, resigned, swallowing its own sigh. "But no funny stuff. Straight to Sloane Hollow. Promise?"

Cars pass slowly in the street, almost as though in a funeral procession, the sun flashing breathless and hot from their dusty roofs, their motion stirring the little piles of powdery red dust that lie calm along the curbs.

"C'mon," I say, starting away. "You worry too much.

Everything's cool. Hardly anybody goes that way. C'mon."

She shrugs, a little helpless movement of her shoulders beneath the white calico, and follows me as we turn off St. Catherine Street and start down a small dirt road that dead-ends at the railroad tracks. At the path leading into the woods Parnell hesitates again and I stop and look back at her.

"C'mon," I say. "Don't be afraid. There's nothing in there that'll hurt you."

ZENOLA

Time happens anyway. Zenola. Cold broom handle. Zenola singing: "Sweep, sweep. Sweep, sweep." Jail cells silent. Piss buckets stinking. Zenola into broom closet reading. Book heavy, sad, secret. Zenola into dictionary, reading: *Ambiguous—capable of being understood in two or more possible senses.* Zenola into inner ears of goats, hearing: *Yellow next. Then black. First technology. Now white thorns, but higher.* Zenola into toilet, peeing. Flushing. Bitch yellow gone. Zenola, black king of the mountain. Cold broom handle. Time happens anyway. Zenola singing: "Sweep, sweep. Sweep, sweep."

A few miles out of town he came upon a familiar stretch of highway. It ran for perhaps a mile or more without a single bend or crossroad. He shifted out of fourth into third gear and pushed the gas pedal hard against the floor. The car surged forward instantly. When the engine seemed to strain at the very edge of its potential, he shifted rapidly into top gear, his foot still pressed hard against the accelerator. For a fraction of a second the rear wheels lost traction, emitting a small, urgent cry as rubber burned on concrete, then bit in again and sent the Plymouth lunging ahead faster. Now the highway rushed at him, defied him; became his sole adversary. Wind ripped at the windows. Small vibrations shivered up through the steering column to the wheel. Still he kept the gas pedal flat against the floor. The speedometer said one hundred. He fought the impulse to keep his foot pressed against the accelerator until he or the machine broke. *He* felt indestructible. The speedometer said one hundred ten. Suddenly his tension left. He lifted his foot off the gas and the speedometer needle began its slow backward fall. At seventy he down-shifted into third and heard the argumentative attack of the exhausts. The car slowed rapidly, and Cal smiled to himself, feeling the satisfaction flow through him, the Plymouth performing flawlessly in his hands like a great steed; its engine winding down now, sucking back on itself, muffling deep and resonant beneath him. He sat immensely proud, in love, as high as on fine whiskey. Now, he thought, I can face the bastards—the Uncle Tom motherfuckers. At the first crossroad he turned the car around and headed back toward town, driving again at precisely the speed limit.

We heard him pull up outside, his damn mufflers popping and crackling. No law-abiding colored man could get away with it. But just act crazy and white folks'll let a niggah get away with murder. It don't make sense.

So we heard him pull up—me and the three board members. Our chapter is the newest in the League—National Negro Advancement League—biggest civil rights outfit in the state of Mississippi. And I head this chapter. We've agreed to cooperate with Calvin Drew's group on Duncan Park. Black children have no place to play, except in the street. So we're doing it for the children; not for Calvin Drew and his band of renegades. We're in total disagreement with their guerrilla warfare tactics. They call us Uncle Toms, but it don't cut no ice. We represent the respectable folks—not some rabble lot. They're just wild kids: students, irresponsible, dirty-looking, long hair, and beards. They couldn't get fifty people out there tomorrow without our help. Nobody in his right mind would follow them to a cold soda machine on a hot day. I've witnessed their little demonstrations—a dozen or so blacks and whites sitting-in at some two-bit lunch counter downtown, trying to integrate it. And them getting dragged out and whipped to within a inch of their lives. Carted off to jail. Fined. I've also witnessed them tramping up and down these hills, coercing black folks, trucking them off like cattle to register to vote. We got a voter program too; but we know what happens when you lead a horse to water and it don't wanna drink. So we don't push too hard. We lead gently. You might as well. You cain't change folks overnight, disrupt their lives, uproot them. It's against human nature. Our organization has history and tradition behind it. Over fifty years. Folks trust and respect us. They know we're not like these fly-by-night, scatterbrain kids. Freaks. *Freedom house freaks!* Here today, gone tomorrow.

So we heard him pull up. He came up the stairs and my secretary, Cora Battles, opened the door for him and the arrogant sonofabitch strutted in like it was his goddamn office—like he called the meeting instead of me. And here we'd been waiting twenty minutes for him while he was probably sitting on his ass somewhere, reading a comic book and picking his nose. "Good morning," I said. "Have a seat. We been waiting for you."

"I had business," he said. "Sorry."

Nothing else. Then he sat down. I took out a cigar and lit it. He scraped his chair over near my desk where they were all sitting, and looked from one to the next, his eyes going quick, hateful, light-colored; and his long nappy hair not even combed, and them damned sunglasses slipped down on his nose like they'd fall off the tip any minute. I blew out some smoke. Cora sat down and picked up her notebook. I saw him look at her and something flicker in his eye like he knowed her good. Then she looked down at her notebook and wrote something. We began to discuss plans for tomorrow and everything went smooth 'til Ross Catlett suggested we drive to Duncan Park 'stead of marching. Catlett's the only black doctor in town—he's in his seventies.

"It's my feeling," Catlett said, drawling his words, "that the element of danger is too great to risk our women and children by marching them a mile and a half through the streets. Sure, there's bound to be trouble in any event. But at least if we went in a motorcade, we'd have some protection. If the police go wild, I wanna be sitting in my car with the windows rolled up."

We laughed. Drew didn't crack a smile. He was stewing, burning up; and when I saw that, I nodded my head, agreeing. I blew out some smoke. "Sounds damn reasonable to me," I said.

"A very good idea," Reverend McIver said. He's our biggest minister. "Why didn't somebody think of it before?"

" 'Cause it's a terrible idea," Drew said. " 'Cause it stinks. You just gonna foul up the works," he said. "You gonna confuse folks. All week we talk 'bout marching. Now y'all wanna ride through the streets holed up in cars like a bunch of monkeys on the way to a zoo." He turned those eyes around at us, smoldering, hateful, but trapped. The room seemed hotter. Cora started writing faster. I got up and turned the floor fan up to high speed and sat back down.

"Brother Drew," McIver said in a calm voice. "If we try marching to Duncan Park we'll be fish bait for the Ku Klux, the police, and any local hoodlum who wants to molest us."

Drew was burning. But we had him. Without us his group couldn't get fifty people out there tomorrow, much less two hundred.

McIver said, "I think the motorcade's an excellent idea."

"Me too," I said, Drew staring at me. I looked straight at him. "Your bunch is wild," I said. "Young. Impulsive. Irresponsible when it comes to other people's lives. You got nothing at stake. We got jobs, families, responsibilities. It's our duty—"

"It's too late to organize a motorcade," he said, slow, quiet, pushing his glasses up on his nose. "You gonna confuse folks."

"Better confused than dead," Kyle Moody says. He's the local undertaker.

"Why the hell y'all making so much of it?" Drew said. "Damn, it's only a demonstration."

McIver looked out the window.

"Let's decide now," I said quick. I ground out the cigar. "I say I'm against marching tomorrow. I say let's go in cars."

"Me too," Kyle Moody said. "I'm against marching."

"Against," McIver said without looking at Drew.

"Against," Ross Catlett said.

"It's unanimous," I said. I looked at Cora. She was looking at Drew. Then she saw me and went back to writing, fast. I looked at Drew, then back at her.

Drew stood up. "Let the people decide," he said. "Tonight

at McIver's church. At the freedom rally." He looked at McIver. "Put it to a vote. It's the only fair way. Ain't no safe route to Duncan Park, you know that. Freedom comes high, brother. And this is war. Black folks been dying like flies 'round here long as I can remember. Dragged out and lynched. Starved to death. Beat to death. Violence and death ain't new words. Y'all know that. So let the people decide. Let them make up their own minds." He sat back down.

McIver was still looking out the window.

"It's up to us to lead," I said. "The people don't have enough information to make decisions like that."

"What about you?" Drew said to McIver. "It's your church."

"Well . . ." McIver said, still looking away. "I just don't know." Then he turned slow and faced Drew. "I 'spose it's fair as any other way of deciding. Maybe it's the only fair way."

"I think it is," Catlett said. Cora was writing fast again. I could hear her pen. "It's the people who'll be facing the danger," Catlett said. "So let them decide."

"All right," McIver said. "I'll agree to it. After the regular prayer meeting. Let the brothers and sisters decide for themselves. Let them vote on it."

"A mistake," I said. "An outright blunder!"

"But let it be remembered—and put it on the record—" McIver said, "that this board unanimously felt the people should *not* march to Duncan Park."

"You get that, Cora?" I said. I caught her. She was watching him again. I decided to speak to her about it.

"Yes, sir," she said, writing again. Then she read it back.

Drew kept pouring his eyes into mine, hateful, hot. I held mine to his for as long as I could, then I looked away. "What's next, Cora?" I said. "Dammit, it's too hot to argue."

# PLOWERS

Hell, I hate niggers much as Worden does, maybe more. With thirteen years on the force—five years a sergeant—I was ready to quit two years back when Worden and the commissioner put that nigger Peters on. Couldn't see working with a damn coon—'specially one carrying a loaded pistol. Worden talked me out of quitting. He knows how I feel. So today when he calls me on the carpet 'bout this trouble we're having I figger the sonofabitch was kidding, but he was serious. Hell, I was thinking, standing there, wasn't I the one who told him way back then—when the niggers and communists first started trying to take over the country—that we ought to kill a few right off? If we'd done it, we wouldn't be in the mess we're in today. But then he said that niggers were bound to get some of their rights and us white men just had to learn to accept it. Now he's whistling a different tune. Now it's all turning against him and he's looking for somebody to blame. That's me. Not that I care 'bout getting chewed out, but when he asks if I was a *white man,* well—"Sir," I tells him, standing there in front of his desk with my hands folded behind my back and the sweat running down the crack of my ass, "there ain't a mother's son in this county who'd tell me to my face that I ain't," I says.

He sort of smiles crooked out the side of his mouth. "If you was a *real* white man," he says, "if any one of you out there was worth the money the City pays you in salary, you'd of found ways to keep this trouble at a minimum."

I just stand there, burning. Hell, *he* was the Chief. And if he'd of listened to me three years ago, there wouldn't be this trouble today. With niggers you gotta hurt a few real bad—right at the git-go. That lets the rest know you mean business.

'Cause if you play footsy with them, they'll run over you every time. You give a nigger a crumb and he'll want the whole loaf. Give him a inch and he'll take a mile.

"Stop cracking those goddamned knuckles!" Worden says, shouting.

I look down at his thin red hair and don't say anything. My hands are itching to get hold to somebody. Some nigger.

"You let a handful of fucking kids run us crazy," he says. "A goddamned handful. What do they have to do before you act like a white man—drag our sisters and wives into the woods?"

"Sir. You know better than to say—"

"Shut up," he says. He just stares at me, like it's my fault.

Niggers, I was thinking, trying not to squeeze my knuckles loud. Niggers. Goddamn them. Pull one out the woodshed and beat his ass good for exercise when Worden gets through, I was thinking.

"I'm putting you back on patrol," Worden says. "McClaren can second me tomorrow. Maybe he's more of a white man than you." He looks down at some papers. "That's all. Get outta here. And send McClaren in."

The one thing I cain't stand is to be called a nigger lover. I cain't stand it. This badge won't keep me off anybody's ass who says that and means it. "Chief," I says. "These ain't regular niggers we're dealing with. They ain't the ordinary. They don't scare 'less you hurt 'em bad. You know yourself we ain't had no trouble out of our others; not 'til these new ones came along. They're bold and uppity and need a good lesson. We been babying 'em. Arresting 'em, feeding 'em, letting 'em out on bail. Holding real court trials for 'em. Wasting the taxpayers' money. The onliest way is to maim a few of 'em and then you see how soon this trouble stops."

He looks up at me slow, like he's disgusted, and his eyes look tired. "Send McClaren in," he says soft.

"Yes, sir," I says. I wheel hard, feeling my face burn, and walk out of his office; not knowing or caring which nigger it'd be, but knowing whichever it was would sure as hell know me for a white man when I got through.

CAL

He waited outside for Cora. She came down the steps, walking toward him slowly, almost shyly, her big breasts bouncing. Then she stood in front of him, hands on her hips, fingers drumming lightly against the seam of her short skirt. Cal leaned casually against the fender of the Plymouth, not believing her.

"Let's go get something to eat," he said. "I'm hungry."

She watched him steadily, her face partly in sun, the eyes brown, irisless in the shadows. "Why didn't you call?" she said. "It's been over a week." She rolled her eyes at him in mock anger; the face first turning off to the side and the eyelids closing; then her face turning back to him again and the eyes opening as they rotated toward him.

He laughed. "Don't roll your damn eyes at me," he said. "I ain't done nothing for you to be mad 'bout."

"Why didn't you call?" she said again. "I waited home every damn night."

Cal shrugged, expecting her to stamp her foot next. "I been busy," he said. "Been organizing. You think all I got to do is call up folks? Get on in the car," he told her. "I'm gonna buy you a hamburger."

"Since when a po'-assed niggah like you got some money?" she said. "You usually crying broke. What you been doing, hustling them white bitches at the freedom house?"

Cal suppressed a laugh. "Now you got no right to talk that way 'bout folks you don't know," he said, looking at her legs. She wore no stockings and her legs were a rich brown in the sun. He looked into her eyes again. "Get in my car," he said, "Go 'head." He opened the door and waited.

She rolled her eyes at him again. "You ought to have called me," she said. "You know I was worried. That's the least you coulda done. You don' care 'bout nothing 'cept yourself." She stepped past him and got in the car.

He got in on the other side and started the engine. Cora said, "You been sleeping with them white bitches, ain't you? Bitches. White skunks. Anything to get our men." Then she fell silent for a few moments. Finally she looked over at him again. "You niggah men don't fool us. If you think *they're* so damn special why don't you—"

He leaned over suddenly and kissed her. "Shut up," he said softly. He laughed. "Why you working for them Uncle Tom motherfuckers?"

Cora stared straight ahead. "Least they take baths and shave and don't say motherfucker every other word."

"They's a bunch of fags," he said, sliding his hand under the edge of her skirt. She squeezed it gently between her thighs.

"I ain't feeling so hungry now," he said. "You?"

She shook her head no, increasing slightly the pressure on his hand. "But I only got a little while," she said, her almost pretty face softening and the nostrils flaring thinly as she breathed.

"It ain't far," he said. "You know it ain't."

She looked straight ahead again out the window, her makeup running slightly from the heat. "You promise you'll drive me back this time?" she said. "You won't get mad again? Promise?"

"Sure," he said. His hand edged farther up her leg.

"All right," she said, her face pouting again. "All right. But you ought to have called me."

"Sure," he said. He drove her around the block and headed down Franklin Street toward the freedom house, which he knew would be empty now except for Cates. He'd probably still be fiddling with the radio. Poor bastard, he thought. Too damn bad about the good ones.

CATES

Be durned if I can figger out what's wrong with this radio. I've checked every fucking circuit, every goddamned tube. It's just no fucking good, wore out, finished. Like everything else around here. And the truck's got a flat tire. I can fix that after lunch. But replacing the head gasket's got me worried. I'll have to pull the head. That'll take time, and I'll need to borrow a torque wrench from somewhere. The truck is more important than the radio. They'll need it tomorrow to haul folks in from the country. I swear, if I ever get back home to North Carolina in one piece, it'll be a freezing day in Hell before I come back to Mississippi. *Ditty-ditty dum. Ditty-ditty dum. Ditty-ditty dum. I swear it was the damndest feeling to sit there in the dark listening to it. Like something in me walking slow. Or something slow-walking me. I was just a beat somewhere—a simple rhythm among so many.*

It was past noon when he drove Cora back to work. Then he went directly to police headquarters. The duty sergeant sat at his desk hunched over a newspaper. The desk was behind a wire screen. Finally he looked up, his face surly under a bristling brush of close-cropped hair. "Yeah, whadda *you* want?"

"Sergeant Plowers," Cal told him.

"He's in with the Chief," the other said. "Sit down and wait."

"I appreciate your kindness," Cal said, his tone patronizing, his eyes leveling at the other, cold, steady, with nothing in them to betray his dislike.

The other looked up annoyed, silent, vaguely suspicious. Then he returned to the newspaper. Cal crossed the large open room and sat down on one of many wooden chairs arranged around two sides of the room. He sat beside another policeman who was also reading a newspaper. The man smelled of aftershave lotion and hair pomade.

"Good morning, Officer," Cal said.

The other said nothing.

After a while Cal said, "Can I see the funnies, Officer?"

Grudgingly, the other separated the paper and let a section of it fall to the floor. "Get it yourself," he said. "If you can read."

"Thank you, Officer," Cal said. He bent and picked up the paper and began reading. After a while he turned to the other again. "Officer, can I see the society section?"

Abruptly, the other brought his hands together, trapping the newspaper so that it squashed in on itself. "Goddammit," he said, his lips barely moving, the initial sound rushing from his mouth where the tongue had flattened and suspended it like a quiet sustained gargle. Then he said it again. "No, god-dammit! Bug off!"

"Thank you, Officer," Cal said.

The other rose and crossed the room and sat down in another chair. He looked once at Cal, then opened and smoothed out his paper and began to read again.

A door across from Cal opened suddenly and a third policeman entered in a rush. He was a big, powerfully built man with shoulder muscles bunching into his neck so that he appeared to possess no neck at all, but simply head and body rammed together gracelessly. He wore a short-sleeved shirt and a .38 pistol was strapped to his chest. He stopped short when he saw Cal and stood for a moment with his fists on his hips, his broad forehead unknotting slowly.

Cal looked at him but said nothing. He put aside the paper.

"Well, well," the other said. "Look what's here. When the wind blows, it blows in anything."

"How you doing, Sergeant?" Cal said, his tone now slightly diffident, shaded with caution and a certain grudging respect, though still in its basic inflections patronizing.

The other looked at the desk sergeant. "What does this nigger want?"

"He comes here every day to read the funny papers," the other said.

"I didn't know they could read," Plowers said.

"Next thing you know they'll want to come down outen the trees and eat people food," the other said. All three policemen laughed.

"The Chief wants you in his office, McClaren," Plowers said. Still laughing, the policeman across the room got up and left.

"All right, boy. Now what is it you want?" Plowers said.

"Sergeant, you know you's wrong calling me out of my name like that," Cal said. "I ain't no damn boy. And we ain't niggers. So you got no right calling us anything except by our names."

Plowers moved forward a step, immense, swaggering. "We 'bout had a 'nough out of you, Cal. You walking on thin ice. State your business and get out."

"All I want is our parade permit," Cal said. "It's been near a week since we applied."

"It might be another week 'fore you get it," Plowers said. "Come back Monday."

"We march tomorrow," Cal said.

"Then come back tomorrow. Maybe it'll be ready. Maybe it won't. We're a little shorthanded. Some niggers up on Franklin Street are keeping us busy."

"Now there you go again. How many times do I have to tell you we ain't niggers?"

"You arrogant—you let me get you in the woodshed. It'll be your ass."

"You know the law as well as I do," Cal said, speaking slowly, quietly. "And you got no right denying us the permit when we made proper application."

"Get out of here," Plowers said. He took another step forward and stopped. "Come back this afternoon. Your damn permit'll be typed up. It ain't gonna do you no good. You coons ain't getting inside Duncan Park."

"We'll see," Cal said. But Plowers no longer seemed to be listening. He had already turned his back to Cal. "Where the hell is Zenola?" he said to the desk sergeant. The other jerked his head up from the newspaper. "Out back," he said. "Cleaning up cells in the woodshed."

Plowers moved away, immense again, but agile, his broad shoulders turning smoothly in opposition to his stride. Cal watched him as he crossed the big room and passed through another door at the far end and slammed it behind him.

"Anything else?" the desk sergeant said, folding the newspaper.

"No, Officer. Thank you for your kindness," Cal said. He forced a grin, then turned and walked outside again to the parking lot, and got in his car and drove off in the direction of Duncan Park.

 **ZENOLA**

Jail cells. Zenola singing: "Sweep, sweep. Sweep, sweep."

"Hey, Zenola, you simple-assed sonofabitch. C'mere. Right now."

Plowers looking curses. "Yeah, boss. No more trouble. Broomstick. Boomsticks." Cold broom handle. Zenola mumbling curses.

"Fetch me one of them niggers, you black bastard. And hurry up!"

Plowers waiting, jaw working.

"Yas, suh. Which?"

"Any'll do. Just hurry up."

Zenola looking. Jail cells sighing. Bars, monkey paws, eyes, and teeth. Zenola into dark cave. Piss bucket stinking. Bubbles shaping continents. Josh flat against the wall. Eyes and teeth.

"You dassent. You dassent," mouth hissing say. "You Judas. You no-good motherfucker. What I ever done to you?"

Plowers slapping club to palm. Slap. Slap.

"Zenola! Zenola! Goddammit. What the hell's taking you so long?"

Broom handle poking. Poke, poke. Josh barefoot going.

"Lawd. Mercy, Jesus. Please, boss, Sergeant. What I done?"

Plowers going away with Josh. Slap, slap, slap, slap.

Zenola. Cold broom handle. Jail cells silent. Monkey paws gone. Zenola singing: "Sweep, sweep. Sweep, sweep." Black king peeing continents apart.

 **CLARICE**

He comes and goes as it pleases him. Not that I care, or that I miss him being here; or even that I still love him—it's that he doesn't even think about bringing us food, or paying the rent until he's spent up most of his pay on white lightnin'. It's ruined his mind. He used to be a smart man, an upstanding man. But that corn likker—He doesn't care anything for me or his children anymore. Just the likker. And this place, his home, is just somewhere he can come to lay his head, or hide when he thinks the world is after him. I don't rightly know why I bear it; why I suffer him year in and year out. I used to say it was for the children's sake; that when little Angie—our youngest—was old enough to work and help me, I'd pack my books and the rest of our belongings and we'd leave Zenola for good. But Angie'll be fourteen come next month, and Wilber—our eldest—is already two years in New York City. And the three between Angie and Wilber don't much need anybody, they're so independent. So I can't rightly say what's keeping me now.

Some days, sitting out on this porch sewing and the sun boiling down on this miserable and rotten alley, I say to myself: Clarice Pritchard, neither your dead mother nor father would recognize you today. Nor would they accept your fallen state. You're barely the shadow of that woman twenty-five years ago who married out of love; who ran off with Zenola on a Greyhound bus up to Jackson—waking up a preacher in the middle of the night. Couldn't wait another day! Ran off without even leaving so much as a note to them. And after all they'd done for me. After they spent their hard-earned money on me, making me ready to be a school-teacher, and I studied hard and read so much, and my mother and father were so proud of me. So very proud. And then I met him. He was climbing trees for the town, pruning the rotten limbs. And he looked so strong with his chest bare and all those leather straps and belts and hooks hanging from him. He seemed daring and brave, and I thought him a good man. A sensible man. And I loved him. So I ran off with him, to their everlasting despair. To their deep, deep despair. We settled in this shack, here on Long George Alley—here on this foul and cursed hill. And we haven't budged a minute since. Now Zenola cleans up down at the jailhouse and runs errands for the white folks; and when he isn't doing that, he's drunk on white lightnin'. Sometimes sitting out here on this porch and looking out on the hill, looking at the pigs rooting and chickens pecking away at the collected and abiding filth, I say to myself: Clarice Pritchard, you're a fool to have stayed so many years in this corrupted and doomed place. You must have been cursed by Almighty God to abide here on this destitute ground—a Jezebel to be eaten by pigs and chickens instead of dogs. It is then that my faith slips away from me and I cry senseless tears, sitting there in the sun with folks passing up and down the alley not ever knowing. Then, when I cannot stop the tears, I open my Bible and read from Job: *"Wherefore is light given to him that is in misery, and life unto the bitter in soul. . . ."* I close my eyes and pray to the good Lord to spare my children and my poor crazy husband; but ask that in His bountiful mercy He take me one night sudden in my sleep; that He release me from this pitiless life. And this morning I said to Zenola, "I'm going with those freedom riders to Duncan Park tomorrow. No matter what, I'm going to be at the front." He looked at me and gave me that wild, knowing look of his that said, "This time the Lord answer your prayer." But I'm going with them, for I believe in my heart that they are our salvation. They have come to help us accomplish in deed what has always been promised in word; to help us love and help one another as we have preached. Bless them, Jesus. Bless them. For they are truly beautiful.

▦ B. JACKS

I got this little ole gal, see. She lives on the Louisiana side of the river. A honest-to-goodness dyed-in-the-wool cracker. Never been out the South in her life. Never fucked a niggah before. We's both married. Her ole man works nights here in town at the rubber tire factory. I drive over the bridge to Vidalia, the first town on the other side, and meet her at this little colored club. Everybody there knows me and don't nobody pay us much attention. Peggy's her name. She likes to get high, so we meet in the parking lot and she gets into my car and we smoke a couple of joints. Then we go in the club and dance and drink 'til closing time. Then we leave her car there and drive back in mine across the river to here, where I keep a rented room on the south end. Hardly nobody knows I got it, 'cept Peavine and a couple of my close running partners. I got to be real careful, see, 'cause last time Lil—that's my wife—caught me playing she pulled my own stove on me. I believe she woulda shot me 'cept I wrassled it out of her hand and whipped her ass good. Damn near put her in the hospital. Don't 'low nobody to pull a gun on me—'specially my own.

Well, this other little ole gal, Peggy, she wants it all the time. Going crazy over it. Says nobody ever done it to her so good before. Says I took her soul. I don't know 'bout her soul but I have sho took a lot of her pussy. One night she come sixteen times, one right after the other—us counting. We was doing it to music. "Go high as you can," she says. I kept going higher 'til she was hollering and sliding backwards up the bed. I thought sho somebody would call the police. But I ain't 'bout to go to jail in this town over no white bitch. No, suh. All the time I was giving it to her I had one hand up under the pillowcase, holding on to my stove, a pearl-handled .38. I don't carry it for show. I'm a marksman. When we go to Duncan Park tomorrow, it'll be on me. I'll be ready. See, I don't take shit from nobody, black or white. If I say so myself, I'm a *bad* motherfucker.

CAL

"**S**omething's wrong with Cates. Something serious on his mind. He takes twice as long to fix what he used to figger out in no time. We need that truck bad tomorrow. There're country people depending on us to pick them up and bring them to town. And the radio oughta be working by now. But the truck. . . ."

He lit a cigarette and stared out the car window as he made a first pass by the entrance. Beyond the high wrought-iron gates a carpet of neatly mowed lawns retreated in the distance.

He saw a baseball diamond and part of the golf fairway. He could not see the swimming pool—a prime target tomorrow. He stared again at the towering iron gates, and drove now with his foot barely touching the gas pedal. Tomorrow the Klan would probably try to block the entrance, and the police do nothing to stop them; indeed, if anything, they'd help them. It was this likely confrontation that worried him most. For here, if anywhere, he and many of his people could be seriously hurt.

He turned the car around and made a second pass by the entrance, again driving deliberately slowly, ignoring the stares of the curious entering and leaving the park. Satisfied at last, he headed back toward the freedom house. It was a hell of a time for Cates to be acting strange. Maybe it was a woman. That could fuck a man's mind up fast as a rabbit could jump a ditch. But he hadn't seen Cates with a woman in weeks. Maybe that was it. Maybe all he needed was a piece of ass. Cal smiled. Hell, he decided, Cates was all right. Probably just tired. Like himself. Battle fatigue. It would pass with rest. Or would it? Again, as though to etch it permanently on his brain, he swore out loud to himself that it would be his last summer in the Movement.

 **CATES**

I oughta walk out now and leave this damn truck for them to fix. Why the hell bust my ass? It don't make sense. They don't want me anymore. They've as much as said it. You're a god-damned outcast, Pete. Face it, that's what the hell you are. And *she's* one too; Aurabelle sitting up there on that porch day and night and hardly nobody speaking to her—'cept those who come for business. The other black folks stick their noses up in the air at her. *Ditty-ditty dum. Ditty-ditty dum. Ditty-ditty dum.* Right at the beginning of the summer I said to myself I oughta tell her how we were the same. But she wouldn't hardly open her durn mouth to me then. Just would look at me when I passed, and turn her head away like I was a tree or something. Arrogant as she could be. But I knew damn well it was a front. Like my own was a front—me going 'round acting as though nothing had changed; as though I wasn't being eased out. *Ditty-ditty dum. Ditty-ditty dum. Ditty-ditty dum.*

And lately I've been thinking that I shoulda had my head examined when I first thought 'bout joining the Movement. Not that I regret what's been accomplished, but I musta been living in a dream world to think black folks would accept me completely—that in the end they wouldn't want all the credit and power for theyselves. I sure was blind. But it was the memory of Lester Hutchins that weighed heavy on me then—this colored boy I'd known since a kid. His Pa worked for mine—crapping tobacco. Lester'd come to our place with his Pa and we used to play together a lot; go off hunting in the woods or fish in the big ditch behind the curing barns. My Pa, he didn't like it from the first, but never said much against Lester 'til I turned thirteen. Lester, he was twelve. Pa said I was getting to be a man—a *white* man—and I couldn't keep on associating with a nigger like he was an equal. He said it right in front of Lester, and Lester, he ran off down the road toward his house and never came back to our place again. And Pa forbid me to go to Lester's.

Then four years ago—when I was just turning eighteen—I heard the news: Lester and two other boys got killed in a car accident. And unbeknownst to Pa I went to the funeral, and I went to the graveyard too—the only white man there. Afterwards his people took me home with them and I sat at their table and broke bread with them, and we talked 'bout Lester. Even back then there was a lot of civil rights stuff going on. And when I'd watch the television at night and see the colored getting beat by the police, or bit by them fierce dogs, or being dragged off to jail, I just kept thinking 'bout my old friend and 'bout his family and the way they had to live—and the way things were in this country.

Well, 'bout a year passed and I commenced to feeling worse and worse 'bout the situation—and I knew I oughta be doing something to help change things. So I wrassled it out in my head, and one day sitting in the barn grading tobacco with Pa, I told him my decision to join the Movement. He said he'd see me dead first. Me, I was thinking 'bout my oldest brother, Luke, who was killed in the Second World War. And I was thinking that this other—the civil rights business— was really a war too. So I left home against my Pa's will and joined the Movement; and here I am. Yep, here I am—a goddamned outcast. Ain't that a bitch? See how folks'll do you when they don't need you anymore? And Aurabelle, she's an outcast too; and one of these days I'm gon' tell her how we're the same. Damn near told her last Wednesday night when I got up the nerve to go up the hill and ask her if she'd ride to Jackson with me. *Ditty-ditty dum. Ditty-ditty dum. Ditty-ditty dum. "Anytime you want to, Pete. Just pack up and leave. . . ."*

▧ AURABELLE

They don't buy no pussy here. Don't buy no liquor neither. Freedom talk's all they good for. It's bad for business; all this demonstrating, marching, voter registrating. Me, I look out for myself. Duncan Park can kiss my black ass. I ain't going to jail for nobody 'cept myself. Been there once already. Had to give some pussy to get out. Lord, but I'm tard of this shit. Tard of this alley. Tard of Mamie Lee. She ain't hardly been no momma to me. She don't care nothing for me. I work hard as she do to help pay the rent. Laying on my back with my ass stuck up in the air like she show me two years ago when I turn fourteen. Sho, I'm tard of fucking every niggah what walks up this alley with two dollars and his dick hard. The last niggah was still hard when he left here. Never did take his hat off, the big-head motherfucker. He gets off and pulls his overalls up and looks at me sly. "Why should I?" I says. "You come once. I know it 'cause I felt you. You cain't bullshit me. Kiss my ass if you think. . . ." He kept looking at me, with his pants front still unbuttoned. Some you cain't please noways. "Go home and stick it in your Mammy," I says. One day I'm gon' sky outta here. Chicago maybe. Or Detroit. And when I get up North, I ain't never coming back. Not sending for Mamie Lee neither. She have me right back on my ass looking up into some groaning niggah's mouth. Naw, when I get out of here, I'm gon' get a job and straighten myself out. Find me a man that loves me. Ain't never had one yet. Shit, ain't nobody ever cared for me. 'Cept Cousin Josh. And 'cept maybe *him*, that simple-assed white boy down the hill; the one what fixes their truck. Pete's his name. I believe he really do care for me. He give me a five-dollar bill two nights ago, and all he wanted was for me to hold him tight. Guess he ain't never been with a black woman before. Shit, maybe I shoulda charged him seven.

⧈ MAMIE LEE

That no-'count hussy sitting out there. All she wanna do is daydream. That don't pay the rent. Weren't for me staying on her, she'd sit there from morning 'til night. Long as the sun shines. Don't she know it's Friday—the beginning of the week-end and payday? Today and tomorrow—our biggest. You think she 'preciate the sacrifices I have made for her? She don't. Not so much as a kind word or gesture. Just sullen. The bitch sulks and mopes 'round like she's the woman of the house bearing the worries, and I is the kid. Shit. What 'bout the years I worked my ass off to keep 'nough meat and 'tatoes on the table to feed us. What 'bout the years 'fore she was grown 'nuff to help pull the cart. Who pulled it by herself? Mamie Lee did. And when that no-'count daddy of hers rode off and left me big—rode off on his red motorcycle with his cap cocked and them chrome lights glistening—who was it who suffered through the hard months with her in my belly? I did. Me, Mamie Lee Henderson, her Momma. Doing the best I could. Scrubbing floors for the white folks. Doing they laundry. Tending they bad chil'ren. All I knew then was hard work. Nothing but hard work. Worked for two dollars a day—every day 'cept Sunday. Then I was getting my clothes decent to go back to work on Monday. And I was so tard in my soul; so tard I could hardly get up mornins and go out on the job. Then I met this fella Jake; a real nice guy who worked down at the lumberyard. Older than me. We started going together. Aura-belle no more'n four or five. One day he says to me, "Honey, you ever consider selling lightnin' on the side. It's illegal and you won't get rich from it—and you'll sho have to pay off the police. But then you can stop cleaning for the white folks." Well, I was ready to do anything to get off my knees. So I turned my house into a after-hours joint—selling white light-nin' and providing a safe place for the fellas to drink it. Then, one thing and another, and it wasn't long 'fore I was providing more. The other sorta grew nat'chel out of serving the light-nin'; the fellas getting high and wanting a little sport. So, one thing and another—and here I is.

But that little hussy sitting out there pining down the alley for Lord-knows-what don't understand none of it. All she thinks 'bout is her Momma being a whore. And herself being a whore. I never have called myself that, but once that bitch said it to my face. To my face! I struck her hard as I could—my own flesh and blood calling me that. I never have been called a whore to my face, not even by the fellas. But that little bitch. . . . Who do she think she is? I despise her. I never believed I could come to despise my own flesh and blood; the onliest fruit of my womb. And never before did I feel like a sinner; since what I do I does not for pleasure but to get through this terrible life. But now she drove me to feeling sin. Despising your onliest born is sin. So I go to church meeting every Wednesday night and get down on my knees and ask the Lord's forgiveness. I withstand the stares and sniggles of all them hateful pious bitches just to ask the Lord's forgiveness. And she drove me to it; I declare she drove me to it. And just lately she's got to noticing that white boy down the hill, Pete; the one what fixes their truck. I see him passing here, three, four times the day. See how he looks at her. And her trying to act like she don't notice him; then after he pass I see her steal-ing glances at him. No good can come of it. She'd bring the police down on us for sho. They don't 'low whites in this house. Maybe that's what she wants; to see me ruint.

Lemme go find out what's ailing her. Today's Friday. I cain't 'low her sitting 'round looking sad. It's bad for busi-ness. The fellas don't like no sad woman. "Honey," I says, opening the screen and stepping half out on the porch. Soon as my foot creaks the wood she jerks her head up at me mean. "Baby, daydreaming out here don't pay no rent," I says. She just looks at me. I stand with the screen partly open, resting on my leg. "Ain't you doing no business today?" I says.

"Done one 'fore noon," she says, "and two mo' 'bout a hour ago. I'm tard."

She looks back down the alley, sullen and mumbling something under her breath. "What's that you said?" I says loud.

"Nuthin'," she says. "Leave me 'lone."

"You said 'Fat funky no-good bitch,' didn't you? I heard you. Ain't that some way for you to talk to your Momma? That's what you said, now ain't it?"

She turns hard on me, quick, her tight little fists balled up in her lap, her eyes flashing hate. "How you like to kiss my ass?" she says.

I don't say nothing. When she gets thisaway I don't push her; she's a wild bitch then, like something cornered. 'Sides it's Friday. So I lower my voice and speak nice as I can. "Why you frettin' so?" I says. "You can tell sweet Momma Mamie Lee anything's on your mind. Smile now, honey. C'mon now. You know the fellas don't like no sad woman. You be seventeen next month. You's grown now and you have to face responsibility. So go 'head in the house and comb your hair nice and put on a purty dress. Let's get ready for the fellas."

She gets up and walks toward me hateful, mean, without a word, and I move aside and she goes on past and into the house, still not talking. I look at her and shake my head, wondering what makes that youngun so honery. "Shake your hips," I says gentle. She whips around, standing inside near the bed, her cheeks shiny like polished apple skin and her eyes dancing evil in her head. But she don't say a mumbling word, just unzips her skirt and steps out of it. "That's my sweet girl," I says. "You sho got a purty figure on you. It's Friday, honey. C'mon now. Smile. The fellas don't like a sad woman. It's bad for business."

I let the screen fall to and go sit in the chair she had.

Down the alley I can see the heat wiggling over the tin roofs, and a lot of chil'ren playing in the road. I keep looking down the alley feeling good now, 'cause in a few more hours the rubber tire factory and saw mills'll shut down—and the fellas'll be coming up the hill eager for a belly full of lightnin' and a little sport. What's causing me worryment though is that business could be bad tomorrow on account of that damn demonstration. I swear, if I had any say in it, I'd sic the Ku Klux on those freedom riders and run each and every one of 'em out of here for good. They ain't brought nothing but tribulation, and if you ask me that's all they'll ever bring.

RICE

Until I was five I traveled through the South with my mother. She danced in a vaudeville show and I can remember lying on a folding cot in the band pit, pretending sleep and watching her in the *Midnight Review*. The South has brought it all back—the big tent and Sparky-the-Clown forward somersaulting seven kneeling men and landing on his feet. And my other friend, the amazing Chinaman who played tunes dropping metal coins on a marble tabletop. And all those daddies . . . the trumpet player, the sax player; and our last summer together the bass drummer: a man I liked and nicknamed Daddy Boom-Boom. Then I was not yet a nigger. Then I did not understand this place or see the suffering of my people. In that time there was only the swirl of colored light gels, the midnight blare of bright brass bands, and the sad-happy glitter of greasepaint lives—the sparkling stage-prop people who opened me forever to the world of unrooted things.

When I was five, I got adopted and was brought north to live, leaving mother and our friends behind. And one day not long afterward someone called me a nigger: a white police-man directing traffic. It brought me down, and I felt clearly for the first time that enormous and diamond-hard mountain of reality. And not again could I completely reenter the old bubblepipe world of June bugs and angleworms and cap-tured fireflies flickering in punched-top Mason jars. I simply hovered above it all like a wounded hummingbird, my wings truncated and my self not knowing how or where to land. But being here in this now strange place, here in this foreign but quite familiar land, I have found my way again. All options have been removed; I must be what I am. Yes, at last I'm a nigger. And that will be my salvation.

 **BENJIE**

It was almost lunchtime. Momma still with Daddy Ross. Ludy came back with some bacon and a jar of molasses. Then she went away again and said, "I be back to fix lunch. If the insur-ance man comes while I'm gone, knock on Momma's door or tell him come back later." And then she ran on up the hill. Benjie watched the bottom of the alley for the white man to appear; for his long skinny self to come panting like a hunched dog with red hair through the dust, walking slow up the hill, past the pigs and chickens and the big boys shooting marbles. Once Mr. Tate gave him a quarter to go outside and play while he talked private with Ludy. He always rubbed Benjie's head for luck. But Benjie wished hard against the luck, and from how bad Mr. Tate still looked, he musta never got it. Ludy said she was scared of him 'cause he mostly came when Momma was gone. Ludy said she hated Mr. Tate more'n anybody in the world. Even more'n Daddy Clark.

Benjie heard feet moving in Momma's room. She was up. He heard her voice singing one of her happy spirituals—Benjie swinging his legs happy too. Momma's feet came across the loud boards.

"Benjie! Benjie! Where you at?" The screen door squeaked open and there Momma stood, smiling down through the trembly heat. "That insurance man come yet?"

"No, ma'am."

"Where's Ludy?"

"Her gone off, Momma."

"And you sitting here like a good boy. Waiting. That's my sweet precious. Waiting like Momma told you."

"Yes, ma'am."

Another face came in the door behind Momma. It fell on Momma's neck like a chicken pecking. Then Momma pushed it away and it grinned like a horse.

"Not out here, Ross," Momma said. "Don'cha see Benjie? Ain't I told you—"

"Aw, c'mon, baby. He just a kid."

Then Momma pushing him away again and taking two steps on the porch. "You hungry, Benjie?"

"Yes, ma'am." Benjie's eyes down but knowing the face was grinning, and hard hands touching Momma deep where it's secret.

"Where you going, Momma?" Benjie said.

"With Ross," Momma said. "I be back soon. You keep watching for the insurance man. That po'-trash sucker oughta have been here Monday. I don't want my policy to lapse."

Benjie felt the colors running.

"Aw right," Momma said. "Don't cry. I be back soon. You Momma's pumpkin?"

"Puddin' pie too?" Benjie said. Momma and Daddy Ross across the porch and down the steps.

"And puddin' pie too," Momma said. She came to the edge, took his face in her hands, and kissed him on the mouth. Daddy Ross frowned and walked away and stood in the road and looked down the alley. Benjie reached out and took hold of Momma's wrists and held them with all his might. Momma lifted his chin.

"Where's my big boy, Benjie?" She wiped his eyes with her thumbs. Daddy Ross shuffled his feet in the red dust.

"C'mon, Bertha. Ah's thirsty for a beer."

Momma looked right at Benjie. "What's your name?" she said, smiling. Benjie swinging his legs again, happy. "Puddin'-an'-Tame. That's my name. Ask me again and I'll tell you the same." Momma laughed. Benjie laughed.

Daddy Ross turned and looked at them, then started ahead up the hill. Momma ran after him, waving back at Benjie. Benjie watched her go.

 **RICE**

We walk through the quiet woods, through the dappling slices of sunlight slanting past the high oak limbs. Parnell stoops and picks a flower. I wait for her. We say nothing. My head is going very fast; like a camera's inside going *click, click, click*. It goes *click:* a picture. And it goes *click, click:* more pictures. Old pictures. A head full of them.

Click . . . I'm four and a half. Mother is sick. She wears a velvet robe. I walk beside her, helping her, one arm around her waist, my other hand pressed against her stomach, cupping the front of her robe where the round secret mound moves beneath the velvet cloth. She vomits green stuff and flushes the toilet. I am crying. I help her back to her room, my hand again on the round mound under the soft cloth.

It goes *click* . . . I'm nineteen. A soldier. It's my first fuck. I'm scared. My hand is on a prostitute's cunt. It's a round mound under my hand; soft as velvet inside, wet under my hand. My hand slides deeper into it. My hand goes all the way in . . . help! . . . help! "Don't cry, baby," she says. "You've just swallowed a little pussy."

It goes *click* . . . I'm twelve and in over my head in deep water at summer camp. Hands grasp me, pull me to the surface. The sky swoops down to the lake's edge and the clouds look like the hands of a clock. Mr. Bruno, our tribe leader, sits on top of me, pushing me into the sand. His face tips out of the clock hands and kisses me in the mouth, then goes away into the sky again; then comes back down with the mouth open. "Don't cry, kid," he says. "You've just swallowed a little water."

It goes *click* . . . I'm seventeen. I'm fast asleep. Fists pound against my bedroom door. I awake in terror. "Get up. Quick!" someone says. "Mother's dying. Hurry, she's asked for you." I get up and open the door and it's Aunty's daughter standing there; my stepsister. Twenty. "Why do you always lock your door?" she asks angrily. "Nobody's gonna steal your little ass." I follow her downstairs. The big house is cold, silent except for the sustained hiss of radiators. The relatives stand around her bed. A doctor is there. The Man is there, too; Uncle. A rattling sound comes from Aunty's throat. She looks at me and lifts her hand weakly. "Take it," the Man says. "Be a good boy." I take it. It is blue and dry and cold; the nails thick and ridged. "Look after your father," she says. I can barely hear her. I lean down. "He needs you," she says. "He needs you now. Call him Father.

Promise you'll call him Father." The Man takes her hand from mine and puts it gently back on the bed. Her eyes are closing. The Man looks at me. The relatives look at me. I feel pity for the Man, for her, for myself. There were times when I had actually loved her, times when I almost forgot the adoption and her insults about my mother. The rattling sound grows louder. "I promise," I say. "I promise. . . ." The sound hangs suspended, then grows faint. Then it stops completely. After a while the doctor lifts the edge of the sheet and pulls it over her face. In the kitchen the Man says to me, "You don't have to, you know. You never have, so why should you start now?" His eyes are angry, sad, tired, anguished. "You really don't have to," he says. "You goddamned little ingrate. You broke her heart. You helped put her in the grave. You could have called her *Mother;* just once in these twelve years—ungrateful little bastard." I go out and sit on the porch in the swing; sit there with the warm spring morning breaking across the gray sky. I sit in the gentle morning, cursing him, cursing her; all of them who have conspired to keep me from her, my real love. I sit in the gentle morning where death has been; and I hate the nice street and the nice house; and I hate the other nice colored family down the block. I think of all those circus people I loved—Sparky-the-Clown and the Chinaman. I sit in the gentle spring morning, listening to the undertaker wheel Aunty out; not moving, just sitting there listening to last winter's sparrows chirping brightly in the leafless trees. I think of my own mother and wonder what's become of her, whether I'll ever see her again.

And it goes *click* . . . I'm twenty-one. A cold shabby room somewhere in southern New England. Mother, not yet forty. Dead. He found her not long ago; an old boyfriend. Notified me. I borrowed train fare and left New York at once. "We don't see Tessie around the joints all week," he says. "When you don't see a regular, you know somethin's wrong." I look at him: high-yellow bastard, dense-looking sonofabitch—small hunched shoulders and long-nailed fingers like rat's paws. My last Daddy. "Get out of here. Leave me alone," I say. The bare mattress is slate gray with blue stripes running lengthwise. The iron bedposts are painted white. Dust coats the single window. The undertaker arrives. "I understand this is to be on the State," he says. I look at him. Fat, dumpy, slicked-down hair, a pink carnation in his lapel, a tiny gray mustache; round black cheeks dusted with white talc. The voice and manner grave, contrived, but indifferent. The odor of fried chicken lingers on his breath. "The State provides the following. . . ."

They put her in a plain pine box and the next day hold a brief service for her in the tiny chapel of the funeral home. A few of her friends attend. There is a lot of weeping—they seemed to have liked her. Then we drive to a small cemetery on the edge of town. They lower her into a fresh grave. Two groundskeepers stand ready with spades to cover up the hole when we leave . . . *no money for a stone*. The edge of the grave is wet with shadows. I grow dizzy. They rush to meet me.

And it goes *click* . . . last spring and I stand at an office window—a Manhattan public relations firm. I'm dressed in a Brooks suit, I'm clean-shaven, my hair is short. I'm a *first spade* hired. Well salaried. A *visible nigger*. An *Apple-pie Dancer*. I have everything I asked for. I have nothing. I'm miserable. Inside I'm neither black nor white but *gray;* drifting in a sub-twilight between two worlds, with one world vanishing rapidly, growing ever more vague; furling behind me like a shriveled placenta—and the other world remaining indifferent, aloof, alien; as though having added an undesirable to its periphery by simple accretion, it is then free to turn its back and retreat once again to the comforts of those deep and private centers where it need embrace only its own.

I stand looking down forty stories at a cramped muscle of traffic on Madison Avenue, and hear again that roar, that rush of time and events that I have been hearing for almost a year— a steady roar as ceaseless as sea sounds in a conch. I stand decked out in false symbols, amid enemies, feeling and seeing the decade awake from slumber, awake into its own time, gathering its wide wings and powers, unfurling out of the South on the wings of an electronic picture window; hurling high-winded out of those bastions of slavery, out of the lairs of haints and conjurer doctors; out of the arcane smells of liniments and root salves and sweet oils—gathering its wide wings, catalyzing itself; impelled by time and serendipity, by a young black preacher who tested the climate, who sensed its new permissiveness; its ability to bear a great and sudden new weight. I stand there at the window hearing again the sixties scudding out of slumber and spilling over the lip of its decade into all those sequestered lives like mine—those unconvinced and frightened little lives—shocking them to wakefulness, to sensibility, to rage. So I was already a part of it without really knowing it; and there was nothing left to do but act.

The resignation note was short, polite. The rest took even less time. The jet plane ride to Jackson was only three and a half hours.

It goes *click*. . . .

 **DUDLEY**

About fifteen minutes ago this crazy nigger comes in my hardware store—me standing behind the counter talking to Earl Baskerville about some manure he was interested in. Well, he comes in and don't say nothing at first, just stands near the door looking around at the shelves. I was wondering what business he had in my store, since they got their own where they live. And besides, this one had never set foot in here, though I knowed him by sight. Hell, everybody in town knows him—he's loony'r'n a bedbug. His name's Zenola. He walks around all day with his shirt wide open and the tails flapping out and a chest full of scars from tree limbs. They used to catch him when he'd fall while pruning for the City. Now folks say he's a informer for the police. If he's informing on those civil righters like they say, it's sure a favor to us. There's been no end of trouble since the civil righters came to town. And now, to top it all off, they're marching on Duncan Park tomorrow. Imagine having niggers in our swimming water, playing on our golf course. Drinking our liquor at the club. Folks're real mad. Everybody's just itching to go out there tomorrow and beat their brains out.

Anyways, I finish with Earl Baskerville and ask the other what he wants. Earl goes past him carrying the bag of manure under one arm and an axe handle under the other. It was the last axe handle in stock—sold every damn one this week. "Good day," he says, going out the door. "See you tomorrow at the *picnic*, Dudley. Don't forget your baseball bat." And he winks at me and goes on out.

"What can I do for you?" I say to the other. He's standing there with his head nappy enough to scrape cement clean, and them great angry whelps burning on his bare chest. He has a narrow little pinched face with warts all over it, and big wild light-colored eyes that're set high up in the face. He's barefoot and the britches he's wearing come up around his calves, like they belong to another. I ask again what he wants, and the damn fool goes to laughing. Right then I know he's whacked like they say. I turn and go back behind the counter and start weighing up some ten-penny nails. He comes over and watches me for a minute, then digs in his pocket and comes out with a twenty-dollar bill and puts it on the counter. "Where'd a nigger like you get that kind of money?" I say. "And what you intend to buy with it?" I'm fed up with him by now, and fixing to tell him to get the hell out of my store and stay out. Then he latches them wild gray eyes on me, like a haint would, and I feel a strange sensation run through me, like I was spooked by a conjurer doctor or a witch.

"Take your damn money and get out of here," I say. "Or speak up and tell me what you want."

"Boom!" he says, just like that; and still laying them eyes on me so that I have to look off for a minute, pretending to check the register. "Boom! Boom!" he says. Then the damn idiot falls flat out on the floor and lays there not moving a muscle. I lean over the counter and look at him. They're given to fits and I didn't want him having one in my store.

"You all right?" I say. "What the hell—"

Them eyes pop open wide again and he stares up at me. Then he jumps to his feet and reaches in his pocket and comes out with a book of matches and strikes one. Despite myself I'm getting curious as hell as to what he's up to. Maybe just something crazy, I think. Maybe he carries on like that all the time. Then he holds the burning match up in the air, pretending he's lighting something. Then he blows out the match and sticks his fingers in his ears. I'm watching the fool now, wondering if maybe I oughtn't go next door for some help just in case. Well, he's got his two index fingers stuck in his ears and he's looking at me. Then he bares his teeth and makes a sound with his mouth; like steam escaping from a radiator valve.

"S-s-s-s-s-s-s," he says. Then: "S-s-s-s-s . . . BOOM!"

He makes the boom so loud I flinch. Then it dawns on me. "You mean you want. . . ."

"Das right," he says. "Das right." He's nodding his head like it was bobbing in fast water. I didn't even know the fool could talk 'til then.

"You mean you want some dynamite?"

"Das right," he says. "Me Zenola. Boom! No more trouble. You give me boomsticks. Zenola black king of the mountain."

It was dawning on me slow now, but I was getting it. And I didn't want no part of it.

"Where'd you get that twenty-dollar bill?" I say, looking hard at him. "I believe you stole it. If you don't get out of here right now, I'll call the police. You take that money and go some other place and get your dynamite," I say. "You liable to blow me sky high 'fore you even get out the door, crazy as you is."

"Naw," he says, hammering on his bare chest with his firsts. "Me Zenola. Boom! No more trouble. Boss man say okay black king of the mountain. You give Zenola boom-sticks."

"Who said it was okay?" I ask him.

He shuts his mouth tight as a drum and looks at me.

"Take your damn money and go," I say. "I don't want no part in it." I snatch up a hammer laying on the counter and start around the other side at him. He watches me 'til I'm almost around, then picks up the twenty-dollar bill and bolts for the door, not even hesitating to look back after he closes it. For a minute I just stand there, leaning against the screw-driver display rack, breathing hard from just that little effort and knowing I'm putting on too much weight. I watch him cross the street, scrambling between cars. Then when he gets to the other side, he heads down Main toward Percy Thompson's hardware store. Then the traffic blocks my view. He's determined, I say to myself. Damned if he ain't determined. I go back behind the counter and pick up the telephone and call down the street to Percy's.

 **CLARICE**

I haven't been well enough to go to church in a mess of Sundays. My knees are swoll double from rheumatism and there's a touch of the gout in my feet. But as God is my witness, come tomorrow I will stand and walk with these young folks through the gates of Duncan Park. I have determined this, and I will do it; for I believe in my heart they have come to save us. And their long hair and unshaven faces is a sign; a sign of their goodness that only the wise will see. I admit that when they first came at the beginning of the summer, I did not believe they had our best interests in mind; or that they were old enough to be trusted. And as with all of us on this alley, I was not accustomed to their looks. To me, a young man unshaven and in need of a haircut always meant he was not of good character; that if he did not so much as care for his own person, he could not possibly care for someone else's.

But our shack is at the foot of the hill—right behind the freedom house. And just sitting on my porch, I could watch them come and go; watch them treating us poor folks like we were important. And the way they were so polite and considerate to one another—that impressed me too. Then they gave my daughter, Angie, a job cleaning their house in the mornings; and they paid her more than enough for the little piddling she did. So Angie would come home and tell me what went on there; about the hard life of a freedom soldier. She would tell me about their meetings, and how they wanted to get all us black folks registered to vote; and about all the other things they were trying to do for us. So I listened to Angie, and I watched them as they came and went; spoke to them when they passed my porch; as I sat sewing and hating myself for Zenola, or worrying how to keep enough food on the table for my children. Well, one day the colored one, Tom Rice, came to the house and asked if I was registered to vote. I told him no, but that once I had been preparing to be a schoolteacher, and that I knew it was a person's responsibility to vote. I told him how scared I was—how scared all of us were—to go down to the city hall and take the test. But he said he would help me study for it and show me how to answer the questions; that the test was only given to the colored, so it wouldn't really be cheating. He said they were trying to get rid of the test. I told him I had finished high school, and that my father had once owned one of the biggest farms of any colored man in this county; and had spent his good money to educate me, and that he would not recognize me today. And, yes, I would go register to vote. I don't know why I felt like telling him all that, except there is a quality about these young people—a fineness of character— that makes me believe they truly care about others. I don't talk much to folks around here, though, because they have never accepted me; saying, even to my face, that I was full of proper talk and white folks' airs. Their snubbing me was not a burden at first, but with the years I feel it more and more.

Well, I went and registered—Tom Rice driving me to the city hall in that truck of theirs. He stood in line and waited with me—the white folks hanging around looking mean at us, calling out curses and threatening those of us they recognized. But afterwards I felt so proud, and so much stronger in my heart. Just doing that one little thing made me feel freer. And it was that day that I knew for certain these young people had come to save us; and their long hair and unshaven faces was a sign; a sign for the wise to see the true Christ lives in them—that they are truly ready to give and receive love; truly tired of words and ready to replace them with deeds. Yes, my knees are swoll from rheumatism and there's a touch of the gout in my feet. But as God is my witness, come tomorrow I will stand and walk with them through the gates of Duncan Park. Bless them, Jesus.

We stop to rest, lying on our backs in the cool green moss, looking up into the treetops. The little creek still follows beside the trail.

"What's the difference?" I say to her. "Baby, who'll know? Nobody ever comes this way. Everybody takes the main road. Besides, we'd hear them coming through the woods. C'mon, please."

"We better go on," she says. "We should be in Sloane Hollow by now."

The creek trickles loud. The air is damp, hot, heavy. I hold her close, kiss her long; my hand on her knee, on her thigh, inside her drawers. There she is like the air. "Take them off," I say. "Please."

"I didn't come south for this, Tom," she says. Tom she's calling me. "Tom, we oughta go. Tom, please. . . ."

"I can't help it," I say. "The heat." I kiss her again, softly, prolonged. She reaches between us and takes hold of it with one hand, and with the other keeps pushing me away. Then she stops. I no longer hear the birds, only the creek. We kiss again. "Please," I say. "Please, darling." She raises herself slowly with a sigh and pulls them down. The creek trickles like it's happy. Parnell lays back in the moss and kudzu leaves, her thighs stark white against the green. But where they meet is suddenly an eruption of color, a bronze flame, swollen metallic in the sun; darker brown than brows or braid. I remember nothing. I am suspended in a womb older and darker than all other wombs. I flow out into burnished brown, into metal suns. My blood veins at her cave's mouth. I chill suddenly and shiver. We cry out. Echoes. Echoes. "Michael," she is saying. "Michael, damn." I race half-naked through leaves of kudzu, beneath trees spook-limbed with Spanish moss; I crawl along old snail paths barely glistening in dark suns of restless pasts. To now. To now. "Tom," she is saying. "Goddam. Now, Tom. Now. Now. . . ."

I hear the creek again, and bird sounds—sharp, swift, noble, erratic. I put my pants on and Parnell smooths her dress. We gather the scattered mimeographed sheets and start again along the trail. Ahead flows the gleaming river, sequined in the sun. Around us the woods seem more silent, and our imprints on the moss have faded.

PARNELL

Arching with a cry she rose to summits of love. Ultimate suspensions of time burst like flowers. *Michael lying in the dark ditch. Moonlit rain silver against the shining spokes, his hand still on the gas. "Keep it running," he said. "You know how. Don't let it stall, baby."* How lovely now his He against her She, and all herself yielding to that undertow which pulled her slowly down to murmuring depths, to dark beginnings. And the next tide lifted her higher than she had ever been. And it was sustained. And the She and He went faster. Ah, to be sustained. To be sustained by love. *Yes. Now. Michael. No breath coming. Rain on the turning spokes.* Love, sustain us. Sustain us. Now. "Michael. Michael, damn." Now. Higher. Higher. Oh, yes. Now. Oh, my god. "Tom, goddamn. Now, Tom. Now. Now. . . ."

Black lays long, lazy. Sun runs yellow rills in the treetops. Moss roses cool against thighs. I'll write. I'll mail the pecans home. Say, hi. Hi, folks! Christ, I didn't come south for this.

I musta blowed the head gasket yesterday coming back from Jackson. The first I noticed water in the oil was when I checked to see how much oil she had burned on the trip. She needs a ring job, but I figger that can wait least 'til the demonstration's over. Cain't afford laying her up more'n a day or two right now. But I'll have to replace the—*Ditty-ditty dum. Ditty-ditty dum. Ditty-ditty dum*—head gasket today. Just cain't run her like this. I'll have to pull the head off. Gotta remember to get that torque wrench. Last time I put the head back on without one, I tightened down too hard and stripped a bolt. Took two days just to find somebody with the equipment to drill it out and retap the block. But I keep forgetting stuff lately. Don't know what's wrong. *"Anytime you want to, Pete. Just pack up and leave. . . ."*

Aside from the truck, Calvin is pissed off with me and we don't hardly talk. After all we been through together. I know I ain't been a hundred percent myself lately, but I got a lot on my mind; not the least of which is Aurabelle Henderson. And I'm worried 'bout my Pa. Ain't thought of him much since I left home almost three years ago. We own a few acres up in North Carolina, in a little place called George. My Pa grows leaf tobacco. My mother wasn't dead six months when I told him I was joining the civil rights movement. My twin brother, Clinton, had already left home; and my oldest brother, Luke, like I said before, had been killed in the Second World War. So there was nobody left to help Pa 'cept me and the colored day hands he hired for forty cents an hour less than the going rate. For a long time I'd been wrassling with the idea of joining the Movement, and the day I told Pa 'bout my decision we was out in the barn grading tobacco. We'd been working the fields all morning crapping it and sending it back to the barn by horse and sled. We sat across from one another with a big pile of green tobacco leaves between us on a bench. It was hot as hell, and the juice from the leaves was sticky like chewing gum, clinging to our hands and arms and faces. I just couldn't hold it in me another day.

"I seen a lot on the television 'bout these freedom riders," I said, not looking up at him, but keeping my eyes on the leaf in my hand. We were making three smaller graded piles from the big ungraded one. "And reading it in the newspapers, too," I said. "I think they doing a lot of good. I sho do admire them."

"Uh-huh," he said, like he was half listening. He smoothed out a wrinkled leaf and put it in the *A* pile. He picked up another, smoothed it, and laid it on the *C* pile. "What? You admire who?"

"The civil rights fellas," I said. "Those freedom rider boys."

He stopped working and looked at me. "Ain't nothing there to admire," he said. "They oughta be carried off somewhere and shot. Every damn one of 'em."

I didn't say anything. Then finally I said, "Pa, you know Chauncey Summerwell, don't you?"

He nodded.

"Well, he went off yesterday to join a freedom bus ride leaving from Washington, D.C."

"He might cain't find his way to Washington, D.C.," he said. "That boy never had a ounce of brains. What the hell's a freedom bus ride?"

"It's when these fellas get on a bus in the North and ride it down here to the South to integrate the bus lines. When they get here, folks have drug 'em off the buses and whipped 'em bad. Sometimes even burned their buses."

He sat there looking at me, his straw hat tipped back on his head. "They ought to have burned *them*," he said. He stood up. "I'm going in the house for a spell. You finish grading this load. Then tell those niggers hit's enough crapping for today and I'll pay 'em tomorrow." He looked at me and wrinkled up his forehead. "They's lazy no good sonsof-bitches. All of 'em. Every damn last one."

"Pa, I'm gonna join the Movement," I said. "I wanna be part of what's changing things. Like when Luke went off to war."

He just stood there in the door looking back at me; standing there framed against the sun, thin, bent. Then he looked out toward the fields and cleared his throat and spit into the dirt. He walked back inside and stood over me; silent, drawn and old-looking under the brim of his hat. "Them is niggers, boy. Black niggers. You my blood and kin. You was raised proper. You know well as the next white man what a nigger is. You know what they's after. You know what a nigger'll do if he gets the privileges of a white man. I taught you since you was little. Since 'fore you could talk. You know all they want is our womenfolk. And I be durn if a son of mine'll help niggers and communists take over this country. Be durn if you'll bring shame on my head. I'd see you dead first. As your poor mother is my witness. As you were sprung from our mutual loins, I'd see you dead first. Now you finish up that load and stop talking foolish." He turned slow and walked out of the barn and crossed the yard to the house. When I finished grading, I went out to the fields and let the help go, then I went into the house. Pa was sitting by the kitchen window reading from his Bible. He hadn't brought it out since Momma died. He looked weak and old and tired. "I'll write to you," I said. "Pa. . . ."

"Don't you bother," he said, his eyes shiny. "Just don't you bother. 'Cause I'd burn 'em unopened. You ain't no more son of mine," he said. "You ain't no son of mine."

That was three summers and three winters ago. I never once been back. Never once wrote. But here, lately, I been thinking a lot 'bout home. 'Bout Pa. Wondering how he is. How the old place looks. I'm tired now and I think a lot like that. So it's hard to concentrate on other things, like fixing this fucking equipment what's no damn good to begin with. And my memory's slipping. I want to go home in the worse

way, but maybe there ain't even a home left. Damn this fucking truck. It's just like me: ain't nothing right with it. I hope
the hell I can find a torque wrench. *Ditty-ditty dum. Ditty-ditty
dum. Ditty-ditty dum.* I'll walk up the hill to the gas station on
St. Catherine Street. Maybe the mechanic there'll loan me his
if he ain't using it. Maybe I'll see Aurabelle again sitting on
her porch. I sho wish she would forget 'bout Wednesday
night. Give me another chance. My dead mother was laying
heavy on my mind. That was the trouble. I wish I could do
something for Aurabelle. Take her away from this hard life.
Ditty-ditty dum. Ditty-ditty dum. Ditty-ditty dum. "*Anytime you
want to, Pete. Just pack up and leave. . . .*"

PEAVINE

This cold, low-down feeling came over me; like something
heavy had nudged itself against my navel and settled there
for good. Or like the undertow feeling you get when somebody close to you dies and it's fresh on your mind. You keep
remembering them alive so you won't have to think about
them dead. But all the time you feel the undertow dragging
you down, right down to where they're dead.

I was playing cards at Aurabelle Henderson's house when
I first noticed it. Musta been Wednesday night, 'cause Rosalee,
my wife, has her club meeting then. We was playing bid whist
and I was drinking white lightnin'. It was Aurabelle's bid. All
of a sudden I just laid my hand down. She looked at me.

"Why you doing that?" she said. "Now I know what you
got."

"I feel bad," I said. "All this freedom talk. This demonstrating. I feel terrible. I wish things was like they used to be."

"I bid five," she said. She looked over the edge of the cards at me. "You ain't no damn fool. You ain't going on that demonstration. So why you's worried?"

I took another big snort of the lightnin' and picked up my hand again and looked at it; but my mind wasn't on it. I put it down. "Why cain't they let things be? Why they want to start all this trouble?"

"C'mon," she said, disgusted. "You gon' play or not?"

"S'pose I went. It would be the end. The white folks at the bank would call my loans due. I couldn't pay for James's college. I'd lose the house. And Rosalee needs a operation 'fore Christmas."

"I needed one jack of diamonds," Aurabelle said. She picked up my hand and looked at it. "You couldn't of won nohow. Your deal."

"I wish I could get some sleep. I used to never be troubled. Sound asleep six inches 'fore my head hit the pillow; and didn't open an eye 'til the alarm went. Now . . . Good Lord. Why cain't things be like they used to be?"

Of a sudden Aurabelle threw her hand down on the bed and stood up. "They can all kiss my ass," she said. "They don't do no business here. Freedom talk is all they good for. Duncan Park can kiss my ass. I ain't going on no damn demonstration. I ain't going to jail for nobody 'cept myself. Shit. It's your deal." She sat back down on the edge of the bed, breathing hard.

I picked the cards up slow and shuffled them good and dealt. "You is right," I said. "What I'm worried 'bout? They cain't *make* me go. Cain't nobody *make* me go. I bid four."

When he heard the insurance man, he didn't look up. He knew who it was because the white man always cleaned his brogans on the steps, scraping like people did out of the rain or snow, or after they stepped in doggy poops. Benjie sat at the kitchen table sopping molasses with a chunk of cornbread—Ludy at the stove frying another piece of bacon.

"Afternoon," the man said through the screen, through the dusty little squares you could wet with bubblepipe soap and see rainbows. "Anybody home?" He always looked in first and if he saw people, he said, "Anybody home?" 'Stead of "Hi, y'all," like everybody else. Benjie watched Ludy poke the bacon with a fork. Ludy watched the insurance man. Benjie looked. There he was, all right, full of the misery as ever—Benjie making a dimple in the molasses with the cornbread edge.

"Lord, hit's sure hot," the insurance man said. He pulled off the white straw hat and wiped his forehead on the back of his hand. He grinned narrow pucker lips with brown teeth at Benjie.

"How you doing, boy?"

"Fine, suh," Benjie said.

"Lord, that hill ain't nothing but mighty. I dreads the minute I get down in these here alleys and have to start climbing and descending. Hardly ain't worth hit."

Of a sudden, Benjie remembered. "Mr. Tate, suh, what is a insurance man really for?" he said.

Ludy frowned. The insurance man laughed past the shadows at the screen.

"Ah be doggone if I rightly know, boy. Though I could be for a ice-cold glass of water. That's if somebody had a mind to fetch it." He looked at Ludy.

Ludy brought the bacon dripping grease, her hand shaking. Then she went out of the room.

"Your Momma home, boy?" the insurance man said, whispering.

Benjie didn't look. He felt scared. "No, suh. Her not home." Benjie whispered, too. Then he looked. Mr. Tate wasn't mean-looking as Ludy said. But skinny and po'-looking like Momma said. Momma said the insurance man was thirty-five and had a wife and six younguns living in a po'-white-trash house near the river. "No better'n these shacks here on Long George Alley," Momma said. Maybe the white man was po'-looking 'cause there wasn't 'nough food home, Benjie thought. Of a sudden the scared went. He remembered pictures in the face magazine—starving children squatting on the ground like monkeys. Then the insurance man said loud, "You reckon I could get a cold glass of water?"

Benjie started up. Ludy came in the room carrying the money balled up tight in her fist. Ludy frowned. Benjie sat back down.

The insurance man wiped his forehad again. "I'd sho be much obliged if y'all let me come in and rest a minute outen this sun," he said.

"Momma ain't home," Ludy said. They looked straight at each other. The insurance man grinned. Ludy unlatched the kitchen door and handed the money. He took it and counted, then licked his thumb and opened a black notebook and turned the pages. He wrote down something, then scratched in his hair.

"Something's wrong," he said. "This ain't quite right."

"Then you best come back tomorrow," Ludy said.

"Last day of the business week," he said. "You want your Momma's policy to lapse? You wanna see poor Bertha go in the cold ground without a cent t'ward a coffin?" He shook his head side to side.

Ludy dropped her eyes. Benjie felt his scared again. Laps

people sit in, he thought. Why Momma was going in the cold
ground? He reached in the overalls and took out his favorites—
a rabbit-foot key chain Parnell gave him, and two glass shoot-
ers. He liked the marbles in his hand. Hard. Cool. The rabbit's
foot was warm, soft. He put it away.

"It just may be my mistake," the insurance man said. He
poked the ink pen toward the latch. "Lord, hit's sho hot out
here. Lemme come in for a minute and figger this thing out."

Benjie got up and went to Ludy. He looked up through
the screen door at the insurance man.

"Well . . ." Ludy said. "If you promise to sit here in the
kitchen and do it, I reckon it's okay."

"I do hit anywhere you want, honey," the insurance man
said. The lips went out straight and the brown teeth came again.

Ludy dropped her eyes. "I mean it," she said. "I really
mean it."

"I know," he said. "I was just fooling. C'mon now, honey."

Ludy unlatched the door and the insurance man came
in—Benjie smelling him. Like what Momma called *musty*. He
went straight on through the kitchen—Ludy following behind.
Benjie went too. In the living room the insurance man sat
down hard on the sofa propped up with bricks on one end.
He fanned with the straw hat and wiped again. Ludy put her
hands on her hips and looked.

"You promised," she said. "You promised you wouldn't—"

"How 'bout that glass of water, gal?" the insurance man
said. He put the black notebook on the little table by the
sofa. "Put ice in it if you got some, baby." He stretched out his
long legs.

Ludy frowned and went to the kitchen, walking fast.

"Where your Momma, boy?" the insurance man said. He
put the straw hat beside the notebook and crossed his legs.
The knees went high.

Benjie sat on the cool linoleum. He rolled the marbles
together.

"So you wants to know 'bout insurance, eh, boy?'"

"Yas, suh," Benjie said.

The insurance man picked up the face magazine off the table. He licked his thumb and turned the pages. "Well, hit's 'bout taking care of folks after they die. See, boy, all us gonna die one day and when we do, hit's the insurance company what sees to hit there's 'nough cash to get you buried decent. Get you a casket and a funeral." He put the face magazine down and took the notebook. "Now this here little book is where I keep a record of how much folks have paid t'ward getting buried." He patted the notebook. "Yep, hit's all in here, boy." He looked at Benjie. "You understand?"

Benjie shook his head yes.

"Well then, good. Now you go on outdoors and play like a good little nigger. Go 'head and watch for your Momma. Where she gone?"

Benjie lifted both shoulders.

"What you mean you don't know? Didn't I tell you what *you* asked?"

"Yas, suh," Benjie said.

"Then c'mon, boy. Be fair. Where your Momma gone?"

The marbles smooth in Benjie's hand, cold like his dead puppy. "Her saloonin' with Daddy Ross," Benjie said.

Ludy came with a glass of ice water and handed it to the insurance man. He took it. The ice made bells.

"I was telling this here boy 'bout the insurance business," he said. He almost finished the water. "Hit ain't no easy job walking up and down these alleys. Ain't hardly worth hit." He finished the water. "I carry this pistol for the bad niggers," he said. "Ain't never without it down here. I ain't a bit worried." He put the glass on the table.

Ludy sat down across the room. She looked at Benjie long.

"They'd cut me fast as they'd cut another nigger," the insurance man said. "The bad ones are funny that way. Ain't scared of nothing or nobody. But you get to know how to spot 'em. 'Cause all niggers ain't bad. You take a scared one, for an instance. He don't worry me a bit. I can cuss him out in the morning and that night he's liable to get piss-eyed drunk and cut up another nigger. But he wouldn't lay a knife to me. No, siree. He respects a white man. So I carry this pistol for the bad niggers."

Benjie wondered if Daddy Ross was a bad nigger. Daddy Clark sure was. Benjie wondered where the pistol was. He saw the insurance man look up Ludy's dress.

"You take these new-breed niggers, like Calvin Drew for an instance; or that big nigger at the barber shop, B. Jacks. Now there you got two real bad coons." The insurance man looked at Benjie. "I had to kill me a nigger once. A big black buck. Jumped me late one evening right on the next alley. I'd finished my day's collections and was heading home. Of a sudden this buck comes running at me outen his shack, hollering things 'bout me and his nigger woman. Saying I'd bigged her. Now you know that's a lie. Well, he come tearing 'cross his porch and down the steps at me. I saw this switchblade flashing in his hand, and I told him. I warned him. I said, 'Fetch up where you are, nigger. Don't make me have to shoot you.' But he kept a-coming. Before his foot hit the last step I had shot him dead."

Ludy pulled the bottom of her dress down. The insurance man got up and let out a loud breath and wiped his forehead again. His pants poked out in front.

". . . Didn't give me no choice. Just come tearing outen that shack at me. 'Tweren't my fault. I tell you it 'tweren't my fault. He had it coming. Y'all believe me, don't you?" The sweat fell down his face, rolling fast like little rain rivers. "You think I give a goddamn if you believe me?" he said, looking straight at Benjie again. "You'd take the nigger's side anyhow. Boy," he said. "This the last time I'm gon' tell you. Go out on that porch and watch for your Momma." The sweat fell down his face.

"Stay here," Ludy said. Ludy was crying. Benjie had to go to the bathroom.

The insurance man went to Ludy. "Look here, take this fucking money. Y'all need hit. You took hit before."

Ludy stood up and went and put her face on the linen scarf at the mantelpiece. Benjie got up and went to her and laid his head on her hip. He felt her stomach jobbling like Miss Mamie Lee's. Something was always happening. He looked at the insurance man. Mr. Tate's breath went fast, like he just climbed the hill. He came over to them—Benjie smelling him again.

"I don't want this money," Ludy said. "Sho, we's po', but this is for Momma. I don't want it."

"Hit's yourn, too, honey," the insurance man said. Of a sudden he talked nice and soft like at the kitchen door. "Just hang onto hit. Buy yourself a new dress. A pair of shoes. Some food for this boy here and for your Momma. I won't tell a soul. Honest to God. I'll fix up the book so's everything's fine. Just don't you worry 'bout it." He touched Ludy's hair. Ludy jumped quick.

"No," she said. "No." She moved off quick—Benjie alone.

"I never wanna do that again," Ludy said. She covered her face and the shoulders went shaking.

The insurance man pulled off his tie and stuck it in the coat. "Get rid of this boy," he said. His breath went fast again.

"No," Ludy said. "Please, Mr. Tate, suh. Please—"

Benjie was shaking in the knees. Soon it be too late for the bathroom. He squeezed tight but the scared stayed anyway.

The insurance man went to the door and looked through the rainbow spaces. He broke wind. "Send him outside," he said. "I ain't got all damn day."

Benjie turned his face. He didn't want the insurance man to see him cry. Of a sudden he wished he was a bad nigger. He wished he had a knife. He wondered if the insurance man truly had the pistol. The scared came worse. Him and Ludy buried with Momma in the cold ground.

"I never wanna do it again," Ludy said. "Never. Please, suh."

The insurance man looked at Ludy. He laughed loud. "That's what they all say. Let's stop fooling 'round now."

"Please," Ludy said.

"Go out on the porch, boy," the insurance man said. "Don't make me have to get my pistol to you."

"Stay here, Benjie. Please stay."

Benjie stood tall as he could. "No, suh. I gonna stay with my sistah." He poked his lips out.

The insurance man stood high over him. "You sassing a white man, nigger? I said get out on that porch." He opened the coat quick and Benjie saw a brown leather holster and the pearl handle of a pistol. "See that?" the insurance man said. "You see that, boy?"

Benjie's eyes stuck on it. They couldn't move.

"Well, hit'll put a hole in your head bigger'n your mouth," the insurance man said.

Benjie squeezed his legs hard together. He got out the rabbit's foot.

"Do like I told you," the insurance man said. "You don't want to be a bad nigger, do you?"

"Benjie's just a kid," Ludy said, loud. "Please, Mr. Tate. Please, suh. . . ."

The insurance man stooped quick and took Benjie under the arms and raised him in the air. Benjie tried to get loose. The insurance man shook him hard, then dropped him down on the linoleum. It hurt. The rabbit's foot fell away. "I oughta stomp your ass, you little sonofabitch," the insurance man said. "I oughta put my foot through your goddamned head. Be one less nigger to contend with later."

"Aw right! Aw right!" Ludy was hollering. "Anything. Just don't hurt Benjie."

Benjie got up. He tackled Mr. Tate's leg and held it with all his might—like the time he climbed the fig tree; nobody could make him come down. Hot up there with the ripe figs and June bugs. The limb moved quick and Benjie was falling again. That's how he strained himself; and the tall lump came beside his weewee, and Momma marked it with smut from the botton of the spider. "Don't worry, baby, that'll make it go away," Momma said. Benjie got up and the insurance man pushed him right back down. The door to Momma's room opened, then closed slow—Ludy's face in the narrow crack. Then Ludy reaching for Benjie. Then Ludy gone and only the insurance man's blue eye peering at him. Then the door slammed shut in Benjie's face. He stood up. He sat down. He got the rabbit's foot and his marbles. He looked at Momma's door again. "Puddin'-an'-Tame," he said out loud, to nobody, to nothing, to the green dragonfly on the windowsill where the alley went by bright and yellow. "That's my name. Ask me again and I'll tell you the same." Then quick it came before he could get up. He let out a deep breath and sat very still in the final wet; sat quiet in the warm friendly and did not care that Momma would scold. "Puddin'-an'-Tame. Puddin'-an'-Tame. That's my name. Ask me again and I'll tell you the same."

 **CLARICE**

I hate to say it but he's no good. It's true. There's a demon in him violating his soul, eroding him. Something deep down making him lie and cheat and destroy what's good. As much as he hangs around next door at the freedom house—nosing in their business and acting crazy—I think in his heart he despises them. This morning I said to him, "I'm going with those freedom fighters to Duncan Park tomorow." He gave me that crazy knowing look and said, "They be dead." Then he went to his beating his bare chest with his fists like he does when the lightnin' has him feeling crazy. "Me know," he said. "Me Zenola. Boom! No more trouble."

"What do you mean?" I said to him. He gave me that look again, his head cocked to one side and his eyes wild and fixed on me. Then he laughed and put on the clean shirt I'd just ironed for him. Without buttoning it, he went out the door and up the alley, the shirttail flapping behind him and him yelling curses into every house.

When Angie came home from cleaning, I told her what Zenola said and she said, "Yes'm, that's the word. And we living right next door."

And I said, "But you mean they would kill them? They would actually bomb those sweet children?"

"But they not 'fraid," she said. " 'Cause the white folks been saying all summer they'd blow them up."

"But Zenola knows something," I said. "This time may be different."

"Yes'm," she said. "That's the word. But they ain't 'fraid."

I took out my Bible then and began to read from Job. I got down on my knees in pure misery and prayed for them— for all of them who would march for freedom tomorrow.

 CAL

Last time they said they gon' blow us up we believed them. Like we expected, nothing happened. Bluffing again like they mostly do. But you never know for sure whether they will. Like last year in McComb, for an instance. The blasts blew out every damn window in our freedom house, plus one whole wall; plus it put two of our best people in the hospital. Cates was one. If you notice him close, he still favors his left leg. And I still got some metal in me. We was all asleep when the blast hit, and all I mostly remember is the sound of glass flying and breaking. A thin high sound—everywhere that sound. I woke up to it—splintering and shattering against everything. And folks screaming, running in the dark through the plaster dust. I was running too. There was just a lot of dust and noise and feet running. And folks coughing and choking. When we got outside, another blast went off and its wind knocked us down. We heard the ones still inside screaming. Myself and this other guy went back in. We found a girl in the kitchen with her foot blown off. We got a tourniquet on her. And we found Cates. He was still unconscious. The ambulance came and took them away. You notice him now, he still favors it.

The Klan's been riding by this house all day with their whip antennas stuck up in the air like cat-o'-nine-tails, radioing information on us. Mostly it's to scare us. But here if you're a scared niggah, you's most likely a dead one 'fore long. They get them first. Tonight we plan to leave somebody guarding the house while we're up at the church. Probably Cates, 'cause he'll still be working on the truck. What them dumb motherfuckers don't understand though is that even if they blow us to kingdom come, it ain't gon' stop this Movement. They already missed their chance. Ain't nothing gon' turn it 'round now. The wheels are going too fast.

 **CATES**

Ditty-ditty dum. Ditty-ditty dum. Ditty-ditty dum. Ditty-ditty dum. It keeps going in my head like that, this rhythm. Real slow. Like something in me walking slow, making me forget things I know real good. And last night I woke up and sat straight up in bed in the quiet and heard this rhythm again clearer than ever—me and the dark and this beat, never stopping, never once changing. I knew then it was my life rhythm, my self—my basic beat. It musta always been with me but I only started hearing it 'bout two weeks ago. Ditty-ditty dum. Ditty-ditty dum. Ditty-ditty dum. Like something in me walking slow, or something slow-walking me; the first four notes the same and the beat equal on the last note, which dropped off lower. Then a pause, and it repeated: Ditty-ditty dum. Ditty-ditty dum. I swear, it was the damndest feeling; spooky sitting there alone in the dark listening and feeling this great understanding that each and every one of us had it, and it was slow-walking us all. And as I peered into the dark I saw this silver-colored vine growing up out of nothing. The bottom end coming up out of nothing and the top disappearing again into nothing. So the part of vine I saw stood alone, suspended in the air. It looked 'bout six feet long; twisted and tortured and sometimes turning back on itself; then running straight for a little bit, then another hard twist, then a dip, then a hook, then another short straight piece. And near the very top—just 'fore it disappeared into the dark—it turned down sharp, almost bending back on itself. Then it was gone. And all the time in the still that same rhythm kept going, drumming in me, slow-walking, descending on me: Ditty-ditty dum. Ditty-ditty dum.

Ditty-ditty dum. I laid back feeling wide and hollow; as though my self had left my body and I was just a beat somewhere—a simple rhythm among so many. *Ditty-ditty dum. Ditty-ditty dum. Ditty-ditty dum. . . .*

 **PERCY**

"**H**ell no," I said to Dudley. "I wouldn't sell that crazy nigger no dynamite. I don't blame you for doing what you did. I'd have done the same. I wouldn't want a part in something like that either. Thanks for calling me." I had no sooner hung up the phone when the bell hooked to the front door rang and he came walking into the store. I hurried out front to wait on him 'fore George, my helper, could get to him. I didn't want him opening his mouth 'bout the dynamite.

"Good day," I said, going up to him. Then I said, low, "I know what you've come for. Just don't open your damn mouth and I'll get it for you. You understand me?"

He nodded his head and reached in his pocket and came out with a twenty-dollar bill. "Me Zenola," he said. "No more trouble. Boom sticks. Me. . . ."

"Never mind," I said. "Just give me the money and wait right here. Don't you budge 'til I come back. You hear me?"

He nodded his head.

I took the twenty and went to the cash register and rung up a sale. I got his change out and stuck it in my shirt pocket. Then I went back and broke out four sticks of dynamite, some caps and fuses, and wrapped it all up in some brown paper and tied it with string. When I went back out front, he hadn't moved from the door. I handed him the package.

"If you ever so much as breathe a word to anybody as to where you got this, I'll personally see that your balls are cut off and rolled down St. Catherine Street. You hear me?"

He nodded his head.

"Now get out of here," I said. "And don't ever set foot in here again." I opened the door for him and he walked out and headed down Main Street toward nigger town.

When I went back behind the counter, George was filing the rough edges off a key he had just cut.

"Wasn't that that crazy nigger, Zenola?" he said.

"Yeah," I said. "Ain't he funny-looking?"

"He's a sight," George said. We laughed. Then George said, "What'd he want?"

"Oh, he said he was doing some plumbing. I sold him four inch-an'-a-half elbow joints and a Stillson wrench."

"He's sure a crazy one," George said, looking at me funny.

"That he is," I said. Then I remembered his change. I went in my shirt pocket where I'd put it. I took it out and rung up No Sale on the cash register, and stuck the bills back in the drawer. "Yeah, he's a crazy sonofabitch," I said to George. "I wouldn't trust him far as I could chuck him."

"He's lucky you found them elbows," George said. "Last time I looked, we were all out of inch-an'-a-halfs. I just sent in a order yesterday for more." He looked at me funny again and blew the filings off the key.

"You look after things," I said. "I'm going back in the office and work on the books a while." I went into the office and shut the door behind me and leaned my back against it. My chest was going a mile a minute. I took out my pocket handkerchief and wiped the sweat off my face. It had got hot-ter'n hell all of a sudden.

 **CATES**

I went up the hill Wednesday night to see Aurabelle. I'd been working on the truck all day, thinking 'bout her. For twenty-two, I been around a lot but I never been with one like her. All summer I been passing her shack and speaking— she sitting on her porch but barely nodding her head to speak back. All summer. I even bought her a box of candy in the beginning, and took it up the hill and gave it to her. "Here's a little present," I said, standing in the yard by the porch railing. "I hope you like choc'late." She gave me that little-bitty nod again, pushing her hair back out of her eyes and looking at me evil.

"You come for business?" she said. "Don't you know the rules? We don't 'low no white men in this house."

"I came to talk to you," I said. "I want to be your friend."

She wouldn't say another word, just handed me back the candy and went in the house. After that I passed every day and spoke, and she'd nod a little more friendly than before, but still not opening her durn mouth.

Well, two days ago, Wednesday, I had been working on that truck and thinking hard 'bout her and trying not to hear this rhythm going through my head all the time. I knew I could finish the brakes and pack that ailing front-wheel bearing by Thursday noon. Then I planned to drive up to Jackson with our short-wave radio and get it checked by headquarters people. It's been on the blink off and on for a month now, needing parts. Jackson's 'bout a hundred miles northeast of here, and a right nice ride if you got company. And since I was coming back that same evening, I figgered Aurabelle might like to ride up with me. Get away from this stinking hill. So Wednesday night, when I finished the brakes, I washed up,

put on some clean clothes, and walked up the alley to ask her. It took all the nerve I could muster. And before I left the house something said to me, Put some money in your pocket, Pete; just in case. All I had was a fin, so I took it.

PEAVINE

Now I remember good. It *was* Wednesday night when I got that cold, low-down feeling. I remember 'cause it was the same night that white boy, Pete, came up the hill to see Aurabelle. I had just bid four and we'd started the next game of whist when somebody knocked on the door.

"Who's that?" I said, whispering and reaching for my likker.

Aurabelle got up and looked out the window, peeking from behind the shade. "That white boy," she said. "The one what fixes their truck."

"Who's truck?"

"The freedom riders' truck."

"What he coming here for? You don't 'low white men. . . ?"

"Lemme go see," she said. "Put up the cards and make like we's just talking."

"Wait," I said. "I got a business, you know. I don't want none of them seeing me here."

"You just come by to play cards," she said, "and drink some lightnin."

"I know but—"

"Then go out the back door," she said. "Hurry up."

I looked at her like she was my own daughter, and of a sudden I felt terrible; that same low feeling again nudging

against my navel. I took a swig from the quart jar of lightnin'
and started for the back door. I was feeling kinda lit.
"Where'd I park my car?" I said.

"Up on St. Catherine Street," she said. "In front of your
shop. When you coming back?"

" 'Fore Sunday," I said. "Who's winning?"

"I am," she said. Then she laughed.

"Bring me some new ones," she said. "These is ruint. Too
much of your bad dealing." She laughed.

Then he knocked again.

"Bye," she said. "Watch out for the chicken shit crossing
the yard."

"I will," I said and slipped her three dollars for the liquor
and went out the door and made my way across the yard and
up the hill to St. Catherine Street in the dark. "Nobody can
make me," I was thinking. "If I don't wanna go, cain't a damn
soul make me."

CATES

I knocked twice. A light was on. I was 'bout to leave when
the door opened. She stood in it, a kerosene lamp burning
on a table behind her. The bed was unmade. There was only
one window.

"What you want?" she said.

"I came to see you 'bout something," I said. She looked at
me with eyes gone way back in her head, dry, hateful. The
kerosene lamp was smoking.

" 'Bout what? Freedom talk?" she looked both ways out

the alley. "Don't you know the rules?" Then she pulled me by the arm. "Hurry up and come in 'fore somebody sees you."

The room smelled heavy: cooking grease, kerosene. The lamp gave off a yellow light. I looked around: a single chair, an empty china closet, an old television set, some comic books scattered on the floor near the head of the bed. The back door was open.

"Lemme see your money," she said. She went and closed the door and came back.

"It's 'bout tomorrow," I said. "You ever been to Jackson?"

"Lemme see the money," she said.

I reached in my pocket and handed her the fin. Part of me was afraid.

"It's only two dollars," she said. " 'Less you want some lightnin'. Liquor's three dollars more."

"No," I said. "But just keep it."

Suspicion on her face. "What you pulling?" she said.

I said nothing. She put the money in the roll of her stocking.

"Aw right," she said. "You ready?"

I said nothing.

She started taking off her clothes, slow, blouse first. Shoulders. Smooth. Black. She never took her eyes off me. She slipped her skirt down and stepped out of it and stood in front of me with only her stockings on.

"Wait a minute," I said. "You ever been to Jackson?"

She moved to the table where the lamp was. "On or off?" she said. That part of me was still afraid. I had never been with one like her.

"Off," I said.

He comes up the alley Wednesday night and knocks on my door, standing there looking scared when I open it. So I tells the damn fool to come in 'fore somebody sees him. We ain't 'lowed no white men inside the house, but I figger I could turn this trick quick 'fore Mamie Lee got home from church. Her go every Wednesday night. Lord knows why. She's sho going straight to Hell when she die. Well he comes in and stands in the middle of the room looking 'round like he ain't never been in a poor-assed niggah shack before; standing there, big, dumb-looking, and needing a shave. Something in me is saying, Give the motherfucker the pussy and send him outta here. And something else in me is feeling sorry for him, saying, He ain't a bad fella, as they go. And he do truly like you. Why you so hateful to him?

"Lemme see the money," I says. He looks straight at me with them piercing eyes like a bird's. Something in me goes soft and I says to myself quick, Don't let this motherfucker fool you. They's all no good. A man's a man. I go and close the back door and come back.

"It's 'bout tomorrow," he says. "You ever been to Jackson?"

He's looking at me like I ain't never been looked at. Something in me say, Aurabelle, you ain't even combed your hair all day. Then I cain't hardly stand the way he's staring with them eyes like a eagle's. 'Course I been to Jackson, I'm thinking. Momma Mamie Lee take me six years ago when I'm ten. We ride the Greyhound all the way; me sitting next to the window in the last seat. What he think, I never been off this hill? Shit.

"Lemme see the money," I says. He reach in his pocket and come out with a five-dollar bill; crisp and folded neat, like that's all he got. Then I think, Maybe he want some lightnin' too.

"It's only two dollars," I says. " 'Less you want some lightnin'. Liquor's three dollars more."

"No," he says. "But just keep it."

I take the five-dollar bill and I'm thinking, Maybe this slick motherfucker made it hisself.

"What you pulling?" I says. He don't say nothing, but looks at me with his face gone soft, and his mouth half open like he's 'bout to say something. Remind me of the way some fellas look when they gon' do it for the first time. I fold the five-dollar bill tight and roll it in my stocking. "Aw right," I tells him. "You ready?" I starts taking off my clothes, real slow. He just stands there watching. He don't make a move, not a finger or a eye-lash. But he's breathing hard. I'm thinking, Maybe it's the first time with a black woman. I oughta charge him seven. Then something say, But he do like you. And he brung you that choc'late candy at the beginning of the summer. And you do like him a little bit, don't you? Then something in me say quick, Hell no. I don't like no motherfucking man. They's all no good. Then I'm standing in front of him naked 'cept for my stockings. He still got all his clothes on. He's breathing real heavy, but there ain't nothing showing in front. I know then for sure he's scared and I'd better turn out the lamp.

"Wait a minute," he says. "You ever been to Jackson?"

I don't say nothing but move to where the lamp is. "On or off?" I says, knowing. He looks at the bed. "Off," he says, his voice high in his throat. I blow out the lamp and go let the shade up a little, then lay down on the bed, listening to him breathing hard, pulling at his brogans in the dark. I feel tickled, but something in me say, Don't laugh him down. Give him something he'll never forget. Then he comes to me in the bed and puts his arms around me and holds me tight— and something say, Aurabelle, honey, you ain't never had one like this; he truly cares for you. Don't hardly nobody care for you. Then I get a hold of myself and I say out loud, "You put a rubber on?"

"Hold me tight," he says. "Please hold me tight." Then he don't say nothing and I hold him tight. I believe he's crying. I just keep holding him tight. In the quiet I hear a spigot dripping in the kitchen and a hen clucking under the porch, and the crickets loud outside in the grass. I hold him tight. Then something in me say, That better not be no counterfeit five-dollar bill. And why the hell he keep asking if I ever been to Jackson?

**CATES**

Heavy kerosene dark. Moonlight coming through the only window. Aurabelle naked on the bed. I held her tight—her eyes wide open. I felt her soften for a minute, then she went hard again, her body stiff and unfriendly against me. Then my dead mother commenced to lay heavy on my mind. My eyes burned.

"You put a rubber on?" Aurabelle said.

Canvas and rope to lower us, Mother. Case us in wood and soft gray velvet, Mother. Clothe us, cushion us, then send us back forever to the unremitting Mother.

"Hold me tight," I said. "Please hold me tight."

We come out of the woods and stand at the edge of a low bluff overlooking Sloane Hollow. In her hair Parnell has a pale blue flower that quivers in the wind.

"Who's Michael?" I say. She flushes and looks off down the hill.

"A boy I used to know. This motorcycle accident two years ago. They found us in a ditch. Michael was already dead. It was raining."

"I'm sorry," I say. "I should know better. Let's go down," I say. "See how the folks're doing." She nods and follows me along a path down the steep incline to Sloane Hollow; just a cluster of wooden shacks set in a clearing. Above the sagging tin roofs, TV antennae stand rigid, erect, incongruous. Children see us approaching and run to meet us, their bare legs and arms powdered red with dust.

"Gimme chewing gum. Gimme a nickel," they cry. Parnell stoops and hugs two young boys. They giggle, playing with her braid.

"Y'all wanna march for freedom tomorrow?" she says, her voice slipping into a drawl.

"Sho!" they say. "Sho!"

"When do you want your freedom?" Parnell says, shouting.

"Now! Now!" they chant.

"And how you gonna get it?"

"March for it! March for it!" They laugh and jump about.

"Come, then," Parnell says, standing up and leading them off. "Let's talk with your Mommas about marching for freedom." They follow her. She looks back at me. "Why don't you see if *you* can budge Old Man Simons," she says. "We've given up."

I stand a few moments more in the hot sun watching them go, then start down the line of shanties toward the last one. Mr. Simons sits on his porch, rocking. A closed Bible rests on his lap. When he sees me, he waves. I wave back, thinking of the last time I paid him a visit—more than a month ago. We talked aimlessly, offhanded, about his collard patch, the weather, and the termites. We made tentative friends. Yet even then I sensed in him a presumption—that since I was black I should not only understand his reticence, but should also find it justifiable. Of course I understood his fears all too well, for they were my own. But to reinforce them by agreeing to their validity seemed contrary to what we hoped to accomplish. So I had not brought the matter up.

As I approach his shack this time I decide to ask him outright to join us tomorrow. And if he refuses to do that, then perhaps at least he'll register to vote. But since no one has succeeded with him all summer, I don't feel particularly optimistic.

"Afternoon," I say, turning into his yard and mounting the porch steps. He waves again. "Hotter'n a bitch, ain't it?" he says, laying the Bible aside. He leans forward and spits over the railing into the yard, the tobacco juice slipping through the sunlight like a squirt of brown water from a toy pistol. It rolls in the dust, making reddish-brown beads. I look at his hands on the railing. They almost match the wood of the porch—ashen, dusty; like the silver-gray patina of old driftwood. He sits back in his chair, scrutinizing me, his huge anguished eyes rheumy and the lenses fogged with grayish-blue cataracts. His eyes somehow make me feel defensive and I look off toward the bluff and the woods.

"Damn if this ain't a spell," he says. "Keeps up much longer, we'll have them flash fires again. As 'tis you cain't hardly light a match without burning yourself up."

"Even worse in town," I say, wiping the sweat.

"You gotta know how to move in it," he says. "Cain't move too fast or you'll pass out. Best not to move at all. Look here," he says, "where you fellas been keeping yourself? Don't see you 'round much as I use'ta."

"Maybe you've heard about the demonstration tomorrow," I say. "We've been working to get it together."

"Sure I heard. But I don't believe it. I give y'all credit for having more sense. College and all." He looks at me. "Is it a fact?"

"Yes, sir. Tomorrow afternoon. And we need plenty of help."

He nods agreement, then looks out toward the woods. "Y'all need all the luck you can get, too." He leans forward and spits, his hands gripping the banister, his wide, thin shoulders hunching. I can tell he was a big man. But now the plaid sport shirt and baggy trousers hang off him like flags on a windless day. He sits back. "I use'ta could hit a roach on the dead run in the dark at ten feet. Where you from, son?"

"New York City," I say. "Manhattan."

"Never been to either one. You know something? I'd sho like to go to New York City 'fore I die." Finally he notices me standing. "Sit. Rest yourself. Too damn hot to be standing up," he says, pointing to an empty chair beside him. It has only three legs. "Lean back on it," he says. "Don't worry, it'll be all right."

"Got a few minutes to talk?" I say, sitting and tipping the chair back.

"Sure. For a freedom rider, boy, I got all the time in the world. You say you from New York City?"

"Yes, sir. That's right."

"I knowed a niggah once. He left the Hollow and went up to New York City. Come back here lying his ass off. Never did hear lies like that. Telling 'bout all the fine women he'd slept with. And 'bout them skyscraper buildings. Said they's so high you cain't see the ground when you's up on top of 'em."

He turns his enormous eyes on me, then abruptly says, "Let's stop kidding. Y'all keep coming 'round 'cause you wanna talk me into registering to vote, don't you? And maybe now you want me to go on that demonstration tomorrow. Ain't that right? Duncan Park, right?"

I nod yes. "That's right. I came to ask you to help us. We can come get you in the truck. Bring you back here when the demonstration's over. What about it? Will you help?"

"Well, you ain't the first," he says, ignoring the question. "Every damn one of 'em been here trying to get me to register. I figgered they'd of give up by now."

I sigh deep and take out my cigarettes and offer him one. He takes it. I light it and one for myself and we smoke awhile.

"One thing I'll say for you," he says finally. "You don't seem like the others. They're pushy. You know what I mean? Full of a lot of claptrap and drummer talk. Least you don't make a big fuss 'bout how I oughta be doing this and that for the Negro race."

All his teeth are missing and he pokes the cigarette squarely into a tight little hole formed by his lips as they pucker like the mouth of a drawstring pouch.

"What do them white chil'ren know 'bout life for a black man here? A black man *anywhere?* I cain't just jump up and run down to the city hall and register 'cause *they* tell me to. More to it. A *heap* more. Black folks 'round here get killed for less. You're a colored man, you oughta know."

He looks out past the bluff toward the woods again. I look too, knowing. Then he picks up the Bible and opens it. "This is from Job," he explains, his eyes directed at the page but not seeming to focus on the words. " '. . . *Who wast thou when I laid the foundations of the earth?*' " he says and closes the Bible slow and looks at me. "Where you freedom riders been so long? Where was you all these years when niggahs was getting lynched in them woods yonder; throwed in that Mississippi, in the Pearl, the Tallahatchie, and the Yazoo? Where was all this civil rights stuff when *I* was a young man?"

He holds those eyes to me, huge, sad, luminous. I say nothing. Then he looks in the direction of the river.

"Throwed in the Mississippi, I say. Chained and beat and dragged. Naw, I ain't 'bout to go to no Duncan Park with y'all. I ain't 'bout to vote, neither." He pauses, excited. Then he begins to calm down. Finally he says quietly, "Look here, sonny. You's colored like me. I know you understand what I'm talking 'bout. But them others—What do they know? Come the end of summer, where'll they be? Right back up North with their feet stuck under somebody's table—eatin' good, livin' good. Where'll the rest of us be? Still right here amongst these hateful white folks. Devils! Don't go deceiving yourself, boy. Ain't nothing gon' change 'til all folks get the hate outta their hearts. And that ain't gon' be no time soon, 'cause people are vile as snakes. 'Specially white folks. Don't you tell me nothing 'bout them. I know 'em. When it comes to us they's the hatefulest things God ever put on this earth."

He sits straight up in his chair, pinching the cigarette butt hard. "Son, I'd really like to help, but I tell you the truth: I just cain't move. I feel like a man froze in his tracks. I cain't even read or write. Ain't never voted in my life. Ain't never so much as sassed a white man, 'cept once. And you talking 'bout voting—"

"We'll be right there with you. See that nobody hurts you," I say. "Just come down to the city hall with me. Just make yourself do it. You'll feel a lot better. Just try. I'll stand there in the line beside you. Look out for you. Just try. Please."

His whole face seems to slump. He looks at me. "I just cain't, son. I cain't move no more. It's too late for me now." He puts one hand on my knee. "But once I was braver than either my Daddy or my Momma." His voice sounds distant, his eyes vacant. "I *was*. . . . Honest I was. Lemme tell you a story. Ain't told none of the rest. But I'll tell you; you's colored like me. I ain't had no spirit for white folks since the year I was twelve—more'n sixty years ago. My Daddy raised cotton. He'd raised seventy-two bales that year. Just 'fore Christmas we carried 'em to market, hauled 'em twenty miles in a mule cart, knowing we was gon' get money to buy food and clothes for the winter. Maybe even get Momma some nice present for Christmas.

"When we get to market the white man says to my Daddy, 'You done well, Jack.' That was my Daddy's name. Well, I felt good then, 'cause I knowed we was gon' get some money. But then the white man says, 'Now you's outta debt.' I knowed then we wasn't getting *none*. The white man commenced to messing with the figures in a ledger book. Then he says to my Daddy, 'How much you think you got coming, Jack?' Daddy didn't say a word, just kept his eyes to the floor. Then the white man says to me, 'Boy, how much you think your Daddy gon' get?' I looked at the white man, my eyes brimming. 'None,' I says. 'He ain't gon' get *none*.' Well, the white man turned red as that rooster out yonder and slammed the ledger shut. 'We's even,' he says. 'You done well, Jack.' And you know he didn't give my Daddy a cent either.

"We rode that twenty miles back home not saying a word—my Daddy not even looking at me. When we got to the house he run right in and told my Momma what happened. She come out and tore the shirt off my back and dragged me into the front yard and commenced to giving me the worst whupping I ever got. She beat me with a birch switch thick as your little finger, whaling it down hard on me—it coming outta the sky like the wrath of the Lord was on it. I never seen her so mad. I never felt such pain from her hand. Every time she hit me she'd holler, 'That'll teach you to sass white folks! That'll teach you . . . ! That'll teach you . . . ! That'll teach you . . . !' It was the last time I ever talked back to a white man."

He pauses and sighs and a whiff of stale breath comes through the charged air. I look away. How could I have come sooner? Our eyes lock again. We say nothing. I get up to leave.

"Wait a minute," he says. "Where you going? Be still. Rest yourself. Lemme tell you another one. I got plenty."

I start down the steps into the yard. Then I have it under control and I look at him.

"Hey," he calls, "ain't you gon' try talking me into voting? Into going with you fellas tomorrow?" He's grinning now, toothless and certain.

"No," I say. "No, sir. I'm not."

"Well, what 'bout letting me hold another one of those ready rolls 'fore you go?"

I force a grin and go over to the porch railing and hand him the whole pack. "Keep it," I say. "I'll get more."

"Much obliged," he says. "You're a nice young fella. Thanks for stopping by. Always enjoy talking to you college fellas."

"So long," I say. "I'll come back. We'll talk some more."

"Anytime. Just don't forget to bring some more of these ready rolls." He grins again, that same toothless, shrewd grin.

I cross the yard and head down the row of shacks, not looking back. Ahead, beneath a tall oak tree, Parnell stands talking with some children. When she sees my face, she knows. We say good-bye to the kids and promise to pick them up tomorrow in the truck. We head back up the slope, this time taking the main road into town. My head is going very fast again. It goes *click, click, click*. . . .

BENJIE

The notebook was on the table with the white straw hat. The door to Momma's room still shut. Benjie licking his thumb like the insurance man, turning the pages. All the pages. *Where Momma in the cold ground?* The book back down and

Benjie into the kitchen. Bacon and molasses still on the table. Ants in the molasses. Benjie climbed on the chair to the shelf where Momma's empty preserves jars. Down again with the jar. Then the ice pick, hitting air holes through the tin lid. Back to the front room with the jar. Benjie looked at the notebook and the hat. Then the straw hat on his head and down over his ears. Benjie put the hat back and picked up the notebook. He turned all the pages. *Where Momma in the cold ground?* Benjie put the notebook down and went looking for Momma's strawberry pin cushion. He found it and pulled out every straight pin. He looked at Momma's door. He looked at the notebook. The colors tried to run but he caught them and wiped. Benjie picked up the notebook. He took it and the preserves jar and the straight pins and ran out the front door into the bright alley. Benjie ran down the hill toward the ghost house, stopping at every hedge, bush, and flower. Soon he had six June bugs in the jar. He put grass on the bottom so they could crawl and eat. He stuck a straight pin through each one's back and screwed the lid tight. The colors again—this time before he could catch them, and them running, and him running too, and looking through the rainbows at the June bugs with the daggers sticking out.

 **PEAVINE**

It musta been 'round ten o'clock when I got home Wednesday night, 'cause Rosalee's club meeting was already over. She was clearing up the dishes, and I was thinking 'bout Aurabelle and that white boy, Pete—and 'bout the civil righters. It was sho aggravating me, weighing heavy on my mind. When I walked in, she took one look and said, "What's ailing you, niggah? You look like you just lost your teeth again." She laughed.

"Nothing," I said. "Where's James Junior?"

"Out somewhere. You think all I got to do is follow behind him? He's a man now, honey. Be eighteen next month."

I switched on the color television set and screwed the dial around. "You don't have to tell me how old he is. Ain't I the one got to cough up a thousand dollars for his college? Don't you think I know how old he is?" Wasn't nothing on worth watching, so I turned it off.

"What the devil is ailing you, man? You come in here looking like who-the-hell-woulda-thought-it and smelling like a damn busted distillery. And you wanna start a argument."

"I ain't starting a argument. I'm just asking where my son is. If a man cain't ask a simple question after he works all day behind a barber chair, then what the hell is there for him?"

She had walked out the room into the kitchen and I heard her slamming stuff. She came back and emptied the ashtrays and piled them up and took them back into the kitchen and started slamming stuff again. I went and stood in the door.

"You keep throwing it like that," I said, "we'll be eating outta our hands!"

She walked past me and back into the living room and I followed her. She began straightening the pillows on the settee, and I waited 'til she finished, then I sat down on it. She put her fists on her hips and looked at me evil.

"Look, niggah. I'm too tired and sleepy to fight with you tonight. Every time you get the least bit likkered up, you get your ass up on your shoulders. You got something to say, say it. But don't follow behind me picking a argument, 'cause I'm tired and sleepy."

I looked at her standing there all dressed up and with her hair looking pretty the way she had it swept up off her neck;

and I commenced to feeling worse. I got up and went to her and put my arms around her.

"I'm sorry," I said. "I don't mean it. It's just that I'm feeling bad 'bout all this trouble—"

"We all feel bad," she said. "Each and every one of us." She put her head on my shoulder. "And this heat ain't helping nothing."

"I sho wish it was over," I said.

Then she looked at me, her face worried. "James Junior says he's going on the demonstration."

I couldn't even speak. I pulled her down on the settee beside me and we just sat there for a little while without talking. Then I took her hand and held it and I said, "It's like somebody is tearing my house down with me still inside. Everywhere I look the walls're falling and there ain't nothing but bad weather past the door."

"I know," she said. "To work and save so long for what we got, then lose it—"

"Well, I for one ain't going on that demonstration," I said.

"It don't matter," she said. "The freedom riders'll keep on 'til they rile these white folks so bad there won't be an end to the trouble. Every one of us'll be in it."

"Damn if I'll be in it," I said. "James Junior ain't really going with them, is he?"

"That's what he said today. And lately he's been hanging 'round down at the freedom house too."

"Damn if he ain't gon' ruin his chances for school." I got up and walked back and forth across the living room. "My own son. After all I tried to do for him. Tried to give him what I didn't have. What the hell can a man do—"

Rosalee got up and went back into the kitchen and I heard her running water in the sink. I went to the door and looked in. "You ain't gon' start doing dishes *now*, is you? Cain't they wait 'til in the morning? Here I'm trying to talk to you and you messing with some damn dishes. Ain't there nobody I can talk to? Here I stand ten hours a day behind a barber chair and come home and cain't talk to a soul. And I ain't going on that demonstration, either. That's all there is to it. That's final."

She looked at me, calm, her hands dipped in the dishwater. "Then don't go," she said. "Why you keep talking 'bout it. Nobody asked you to go. I said James Junior was going."

"Well, I won't," I said, not able to keep my voice down. "Goddammit, I won't."

"Then don't," she said. "Just go upstairs to bed and leave me alone. I'm tired. I don't feel like arguing."

I turned to leave. "They cain't make me," I said. "Nobody can make me. I've a mind of my own."

"I'll be up in a minute," she said. "Your white shirt for tomorrow is on the bureau. Good night, honey."

I felt like a dog. "A man oughta be able to come home to his own house and talk to somebody," I said.

She didn't answer me. I went on upstairs and sat on the edge of the bed for a few minutes, then I got up and went to the bathroom. Then I got in bed and laid there thinking. Rosalee came up and got ready for bed and turned out the light. I laid there in the dark for a long time. I was even thinking, Maybe we should move to another town. I could open up a shop somewhere else. But hell, what guarantee would I have that they wouldn't come there too? This thing was all over. Where could I run to get away from it? Rosalee started snoring and I laid there listening to it rising and falling in the dark, almost seeing it—like chips of wood flying off a buzz saw. It was damn near morning when I finally closed my eyes. Hell, I just wish things could be like they used to be. That's all.

❧ PUDDIN' HEAD

Me and Lollypop Johnson were shooting marbles when we seen him come running down the hill. He was toting this jar full of June bugs and a little black book, and crying; and the beetles had pins stuck in them. Then he goes in the ghost shack and don't come back out, so we go in after him. He was sitting in a corner with the jar on the floor. I had five marbles and a ring that shines in the dark. Lollypop had the slingshot he made yesterday. We wanted the book bad. We went over to him and I showed him my ring.

"You wanna trade?" I say. "Where you get that book? And why you put pins in them bugs? Was they bothering you?"

"Yeah, why you sticking pins in them poor bugs?" Lollypop say.

"They can still fly," Benjie say. "Look."

He chunks one in the air and it takes off out the door and over the trees, flying with the pin sticking straight out its back like a real dagger. He keep doing that 'til every beetle is gone and he's crying the whole time. Me and Lollypop both twelve and Benjie's just a kid. So we wait for him to stop, wishing he'd hurry up so's we could see what was in that book. When he stop, I show him my ring again.

"I'll trade you," I say. "This ring and these here marbles for that book. And Lollypop's got a new slingshot. We'll chunk that in too. Whatcha say, kid?"

He hug the book tight to him and goes to crying again. "This where my Momma's money," he say. "Where her in the cold ground."

Lollypop scratched his head and I just looked at him. "I'm your good friend, ain't I?" I say. "Puddin' Head Jones.

You know I wouldn't hurt your Momma. Lemme see that book. Lemme see where her in the cold ground."

He hand me the book and I look in it and see names of a bunch of folks I know. Folks living right on this alley. There Miss Pritchard was, and on another page my own Momma; and sho 'nough a few mo' pages back there was Miss Bertha. And a bunch of numbers was writ down the side of every page. "Who this book is?" I say. "Where you get it?"

He goes to shaking his head and stops crying. Then Lollypop wants a look in the book and tries to snatch it outen my hand, but I pulls back hard. Then the pages start spilling out and we goes to laughing and jumping 'round and the pages they flipping in the air like the Fourth of July.

Then Benjie say, "It's Mr. Tate's book."

We stopped dead still. Lawd have mercy, I'm thinking, and look at Lollypop who's already down on his knees picking up the sheets, but some are already blowed out the door and tumbling down the alley.

"Oh, shit," I say. "Whyn't you tell us 'fore we tore it to pieces?"

"It's my Momma in the cold ground," he say. "Me and Ludy is shot dead 'cause I's a bad nigger."

I ain't hardly listening to his funny talk now. I'm down on both knees with Lollypop trying to pick up what sheets I can find. "C'mon," I say. "Benjie, don't you tell on us. C'mon and help us get this book back together." Then we's all three on our hands and knees crawling 'round, but it ain't much use 'cause they's blowing out the door fast as we picking 'em up. Then I hear some loud footsteps out on the porch and I say, "Hush, y'all, somebody's coming."

"Lawd, it's the end for us," Lollypop says. "It's Mr. Tate and he's gon' shoot us dead with his pistol."

I grabs Benjie and we all run into the next room where it's real dark and peek back out into the other room.

"Take off that durn ring!" Lollypop say. "It's shining in the dark!"

I take it off and put it in my pocket and we keep peeking. And then I'm thinking 'bout all the times we looked for ghosts here and that maybe one's looking for us now and I start to be afraid. But just then I see a man come in the open door and at first I cain't make him out 'cause the sun is back of him. But then he move further in the house and I see it's Mr. Zenola. And he's carrying something under his arm. Then he comes in more and I see it's a package and its wrapped in some brown paper with a white string around it. I hunch Lollypop in the rib and he look at me and even in the dark I can see his eyes are scared. I still got hold of Benjie and I can feel he's scared too. I'm not scared no more 'cause I see it ain't Mr. Tate and it ain't no ghost. Nobody's scared of Mr. Zenola—he just crazy.

Well, he stand there looking 'round, then he look up the stairs to the attic. Nobody got the nerve to climb them stairs 'cause they ready to fall most anytime. Then he looks t'ward where we're hiding and starts our way. My chest commenced to jumping into my throat, when of a sudden he stop dead still and look back up the stairs. Then he turn and go to the stairs and test them with his hands, all the time looking up into the dark. Then he eases his weight onto one step and tries it, then another one; then he skip two and try another, and soon he's outta sight up the stairs and we hear him moving 'round over our head.

"I don't know 'bout *you* niggahs, but I'm making a run for it," Lollypop say. "Damn if I'm gon' get caught."

"Naw," I say. "Let's wait. I wanna see what he gon' do." I can feel Benjie shaking and I pat him on the head and give him a little hug. Then we hear Mr. Zenola over us again. Then he's coming down the stairs, moving right nimble like he was climbing trees for the city again. Tipping light like a tomcat on a fence. Then he down again and going out the front door. He ain't got the package with him now. When we's sure he's gone,

I creep back out into the other room and peer out the window through a hole in the dirt. I see him going down the alley toward his house. So then I signal back to Lollypop and Benjie that it's okay and they come running out the other room. I go over and test the stairs, figgering if they can hold a grown man they oughta hold me. But they is mighty rickety.

"You ain't gonna climb them stairs, is you?" Lollypop says.

"If he done it, I can," I say. "He weigh more'n me. And 'sides, I seen what steps he hit."

"Go 'head then, fool," Lollypop say. He's back down on his knees at the pages again, Benjie beside him.

"My Momma in here," Benjie say. "Where her in the cold ground, Lollypop?" I start climbing the stairs, tipping light on the same steps he use. When I get up there I don't see nothing at first. Then my eyes get used to the dark and I see it in a corner. I go and pick it up and take it out near the window where it's light. Then I untie the string and take off the brown paper careful so's I can put it back like it was. Inside I see these four little red sticks, like little biddy poles. And there's a roll of thick string and some pieces of metal. I never seen nothing look exactly like it before. I reckon it's something crazy he's up to 'cause he's so durn crazy hisself. Then I close it all up again like I find it and tie the string back. Then I tip back downstairs through the spiderwebs.

Lollypop gets up off the floor and say, "What was it, Puddin' Head? Whatcha see, man?"

"T'weren't much of nuthin'," I tells him. "Just four little poles and some string."

"That's all?"

"Yeah," I say. I practice spitting through my teeth.

"What it look like?" Lollypop say. "C'mon, man."

"Nuthin', I told you. They was red. Look sorta like firecrackers, 'cept no wick or nuthin' to light."

"He sho is a fruit," Lollypop say.

"He sho is," I say.

"My Momma's in here," Benjie say. He's still on the floor. "Where her in the cold ground?" He commenced to crying again.

"Cross my heart," I say. "It didn't look like much of nuthin.'" I get down on the floor. "C'mon, y'all, let's get this shit up and get outta here." Lollypop gets back down too.

"Mr. Tate sho gon' miss this book," Lollypop say, laughing.

"Long as he don't know it's us," I say. "He can kiss my ass."

"My Momma's in here," Benjie say. "Where her in the cold ground?"

 **CLARICE**

He comes walking in here about three o'clock, grinning like a Cheshire cat. I was sitting mending socks when he opened the screen door and walked in. He went past me without a word, and into the kitchen where he hides his lightnin'. I've never understood exactly who he's hiding it from, since none of us touch a drop of alcohol. We've enough to do living with his. Well, he goes back there and I can hear him lift the loose floorboard and take out the lightnin' and swig it straight from the jar. Then he puts it back and comes into the front room where I am. He's still grinning.

"You look like you swallowed a pile of goose feathers," I say. "What's so durn funny?"

He doesn't say a word, but goes to the shelves where my books are. They're my only possessions, the dearest things from my other life. Zenola is forever reading them, but we have never once had a discussion. He never buys his own, but carts mine down to the jailhouse. The only book he owns is a dictionary, and he keeps that with him down there.

Well, he goes and takes down my dictionary. Then he stands by the window where the sunlight streams in bright through the curtains. He stands there turning the pages, and I look at him and feel the pity rise in me—thinking again about the man he was. Now: barefooted, his hair wild, his chest struck out and his shirt front open, and him wearing Linwood's britches (he's our fifteen-year-old) and the pants hitting him up around his knees. He's a sorry sight to behold. I look back down at my sewing, neither hating nor loving him; not even feeling contempt anymore—but just pity and a kind of abiding impatience that's harder to bear than contempt.

He begins to read out loud from the dictionary: " '. . . Made of ni . . . tro . . . gleece . . . rin absor . . . bed in a por . . . ous material. . . .' " He closes the book and puts it back on the shelf, then looks at me, grinning again.

"Me Zenola," he says. "Me black king of the mountain. You woman. Get off my land."

"Zenola," I say. "Stop your foolishness and listen to me. If you'll be coming home late tonight, I won't be here to give you supper. I'm going to the prayer meeting and freedom rally at McIver's church. But your supper'll be on the stove. I'll leave a pan of hot water under your plate. The children'll be at the church with me, so you'll have to make do for yourself. Just heat it up. You understand?"

"Zenola understands all things," he says. "You woman. Get off my land. Me black king of the mountain. Yellow next. Then black. First technology. Me Zenola. No more trouble. Ni . . . tro . . . gleece . . . rin. Boomsticks. Broomsticks."

Then he goes to beating his bare chest, beating those old scars that stay red from his pounding. I look away.

"Angie was here a while ago," I say. "She said she heard Josh Thomas was taken out of jail today and carried to the hospital." I look at him quick. He stops beating his chest and his fists hover in the air, and he looks off and down to the side. I went back to my sewing again, knowing it was true.

"That poor young man. He did nothing more serious than driving his car once without a license. And they threw him in jail. And his ailing mother doesn't have money enough to bail him out. What have they done to him, Zenola? Tell me. You know everything that goes on down there. He just sick or hurt bad? Please tell me."

Zenola turns and starts for the door without a word. Then he stops and looks back at me. "Zenola fix soup now. Slop. Slop," he says. "Josh gone forever. No more Judas calling. Zenola make slop, slop. Singing."

Then he goes on out and I put down the sewing and go to the door as fast as I can, and holler through the screen, "What do you mean, gone forever? Zenola! Zenola!" But he goes on down the steps and heads up the alley toward St. Catherine Street, practically running back to the jailhouse. I watch him until he's out of sight, then I go back inside and sit down again. I sit thinking about Josh and looking at the two shelves with my books. My precious books from that other life. I look around at the wallpaper stained brown from rain leaks. I stare at the big blue roses printed on it—blue paper roses blooming on those walls, faded but unwilted. And then I feel the senseless tears come and I know it's time to read from Job again.

We arrive back at the freedom house. Cal and Cates are seated at the desk, fiddling with the short-wave radio. All I hear is static coming through. When we come in, Cal turns and stares at us, looking Parnell up and down. She walks past them toward her room. Cates and Cal are watching me. Cates wears one of those olive drab fatigue suits with the floppy hat. Cal has on a pair of headphones pushed in front of his ears over his temples. His sunglasses have slipped down on his nose. He turns back to the radio, curses and yanks off the headset and throws it down on the desk and stands up. He pivots and looks hard at me, his eyes angry, penetrating. Then he looks back at Cates.

"I carried it to Jackson," Cates says, his voice diffident. "I swear I told them." Then suddenly he looks off absently. "She could of rode up with me but she didn't wanna come."

"What the fuck are you talking 'bout?" Cal says. "Listen, motherfucker. I want this goddamned radio fixed. You hear me? You ain't done nothing 'cept sit on your ass and mope for more'n a week now. If you got troubles, you better talk up and tell somebody. This ain't no game. You better shape the fuck up or pack your goddamned things and leave. You got it straight?" He stands there breathing hard, staring down at Cates.

"I carried it to Jackson," Cates says, still looking off out the window. "I told them to check it out good. That we'd be needing it. You know when I first heard it, I didn't know what it was. But now I think it's my basic rhythm." He looks up at Cal, then at me. Then back at Cal. Cal lets out a deep sigh.

"Look, man," he says. "I'm gon' take my car twenty miles out. My radio works fine. When I get to Fayette, I'll try calling you. If this fucking thing here cain't reach Fayette, you take it back and tell headquarters to give us a good one or shove it up their ass. You hear me?"

Cates nods. Then Cal whirls and faces me again, his eyes above the rim of the sunglasses fixed, immobile, like gray stones cemented in his head. I hear the toilet flush, then Parnell turns on the shower. Cal listens too.

"Where y'all been all damn day?" he says finally, his voice cool and controlled again.

"Sloane Hollow," I say, too fast. I slow down. "We passed out demonstration notices. And Parnell recruited a bunch of folks for tomorrow. But we'll have to pick them up in the truck." Cates gives a little nervous cough and turns back toward the radio. Cal keeps burning his eyes into mine. We're standing looking level at each other. I return his stare as hard as I can so in case he doesn't already know, he won't find it there. Cates starts fiddling with the radio again. Static crackles between our eyes.

"That shouldn't take you all fucking day," he says.

Still he doesn't move his eyes, holding them to mine like he's waiting for me to do or say something wrong. I hold, too, but feeling anxious to look away.

"C'mon," he says. "I want you to ride out to Fayette with me."

"All right," I say. "Whenever you're ready."

"Soon as *you're* ready," he says, his eyes still on me.

"I'm ready," I say.

"You sure?"

"Sure I'm sure. Whadda you mean?"

He pushes the sunglasses up over his eyes slowly. "Maybe you want to change your shirt 'fore we leave."

"My shirt? What's wrong with my shirt?"

"You got Cut-Sue stains all over the back." He turns abruptly and goes out the door, slamming it. Suddenly Cates turns the radio up loud, then turns it down again. I see Cal

through the window, walking to the car, walking stiff and arrogant like a soldier.

"Damn headquarters," Cates says. "They're fucking up worse all the time."

ZENOLA

Jail cells standing. Monkey paws, tin cups. Zenola singing: "Slop. Slop." Dipper into soup bucket. Soup bucket sloshing. Dipper into tin cups splashing. Monkey paws jerking.

"Goddamn you, that shit's hot!" lips and teeth say.

Zenola singing: "Slop. Slop." Josh's cell silent. Piss bucket stinking. Continents gone. Josh gone too, forever. No more Judas calling. Dipper into piss bucket. Dipper into soup bucket. Soup bucket sloshing. Dipper into tin cups splashing. Jail cells silent.

"Me Zenola. Broomsticks. Boomsticks. Broomsticks. Boomsticks. Yellow next. Then black. First technology. Time happens anyway."

Zenola climbing highest tree, baring chest to sun.

He drives like a goddamn fool. I can't keep my eyes off the speedometer. It says seventy and we're still accelerating. The road into Fayette, just two lanes. Like we're flying low over a narrow highway and he's staring straight ahead, sunglasses down on his nose again. He sits like something possessed; fingers almost caressing the wheel, back stiff, straight; eyes fixed on the road, like in a trance. The speedometer says eighty. We come up fast behind a slow-moving trailer truck pulling a long grade. Then we're out in the left lane passing it. Flying. Ahead another car suddenly charges into sight, its front wheels and grille just nipping the crest of the hill, coming straight at us. Then Cal's foot is flat down on the gas and I hear the extra carburetors cut in, opening wide, sucking the air. The speedometer says ninety-five. The other car rushes toward us, and we're still in its lane. He holds his foot on the gas and at the last instant we clear the cab of the trailer truck and he cuts her back into our lane and the oncoming car blurs by—a *swoosh* of metal and color. We top the crest and rush downhill at over a hundred, dusting red rooster combs of clay off the shoulders of the road. Finally he slows down to seventy again.

"Want some toilet paper?" he says, his face cool, expressionless.

"I'll just sit in it," I say, trying not to show fear. Then he catches me by surprise.

"You're fucking her, ain't you?" he says, just like that.

I look straight out the window. I feel like telling him. "Yeah," I say. "Just once."

He slows down more as we come into Fayette. "You know it's against the rules," he says, his eyes hard again. "You want some pussy, get it outside the project. If you get it on the project, you better not let me find out or I'll kick your ass off. Just trouble. We got enough already. Nothing in the goddamned place works." Then he looks over at me, his eyes for once on the verge of smiling. "How was it?" he says. "Can she fuck?"

PARNELL

Dear Mom and Dad:

Hi. Hope this letter finds you in the best of health. Sorry I've been so awful about writing, but things here are terribly hectic. It's always something. Last week's entries in my diary: *Monday:* picketing. Boycotting white stores to force them to hire blacks. Fifteen of us arrested. One boy's shoulder dislocated by the police. *Wednesday:* Mr. Carter (the black undertaker across the street from our freedom house) dragged off at night by the Klan. Beaten with axe handles, left naked and presumed dead. Not dead but now in hospital. (All because he allows us to use his telephone. Ours has been cut off.) *Thursday:* three of us arrested. Charge: loitering. Actually we were standing in front of the freedom house talking when the police drove up, told us we were loitering, arrested us, and took us off to jail. They beat one of the black guys so bad he had to have his eyes pushed back in. *Friday:* shooting by local whites. We were sitting talking on the freedom house porch when a car stopped out front. Three whites got out. One had a pistol. He started shooting. We scattered and ran for cover. Nobody was hit. The whites drove away. Some of us ran back outside and began throwing rocks at their car. The police came. We told them what happened. They arrested us for throwing rocks.

That's how it goes here. Every day something. I'll write more soon. Love to Sis and tell all my friends I'm okay.

Love always,
Parny

P.S. Mailing the pecans in the morning. Love again.

She addressed the envelope and put it in the canvas shoulder bag to mail later. She sat down on the bed, still dressed in only her panties. Across from her was a large mirror. She looked at herself, imagining again; chiseled high aloof cheekbones, straight indifferent mouth, long brown hair streaming honey rain. But there it was, inescapably the same plain face she had always known and hated; almost the face of a peasant woman; all earth and rock. In its way it was quite attractive, but certainly not pretty; an oak tree wrapped in pink tissue paper. She sighed and thought of Tom Rice. They shouldn't have. She hadn't done it with anyone all summer. There was already enough trouble in the Movement without girls like herself contributing to it. And though the whites in town presumed it went on continually, even orgiastically, there was actually relatively little fucking going on among the volunteers—at least to her knowledge. She sighed, thinking again of Tom Rice. They really shouldn't have. Now it would be harder than ever to avoid.

She got up and went to the window. Her bedroom was situated next to Cal's. On especially hot nights when she couldn't sleep because of the terrific heat, and giant waterbugs—like overgrown cockroaches—clung to the ceiling, she would lie naked atop the sheet, listening through the thin wall to him and the women he brought in from town. And those mornings after, he'd look at her with that special invading look, as though knowing she had restlessly turned and

turned, and listened and longed to be held herself by someone—in those moments by anyone. Now she looked out the
window and up Long George Alley. There they were as
always, those scrawny, tireless, eternal chickens pecking at
the ground; and those sad-faced big-bellied children playing
in the littered road. And the road itself no more than a broad
clay path, bending and straightening its way up the hill,
meandering between two forlorn rows of shacks; their wood
bleached, parched; crumbling in ruin without dignity, without even enough strength for collapse. And all those little
howling lives inside, the infants she had seen lying on dirty
sheets, their tiny pinched faces blanketed with flies. She
winced. Her Dad with forty acres in Vermont. Their other
home outside of Boston—so big it had its own woods, and
they used a jeep to get around. How could things be so dis-
parate? How could she explain Long George Alley to her
folks? There were no words for it; it was an irreducible feeling, a feeling heavier than any word or set of words. It would
be good to leave. Another month was all that remained. She
turned away not wanting to think the next thought. Then it
came: *All of them on that rotting, festering hill will still be there.*

She went to the mirror and combed her long brown hair,
and brushed it and then braided it. She put on a freshly
ironed blouse and skirt, then swung the canvas bag over her
shoulder. She opened her bedroom door and walked back
out into the main room. Cates was still there hunched over
the radio. He looked up as she passed. "Damn them," he said.
"Goddamn them." He pushed his floppy hat to the back of
his head and looked at her legs. She hurried on by, smiling at
him with a mouth she imagined indifferent. He continued to
stare at her. She went on by. He couldn't possibly know or
even suspect. It was absurd to think he might. She went out
the back door and headed up Long George Alley through
the afternoon's trembling heat. She remembered his look
again and shrugged. It was only her imagination.

I know damn well Percy didn't sell him inch-an'-a-half elbows, 'cause we ain't had them in stock for almost two days. I do all the inventory, I oughta know. I bet anything it's to do with that civil rights demonstration tomorrow. I never seen that nigger, Zenola, in here before. And I over-heard Percy talking on the telephone to one of his friends and I know a bunch of them are planning to go out there tomorrow with baseball bats and guns. I know they're plan-ning to park two cars in front of the main gate with the hoods up like they're disabled. Then it'll be up to the nig-gers to get by. And if they do, then Percy and them are plan-ning to jump them with the baseball bats. If it's necessary, they say, they'll shoot to kill. Me, I don't like none of it. I believe everybody oughta be 'lowed to use Duncan Park. But if one like me was to say that down front, well, it'd be taken as though I had joined the other side; which certainly ain't the truth. And another reason I think there'll be blood is 'cause all week long we've been selling axe handles and ain't sold nary a axe. It's hard to believe that in this day and age folks would kill one another over a little plot of grass. But it seems we ain't come far as we think. Now Percy there, he's in the back pretending he's doing the books. I know damn well he ain't doing no books, but is back there stew-ing 'cause I caught him in a deliberate lie. Then to top it off he stole the nigger's change and stuck it back in the cash drawer. I wish I knew what he sold him. I sure wish I knew. The way he ran out front to wait on him 'fore anybody else could get near, he musta knowed what he wanted. And just 'fore Zenola come in the store, Percy was talking to Dudley on the telephone. I could hear him way out here, he was talking so loud. I got a good mind to call up Dudley myself and see if he knows something 'bout what that nigger's up to. I oughta do it now while Percy's in the back. Damn right. I'll do it.

 CAL

Leaving Fayette, Cal said, "Goddammit, I cain't reach the sonofabitch. You try it some." He shoved the mike at Rice. "Push this button to talk," he said. Rice took the mike and began transmitting. Cal eased the Plymouth up to eighty and held it steady. He watched Rice out of the corner of his eye. Now everything seemed to irritate him. He sighed, thinking, This sonofabitch here finished college. Had soft jobs. Lived high on the hog. Now here he is paying his dues, looking for his roots. Fumbling. And getting some good pussy too. The bastard. Cal slowed to seventy. After the rally tonight he'd ask her to go for a ride. Ask her straight out for some. She gave it to one niggah, didn't she? He looked at Rice again. The sonofabitch, he thought.

"All right. Knock it off," Cal said. "That's enough. We cain't get him. We'll make do without it. I'll send it the fuck back to Jackson Monday." He stared straight ahead down the road again. "Maybe I'll ship you and Cates back with it. Neither one of you're worth a fuck!" He laughed, a bitter, dry, contemptuous laugh, and pushed the Plymouth back up to eighty.

Going up the hill to the mailbox, I pass Benjie's house. Ludy's on the porch, sitting in the swing. I wave. She doesn't wave back. I go to the edge of the porch and say hello. She ignores me, looking away toward the bottom of the alley. I call inside through the screen door. "Bertha. Bertha." Soon the door opens and Bertha McCloud comes out on the porch—a thin handsome woman in her middle thirties. She is drying her hands on an apron. Then she smoothes down her long dark hair and smiles at me.

"What you want?" she says.

"About tomorrow," I say. "You know we'll need everybody."

"I know," she says. "Das right. You sho will." She looks over at Ludy, then back at me. "I don't know what's ailing that child. She been sulking like that ever since I come home. Sitting there with her lip stuck out."

"I'll mail this letter and come right back," I say. "We can talk."

"Sho. I'll be here. Ain't got nowhere to go 'til prayer meeting tonight." She frowns down at me. "But I know what I'm gon' say to you. And it'd take a heap of talk to change my mind."

"I'll see you in a little while," I say, starting up the hill.

She looks at Ludy again. "You cain't do nothing to please them," she says. "And Lord knows I try my best. Lord knows I do."

Ludy sits in the swing, moving the shadows and heat, her eyes staring toward the bottom of the alley. I go on up the hill.

I just gave Benjie lunch when Mr. Tate came. One look and I knowed. I commenced to feeling scared. If I won't again, he'd tell Momma I done it before and took the money. He'd swear I was lying if I told her he made me do it. He done it to three other girls on the next alley, too. They told their Mommas and they the ones what got whipped. Not Mr. Tate. Everybody knows he killed a colored man. Shot him dead 'cause the man found out his wife was big from Mr. Tate. Nothing a girl's Momma or Daddy can do against Mr. Tate 'less they ready to die for her.

So he came to the door and looked through the screen. It was latched. I left Benjie in the kitchen and went to get the money. Then I came back and unlatched the door long 'nough to hand him the money. Then he said something was wrong and Momma gon' die and not get buried decent. I told him to come in a minute and figger it out. He walked right by me and into the front room and sat down and started talking 'bout that colored man he had shot dead. Then he tried to make me take Momma's money, but I didn't. I'd see myself dead 'fore I'd take it again. And then he got real mad and grabbed Benjie and lifted him and shook him hard. Then he dropped him on the floor—little Benjie. My onliest brother. My onliest. And he kept on hurting Benjie, and I said, "He's just a kid. Please, Mr. Tate, please. . . . Don't hurt Benjie." Then I said, "Aw right. Aw right. Anything you want. But don't hurt Benjie."

He carried me into Momma's room and shut the door and came at me like a bull; pulling at my clothes and wrenching me 'round. I closed my eyes and didn't move nary a muscle. Didn't make a sound. He grunted and grunted; then he finished and got up and heisted up his britches and stared down at me, cussing under his breath. "You little black bitch," he said. "You coulda tried."

I laid there hating up and he stood hating down. I gave him nothing.

"You'll be sorry," he said. "Just for that I ain't gon' turn this money in. And if she do die, she can just lay on this alley and rot."

Then he reached down and pulled me by the arm and slapped me across the face. Then he walked out the door and slammed it. I put on my clothes slow and came out here on the porch to sit in the swing. Benjie was nowhere in sight. But down the hill I saw Mr. Tate stooping and picking up some papers and shouting something. He didn't look back this way. I was sitting here 'bout an hour when Momma came back without Ross and went into the house and started cooking. Then that white girl, Parnell, from down the hill came by looking for Momma and waved to me. I didn't wave back. She could kiss my ass, the white bitch. Why don't Mr. Tate try to fuck *her?* Why do he pick on us po' niggah girls? Then she called Momma and Momma came out on the porch and talked to her and they looked at me and I just looked back at them and didn't say a damn word. I was thinking then there wasn't nobody any good, and I hated both blacks *and* whites—and maybe Momma just oughta be in the cold ground and Daddy Ross right there beside her.

# PEAVINE

It musta been 'round four-thirty or five o'clock this afternoon when the shop got crowded all of a sudden, and that old sonofabitch Chelsey Perl started lying on me. Too bad he got no place else to go or I'd of kicked him out. But I know he cain't stand hisself alone up in that boarding house.

"I been knowing this niggah twenty years," he said, talking 'bout me and grinning down from his perch in the shoeshine chair. "Knowed him 'fore he got so uppity. So hinkty. Used to chase women. Drink hard likker like it was soda pop."

He tilted his Confederate back and laughed—his face under the brim small and pinched, and no teeth in his mouth. I laughed myself. It was a sight.

"You oughta sit home in that damn room of yours and stare out the window," I said. "Or cain't you stand yourself? That's why you have to come down here meddling. Lying your decrepid ass off. I got a good mind—" I went back to cutting. The old fart. He must be eighty. Hanging 'round here from morning 'til night; minding everybody's damn business but his own.

He took off his hat and slapped it against his knee, laughing again. "I ever tell y'all 'bout the time a snake swallowed Peavine's dick?" he said. Everybody was looking at him, waiting.

I turned and pointed my scissors. "I've told you a hunnert times that's a deliberate lie," I said.

He put his hat back on and grinned 'round. "Well," he said, "one night Peavine went out in the country to screw some ole gal. It was pitch dark. He'd had a lot to drink, and so when he finished, he forgot to take the rubber off. Just pulled up his pants and went 'bout his business. And it pitch dark—blacker than the inside of a stove. Presently he had to make his water. He comes to this outhouse in the woods, and goes in there in the dark and pulls down his britches and commences to do his number. Well, the rubber was catching it and starts filling up on him. It gets heavier and heavier, and bigger and bigger. Then it overflows. And Peavine thinks something's got hold of him and he busts outta there and runs down the road with his pants half down, hollering a snake had swallowed his dick."

They all went to laughing, Perl himself near 'bout falling off the shoeshine stand, holding his belly and beating his knee with the Confederate. One fella got up and walked outside bent over. B. Jacks and Dennis stopped cutting. My own customer stood up with the cloth still on, laughing. I just waited. It died down some, and he sat back down. I unpinned the cloth and dusted him off with talc. He paid me.

"Next," I said.

They all busted out laughing again. I waited. I knew a story or two on Perl that were *true,* but I wasn't 'bout to lower myself. So I just waited. Finally when it died down, B. Jacks said, "Peavine, you is some *scared* niggah."

I snapped the cloth twice in the air, crisp, loud. "Next," I said. Somebody got up and climbed in my chair and I pinned the cloth on him. I looked at Perl. He sat up there like an old owl watching me, his eyes beady under the brim of the Confederate. "You oughta stop telling that lie," I told him. "Old as you is you oughta worry more 'bout where you's heading, 'stead of going around lying on folks. Wait 'till you get to Hell. You'll have plenty of time."

"One thing sho," he said. "When I get there, I ain't gon' be scared. Ain't gon' be shivering in my damn boots."

"The reason I ain't marching is 'cause I cain't afford to go to jail," I told him. "Not even for a single day." I was getting sore. I wanted him off my back. "Listen," I said. "I'm a businessman. I cain't afford to go out there laying in front of trucks and buses and getting my head busted open. I cain't afford going to jail. Not even for a day."

He got quiet and I started cutting again steady. The other niggahs looked at me. I was sore, ready to cuss 'em all out. Close the damn doors. But in this business you gotta contend with a lot; even listening to niggahs talk—talk that'd put you to sleep if you weren't standing up. "Just 'cause I don't participate in demonstrations, it don't mean I'm against progress," I told them. "Hell, ain't I got a lifetime paid membership in the National Advancement League? Ain't I been giving free haircuts to the civil righters all summer? Letting 'em hang around in here talking their Movement talk? Don't all that count for something?" I looked around at them again, then went back to cutting.

"There's just one thing I wanna know," B. Jacks said. He looked at me. I knew what was coming. "You going with us tomorrow?"

I just kept cutting, my stomach churning and that low feeling coming again, like something nudged up against my navel. And my head was beginning to ache. Finally they went to talking 'bout something else and I stopped paying attention. When I finished with the one in my chair I decided I better take a break and go next door to the café—get a Alka-Seltzer for my stomach. Some Stanback for my headache. "I'm taking a breather," I said to B. Jacks. "I'll be next door getting a cup of coffee if you need me." He nodded, hardly looking up.

I turned and went out into the sun, my head hurting worse and my stomach tore up. The screen hadn't slammed behind me two seconds when I heard them in there laughing at me. I went on next door.

 **CATES**

I was pulling the head off and dropped a nut. It fell down through the engine compartment to the ground. I slid under the truck to get it, then laid there thinking—my head just past the edge of the running board, looking up at the sky. The blue sky. And this June bug flew by. Way up. And past that was a bird, a chicken hawk, circling. Way up. And right 'bout then this airplane passed higher up than the bird. All up in the sky. Way up in that endless sky. *Ditty-ditty dum. Ditty-ditty dum. Ditty-ditty dum. . . .*

 **B. JACKS**

I go next door to the telephone and call her up 'bout tonight. She's just being stubborn, that's all.

"I cain't," I says. "I just cain't. Not tonight. Now, honey, listen. . . . Peggy. C'mon, please. I just cain't. We're having this rally at McIver's church. You know how I'm gon' feel when it's over. I'll be mad as hell and hating white folks."

She breathes hard into the receiver and say, "Ain't I white? You hate me? You carrying on with me like I'm some slut? Don't you truly love me?"

She had me on the spot and I didn't wanna argue; least not standing here in a public place, talking on a wall telephone. So I say real soft and smooth, "Now, baby, c'mon. You know I loves you. Honest I do. You's differ'nt from other white folks."

"I'm white just the same," she say. "And if you leave that meeting hating white folks, you gon' be hating me too."

She's almost yelling and I can tell she's 'bout to cry. My dime is near run out.

"You took my soul," she says. "Dammit, Jack, you took my soul. And now you don't wanna see me even for one night. Here I'm risking everything. My marriage. My home. My reputation."

I can hear her crying on the other end of the line. What do you do with a woman when she gets like that? "Whatcha mean I don't wanna see you for one night, Peggy? We been four nights at my place already this week and today ain't but Friday. Honey, be reasonable now. Listen—"

"Don't you honey me," she say. "You niggers are all alike!"

"Now wait a damn minute," I say. "Who you calling—"

"Take a woman's soul and then leave her."

"Wait now," I say. "What you mean *all alike?* You told me I was the first." She don't say nothing and I feel the collar of my barber jacket tight'ning 'round my neck. I say quiet into the phone, "Listen, bitch. You been with some other?"

"No," she say real quick. "I was just fooling."

"Well, you picked the wrong way to fool," I say. I reach my hand up and unsnap my collar and let some of the steam out and look 'round the café. Peavine is sitting at the counter, drinking a glass of something, his back to me.

"Aw right, Peggy," I say. "Let's forget it. But don't play that shit with me."

"You coming to see me tonight?" she say, real sweet again.

"Aw right. Yeah. I'll come to the club after the meeting. You wait for me. We gotta be extra careful. The white folks'll be everywhere looking to start trouble. They're nervous now, and after the rally it'll be worse."

"What time's the meeting over?" she say.

" 'Round 'leven. McIver's gon' preach first."

"I be waiting in the parking lot for you 'round 'leven-thirty," she say. "You got any stuff left?"

" 'Nough for a couple of joints," I say.

"Be careful, Jack. I love you."

I hear the dime fall. 'Fore we hang up I say, "You was just kidding before, wasn't you? 'Bout that other?"

"Honest, honey, You're the first. I just wanted to see if you were jealous. See if you truly love me like you say."

When we hung up, I was thinking what a fool I was to mess with her tonight. Well, I'll sho have my stove ready.

As I go out the door, I look at Peavine again. He sees me but don't say nothing. I figger he's still sore 'bout Chelsey Perl's teasing. He oughtn't be that way. But he ain't got a sense of humor like the rest of us. But what the hell, every-body's got a little sore spot. Like my Daddy used to say, "It's always the *little* stones that get inside your shoe and hurt."

 **SOLLY**

It was after five o'clock and we'd finished canvassing for the day. Six of us were sitting around the freedom house having a damn good conversation when Cal and Tom walked in. Paul Furman, the other Jewish kid on the project, was argu-ing that none of man's acts were essentially important. But that man was burdened with the compulsion to act nonethe-less, and therefore lived with an illusion of importance.

I took the position that action was quite natural to man—based on his evolutionary trip—but that it was the overlay of ego and consequence that gave our acts importance. I argued that man arbitrarily projected his own sense of self-importance onto his actions, and that one tended to maximize the importance of one's own actions while minimizing the importance of most of the actions of others. "Furthermore," I added, "it's the idea of *consequence* that makes slaves of us. Every man is free," I said. "As free as he is willing to accept the consequences of his acts. But we're controlled by fear—fear of consequences."

Parnell said, "Rubbish!" And then in one breath added, "People are as free as the power structure and the social climate allow them to be, and we're here in Mississippi to challenge the power structure by organizing the poor and powerless into a cohesive entity which collectively will wield enormous political power."

Then the screen banged open and Cal walked in and said, "Bullshit! What the fuck is this, a goddamned seminar?" Then he looked at me. "Go out back and tell Cates to get his ass in here. And you get your notebook. We've having a meeting. Hurry up!" He stormed into his room and slammed the door, and they started putting the main room back in order. I went outside to look for Pete. He was lying on his back halfway under the truck, staring up at the sky. I called to him.

"Pete. Hey, Pete." He kept looking at the sky, as though he hadn't heard me. I went over and stooped down. His eyes didn't move. I could smell the engine grease on his clothes. It was on his face and hands too. "Cal wants us inside," I said. "Hey, Pete. You hear me? We're having a meeting." He gave me a queer look, his head turning slowly toward me, but his eyes focused off in the distance somewhere. "Pete. Are you okay?"

"Sure," he said, real quiet. "I'm all right. You know, Solly, it just goes on and on. There ain't no end or beginning to it."

"To what? What the heck are you talking about?"

"The sky," he said. "The sky way up so high. And this here rhythm. *Ditty-ditty dum. Ditty-ditty dum. Ditty-ditty dum.*" He was talking very soft, like to himself. But Pete's quiet anyway. Shy, easygoing, gentle. A really sweet guy.

"You better hurry," I said. "Cal's really pissed. You sure you're all right?"

"Sure," he said. "I'm all right. I'll be there in a minute. Go ahead."

Then, for the first time, he looked directly at me and smiled. I stood up and walked back toward the house. At the kitchen door I looked back at him. He had slid out from beneath the truck and was standing up, still looking at the sky. I looked too, but saw nothing except a few uninteresting cloud formations and the sun still hanging bright and hot. I shrugged and opened the screen and went inside, got my notebook and a pencil from my room, and went back to the main room. There everybody was seated and Cal stood near the desk, staring silently at the radio. Then he looked at me. "Where the fuck you been?"

"To get Pete," I said. "I don't think he's feeling too good."

"Neither am I," he said. "Where the hell is he?"

"He's coming," I said, pulling a chair over near Cal and sitting down. The back door opened and Pete entered. He looked around, first at us, then at Cal. Then he walked over to the radio and flipped the power switch on.

"Not *now*, man," Cal snapped. "Just sit the fuck down!"

Pete looked at him, then at us again. I knew something was wrong. It was like he didn't know where he was; or part of his mind knew and the other part didn't. I turned the notebook pages until I found a clean one, and wrote down the date and the time at the top. Cal lit a cigarette and pushed his sunglasses up and looked at Pete.

"Will you *sit* the fuck down?" he said. "Goddamn. . . ."

Pete sat down. I felt sorry for him.

"This is probably the last chance we'll have to get together before the demonstration tomorrow," Cal said. "I wanna make sure everybody's straight on what's happening." He paused, looking around. "Okay, tonight first. Parnell, you take about a hundred sheets of freedom songs to the church and pass them out." He looked at Tom. "Rice, you and Winston lead the singing." Winston grinned. Rice scowled. Winston is a seventeen-year-old, a local black kid who's been a lot of help to us; a short, bandy-legged, tough-faced boy with a good voice.

"I can't sing," Rice said. "You know that. Man, I can't even carry a tune." Everybody laughed. Pete stared at the radio.

Cal almost smiled. "Ain't that a shame," he said. "And here I thought you house niggahs were trained to sing."

Rice looked embarrassed, then angry. We were all laughing, but knowing our turns would come eventually. Cal just had to do it. "Okay," he said. "As soon as McIver finishes, Crayfield'll take over. When he's finished, I'll take over. We got to get folks worked up right off. No bullshit. Freedom songs. Shouting. Let 'em stomp their feet, clap their hands, feel good." He looked at Rice again. "That's your job, brother. You and Winston gonna get the folks worked up. When you ain't singing, I want Rice, Winston, and Furman to stand guard outside the church. Don't want some Klan motherfuckers busting in, catching us with our drawers down." He looked at Paul Furman. Paul was the youngest volunteer: he was nineteen. He couldn't grow a full beard yet. He stared up at Cal with his baby face. "That means, Furman, you'll be keeping lookout all the time, and Rice and Winston'll be out there with you when they're not singing." Tom looked down at the floor, then up at Cal, then out the window. He slumped down low in his chair.

"Now 'bout tomorrow. . . . We'll assemble folks out back of the freedom house at two o'clock sharp. I'll start making runs out to the country around noon with my car, picking up people there." He looked at Tom again. "Rice, you'll drive the truck. You can haul at least a dozen folks every trip." He looked at Pete. "That's if the goddamned truck is fixed," he said.

"It'll be running," Pete said. "Even if I have to stay on it all night."

Cal kept his eyes on him, level, hard, unmoving. Then he

looked down at me. "Solly, you work with Rice. The two of you together oughta have enough sense to find folks if I draw you a map."

I nodded, feeling my face flush a little. He always had to put us down. He just had to do it. I finished writing the last sentence and sat waiting.

"When we get everybody assembled," he said, "we'll line them up two abreast. We'll march on the sidewalk if we don't get the parade permit. If we do get the permit we'll go in the street, four abreast. No permit, no singing. Got that? If folks start singing, shut them up fast. The police'll arrest."

"I hear we may be going in a motorcade," Winston said.

We all laughed. "Chauffeured," somebody said.

"We vote on it tonight," Cal said. "In the meantime, let's figger on marching—and without a parade permit." He looked at Tom Rice. "I want you, Winston, Furman, and Solly to work as marshals." He looked at me. "After the meeting, Solly, break out those red armbands I brought from Jackson and give one to each marshal. The folks must know who you guys are, in case of trouble. You'll be moving up and down the march line, making sure folks don't straggle or sing. Keeping them two abreast, not letting them bunch up and crowd off the sidewalk onto the street. Soon as that happens the arrests start. Tomorrow I'll appoint some more marshals. We'll break the line up into sections, each section approximately twenty-five or thirty people. Each marshal will take charge of one section. Whenever that section approaches a traffic crossing, the marshal must get them across on the green light so nobody'll get arrested for jaywalking. The police'll be laying for that. When you move your group across, move them *fast*; many as you can across on the green. Soon as it turns red again, anybody caught off the curb gets arrested. I'm telling you 'cause I know their tricks. They'll have men at every crossing watching for it. They can cut us down that way—get a lot of arrests. Another thing, don't you marshals expect regular intervals of green and red. That's another trick. They'll probably reset all the traffic lights on Main Street so that the green stays on only a fraction of the normal time, then switches quick to amber and red. Again that's to catch us jaywalking. Anybody off the curb when the red comes on gets arrested. So if you're pushing a group through, don't figger on getting more than nine or ten across at a time, then cut off the flow fast. You're gonna have to yell your ass off, people move like cows when you want them to run. If you get stragglers in the crossing and you see they're not going to make the other side in time, then tell them to jump! That way if the red flashes on while their feet are in the air, then technically they're not jaywalking." He stopped and lit another cigarette.

"At the end of every block where there's a traffic light, you gotta go through the same procedure. So push. Push hard. Got it straight?"

We nodded yes. Then just as I was starting to write again, the screen door banged open and B. Jacks came in the room, still in his white barber's jacket. He was out of breath.

"What's wrong?" Cal said.

"They've beat him to death! Died in the hospital a hour ago."

"Who?" Cal said, coming erect, the vein in his neck standing out, throbbing. "Who the hell you talking 'bout?"

"Josh. Josh Thomas," B. Jacks said.

"Dead?" Cal said. He pushed his glasses up.

"A fella just came in the barbershop and told us. We cain't let them motherfuckers get away with this. We cain't—"

"Anybody seen his mother yet?" Cal said, cool as ice; but the vein standing out more.

"I dunno," B. Jacks said. "Devils!"

"Then you better go see," Cal said. " 'Fore she finds out some other way. Now calm down, brother. Go up the hill and find out if she knows. When I finish this meeting, we'll go down to headquarters together."

"Solid," B. Jacks said. "I better tell Mamie Lee and Aura-belle too. Damn, I shoulda thought to go see his Momma first. I wasn't thinking—"

"Go on, man," Cal said. "Hurry up back."

B. Jacks went out again, this time through the rear of the house toward Long George Alley. We watched him go.

Finally Cal said, "You marshals got it straight?"

We nodded again, all of us still looking toward the back door where B. Jacks had vanished into the bright sunshine. Then Pete got up and walked to the back door and looked up at the sky through the screen.

"Where the hell you think you're going?" Cal said. "I ain't finished yet. Sit down, motherfucker."

Pete didn't say anything. He pushed the screen open and walked out. Nobody said anything. We were looking at Cal, then out at the alley again and the sunshine into which B. Jacks had vanished.

Cal threw the cigarette on the floor and ground it out under the toe of his sneaker and started out the door after Pete.

"That sonofabitch," he said.

 **CATES**

I walked outside and sat down on the running board of the truck, thinking 'bout my friend Josh. Then the screen door opened and somebody came out of the house. I kept looking at the ground but I could see the shadow moving across the clay. Then I saw his white sneakers come into my vision—the bare ankles and the bottoms of his jeans. Then he stiffened his legs, standing in front of me; spread them apart like he was saying, *C'mon, Cates, get up and take your medicine, motherfucker. Get on your feet.* And I raised my eyes slow up those legs; past the clenched fists and the chest breathing heavy. Raised them slow, not wanting to reach those eyes of his that would look at me like I'd failed. So I held to the mouth, not wanting to go to the eyes. Held to the mouth set hard. And then he reached down sudden and grabbed me by my collar and shook me, and I heard him making sounds. I knew he was talking but the words were just sounds that went away into the air. And I held to the mouth, feeling the heat and damp in the air, hearing and feeling death around me, hearing the wind rattling in the oak tree leaves. And the mouth moved again; faster and angrier. And I saw it, and heard the sounds coming from it. But they all went into one sound with the leaves and the wind. So I didn't hear the words, just watched the mouth moving, pushing out those sounds; the lips turning and twisting, going together like old friends, then twisting and parting again like enemies. Then the lips stopped moving and I heard the same steady rhythm: *Ditty-ditty dum. Ditty-ditty dum. Ditty-ditty dum.* And then I heard him. He said, "Well?" I gathered all of myself that was left and I sent it up to those eyes to ask what the mouth had been saying; and his eyes said, *"When do you want to leave, Pete?"*

"As soon as I can," I said out loud to them. Out loud I said, "As soon as I can." And the eyes folded inward and the meanness seemed to go out of them; and they reached out for me, for my eyes—like a hand stuck out to be shook. *"Anytime you want to, Pete. Just pack up and leave,"* they said. And I took the hand with my eyes, and I held as long as I could; held it until I saw Josh standing in the blur—Josh looking at me, pointing a finger at me; and my foot beating out a rhythm against the ground. . . . *Ditty-ditty dum. Ditty-ditty dum. Ditty-ditty dum.*

"Anytime you want to, Pete," Cal said. "Just pack up and leave."

I dropped my eyes, letting the hand go, and saw the white sneakers move away, back toward the house; and saw his shadow follow him across the red clay. *Ditty-ditty dum. Ditty-ditty dum. Ditty-ditty dum.*

 **SOLLY**

I'd just finished writing the last sentence when Cal walked out. We followed him as far as the back door, and stood looking out through the screen. Pete sat on the running board of the truck, staring at the ground. Cal went over and stood in front of him with his fists balled.

"You fucking hillbilly," he said. "You need your damn ass kicked. Get up on your feet."

Pete looked up slow at him, slow but didn't make a move. Cal reached down and collared him and started shaking him.

"That sonofabitch," Tom said. He stood next to me, a full head over me. "Can't he see the cat's sick?"

"I know," I said. "That's what I tried to tell him," I said.

He held on to his collar and started cursing him out. "You honky motherfuckers should get out the Movement," he said. "Just fucking things up. I coulda fixed that truck myself by now. If it ain't running tomorrow, Jackson can do what the hell they please with you."

Then he shut up and let go of Pete, and they just stared at each other for a long strange time.

Then Cal said, "Well? Well?"

"As soon as I can," Pete said. "As soon as I can."

They kept staring. Finally Cal said, "I told you before. I'll

tell you again—anytime you want to, Pete. Just pack up and leave." Then he turned fast and started back toward the house. He jerked open the screen and shouldered his way past us, cursing under his breath. Tom and I stayed by the door, looking out at Pete. He still sat on the running board, staring up the alley, his foot patting to something.

GEORGE

"Dudley? George. George Hollywell down at Percy's Hardware. Fine. Fine. Yourself? Good. Listen, how do you stand on inch-and-a-half elbows? We're clean out. I was wondering if you could spare a dozen 'til Monday. I got a order in but it won't be delivered 'til Monday morning. You do? You can? Swell. That'll get us through Saturday. I sure do appreciate it. And I'll send the boy to pick 'em up right now. 'Fore closing time. Axe handles? No, we're clean out too. Sold every last one, and nary a axe. Sorry. What? You neither? Yeah, I think there's gon' be blood too. Listen, something else I wanted to ask you: that crazy nigger, Zenola, he came in our store a while ago. Looked to me like he was up to no good. Is that a fact? No, Percy ain't said a word to me 'bout it. But he's busy on the books. Is that a fact? Lordy! Came to your place too? Dynamite? I be damn. No, Percy sold him the last of the inch-an'-a-half elbows. Said he was doing some plumbing. Yeah, I guess he'd lost his nerve by the time he got here. Well, thanks for the favor, Dudley. Anytime, anytime. . . . Sure, sure. Anytime. So long. Good-bye."

I be damn. Percy sold that fella dynamite. He must be

up to hurting other niggers or Percy wouldn't of sold it. I don't like this a bit. I got a good mind to call the police. But what the hell good would that do? They'd just laugh in my face.

 **RICE**

I can't sing. Can't even carry a tune. How can I lead the singing? He's fucking with me on purpose—because of her; despising me because of Parnell. I shouldn't have told him. I don't know why I did. Except I think he already knew. But I won't lead the singing, that's all. Let him get somebody else. Or do it himself. He'd have to kick my ass to get me up there. I wish he'd try. The sonofabitch. We're all tired of his shit. Of him fucking over us. And the way he treated Cates. Who does he think he is? Hell, he's just flesh and bone too.

 **CATES**

Josh's dead. Wonder who got the rhythm? He went: *La-de-da-de dah. La-de-da-de dah.* My rhythm: *Ditty-ditty dum.* Josh, he cain't be dead. His rhythm is somewhere. I gotta listen for him. Cal, he go: *Da-da doom. Da-da doom.* Aurabelle is: *Ta-ta*

tee. Ta-ta tee. And he says to me again, "Anytime, Pete. Anytime you want to, you just pack up and leave." With his eyes he said it this time. I saw it. Heard it. *Da-da doom.* And I said, *"Ditty-ditty dum. Ditty-ditty dum.* As soon as I can. As soon as I can."

I'm gonna fix this truck tonight and tomorow I'll go to Duncan Park with them. But that's all. I'm through. Packing up my things tomorrow night, and come Sunday morning—if I ain't sitting in jail—I'll be on my way to Jackson. First Greyhound leaving the depot. *Ditty-ditty dum.* And if she got good sense, like I believe she does, she'll come with me. *Ta-ta tee. Ta-ta tee.* She likes me. I know damn well she does. The way she held me tight. And Josh being her cousin, and him being my friend, and me out looking for his rhythm—she's bound to come. *Ditty-ditty dum. Ditty-ditty dum. Ta-ta tee. Ta-ta tee.* If Josh's dead, who got his rhythm?

B. JACKS

I went up the hill to Mamie Lee's and said, "I got something bad to tell y'all." Both was sitting on the porch, waiting for business. I stood by the railing. I said, "Maybe you already heard it. Josh is dead."

The young one, Aurabelle, scraped her chair back sudden and stood up and looked down at me.

"What that you say?"

"I said your cousin Josh is dead."

"Dead?"

She just kept standing there saying that, and I said it

again twice more. "Yeah, he's dead. Died 'bout a hour ago at the General Hospital."

"Dead?" she said. "Cousin Josh?"

"That's right. And we gon' find out 'bout it. Me and Cal Drew. Goin' to the police station directly. We gon' find out what happened. Don't worry."

"Cousin Josh dead?" she said. The other hadn't spoke a mumbling word, but took out a little pink handkerchief from between her tits and put it to her eyes.

"I swear, I wish somebody else had this job," I said.

Then Mamie Lee took the handkerchief from her eyes and blew her nose. I didn't see nary a tear. But there weren't none in the young one's eyes either—just her face looking like it would bust open any minute. She turned and walked slow into the house and closed the screen quiet behind her and latched it.

"He weren't but twenty," her Momma said. "How can it be? What did he do? My sister's baby boy. She know it yet?"

"I told her," I said. " 'Fore I came here. There're some ladies with her now."

"I better go myself and see 'bout her," Mamie Lee said. "Her baby boy. Lord, if I lost my onliest. I didn't even know he'd took sick and in the hospital. Lord have mercy."

"He weren't sick. They musta whupped him so bad at the jail they killed him. That's what I believe. He died in the hospital. That's all we know."

I turned and started out the yard. Just then a man came up the alley and cut through the yard, walking past me to the porch.

"You come for business?" Mamie Lee said.

"Well, I ain't jest taking the sun," he said.

I kept on out the yard.

"Honey," I heard her say to the young one. "There's a nice fella out here. Get yourself ready for him. I'm gonna visit your Aunty."

I went on out the yard, looking back once, not believing it. The man had walked up on the porch and was waiting by the screen door. I saw the young one's face come to the door and look through the screen at him. Then she unfastened the latch and I saw him open the door and go in; and the young one waiting there behind the screen, standing still as a statue in the shadows behind the screen. Then she moved away and back into the room and closed the other door, Mamie Lee was rocking in her chair, dabbing at her eyes with the handkerchief and looking down the hill. I went on down, thinking of Josh and how he and that young one used to play together when they was kids. Then I commenced to thinking 'bout the police again. I decided to stash my stove somewhere, not take it with us. I didn't trust myself. The way I was feeling then I'd as soon of shot one dead as to look at him.

 **AURABELLE**

When we stand facing for the first time—stand like dogs in the road—I see that look in their eyes; and I hate this minute more than all the rest. They don't care 'bout nothing 'cept to fill their own pleasure. So I send out the hard part of me for them to use. And I think then always that each on me is like a elephant; and this elephant had lay his belly hard on mine and squatted down to smother out the breath from me and shut off the light from the onliest window. . . .

Cousin Josh. Dead. I could always find him, but most times he couldn't find me. Not in the high grass at the top of the hill, where the sun set low in the sky and the cows came mooing through. Cousin

Josh. Dead. He'd always leave some part of hisself showing. And I could spot him easy, and he would say, "You was peeking." And he would chase me through the high grass and catch me. And we'd wrassle 'til we was wore out, then we'd lay on our backs and look up at the sky, and make up stories 'bout the clouds. And once . . . once he put his hand on me; once in the high grass with the sun hot and yellow and sinking slow behind the piney woods; and I put my hand on his and we kissed in the yellow grass. Cousin Josh's dead. Cousin Josh's dead and it don't matter now what we done in the high grass; what we done under the hot sun in the yellow grass.

"It's two dollars 'less you want some liquor," I says. "Liquor's three dollars more."

"I ain't got but two," he says. He ain't a bad-looking fella. Kinda sad in the eyes. Bow-legged though.

"Lemme see the money. Git your damn hands off me! Lemme see the money. First." He gives me the money.

"Aw right. Let's get it over with," I says.

"What you doing with that comic book?" he says.

"I'm gon' read it. What the hell you think I'm gon' do with it?"

"While we's—"

"Yeah, while we's—"

"But—"

"Look, if you ain't satisfied, you can get your damn money back. Now let's get it on."

"Okay, baby. But what did I do to make you act so hateful?"

"Nothing. Ain't none of your business."

In the high grass Cousin Josh said, "You gon' always be my favorite." And I said, "You gon be mine, Josh."

"I wish you wouldn't read that fucking comic book. That's insulting."

. . . And the weight of hisself pressing on me is like a elephant had lay his belly hard on mine and squatted down to smother out the breath from me and shut off the light from the onliest window.

Zenola. Toilet. Mop bucket dumping. Soap bubbles flying. Thinking: circles—white, yellow, black. White circles falling. Yellow circles rising. Black circles floating. Bubbles. Mop bucket dumping. Zenola into dictionary. Reading: *Technology.* Zenola. Dictionary. Reading: *Applied.* Zenola listening. Plowers coming. Soap bubbles flying.

"Zenola! Zenola! C'mere you sonofabitch," Plowers say, brows knotting. Eagle nose beaking. Plowers going away. "Hurry it up, Zenola. I ain't got all damn day."

Door slamming. Plowers gone. Zenola into toilet. Zenola into dictionary. Reading: *Practical.* Zenola. Dictionary. Reading: *Capable.* Zenola. Dictionary hiding. Plowers coming back.

"Zenola! Get your black ass in here," Plowers say.

"Yeah, boss. No more trouble."

Zenola into dictionary quick. Reading: *Sufficient to meet needs. . . .*

"Goddamn you. What's taking so long back there?"

Zenola. Dictionary hiding. Zenola into Plowers's office.

"Shut the fucking door," Plowers say.

Plowers at desk. Zenola in bare feet. Zenola into inner ears of goats. Plowers, white thorn. Higher. Zenola grinning. "Me Zenola. Me climb highest tree. Bare chest to sun." Zenola beating chest. Plowers frowning.

"C'mon," Plowers say. "Cut the shit. Did you get it?"

"Boomsticks. Broomsticks. Boomsticks. Broomsticks. No more trouble, boss."

"Where's the change from my twenty?"

Zenola shrugging. "Percy cut black king's balls. Roll down St. Catherine Street."

Plowers at watch. "Shit, they closed. Go back Monday,

you dumb sonofabitch." Plowers with pencil and paper. "Look here. This is how you'll do it."

"Zenola, black king of the mountain," Zenola say. "Me Zenola. No more trouble."

Plowers smiling. "C'mere then," Plowers say, marking paper. "C'mere you sweet black king of the mountain. Lemme show you how to do it."

GEORGE

I seen a lynching once. Never 'fore or since seen a nigger run like that. They had sicked the dogs on him and when he first came in sight he was running ahead of them, running 'long the bluff by the river where they'd chased him; running in the bright clear moonlight with his shirt tore and it streaming behind him like confetti; and him breaking through the weeds and thorn bushes 'til he was in the open, then running fast again with his fists beating the air and his head throwed back. He moved swift and easy ahead of them 'til they broke free of the bushes; then the lead hound moved swiftly too, yelping loud and closing fast—and all of them locked together in a furious motion of speed and light and form and darkness. Then I heard a gun fire and the nigger went down with his arms outstretched like a sawdust doll falling.

They pulled the dogs off him and dragged him hollering into the woods 'long the river; and two of them held him spread-eagled whilst another cut it off with a razor blade and poured raw turpentine where it had been. When it didn't matter, they put a rope 'round his neck and hung him. That was twelve years ago and I weren't but nineteen. I remember being sick right there on the ground and swearing I would never be a part of that as long as I lived. But I knew from that day on there was something profound wrong with the ways of the South . . . wrong with the ways of this whole land.

 **PEAVINE**

Yesterday evening we were sitting on the front porch after supper drinking lemonade. I kept spraying and swatting the mosquitoes.

"S'pose I went," I said to Rosalee. "You ready to accept the consequences? Have the mortgage called? The loan money for James Junior's school canceled? You ready to give up your color TV and live in a two-by-four shack on Long George Alley? Answer me that!"

"It's a silly question," she said. "Nobody wants to live there."

"Then you oughta try to understand. You and James Junior both." I swatted another mosquito. "Don't you think I know what's on your minds? I see the looks y'all been giving me. I ain't the fool you think." I was feeling terrible, like I was split in two, and one part was talking whilst the other listened. And the listening part was sick of hearing the talking part, but there wasn't nothing it could do to stop it. I got up and walked the porch twice and came back and sat down.

"If we could drive our cars there 'stead of marching through the streets—You know everybody and his brother'll be watching."

"You musta had too much lemonade," she said, looking at me, her eyes kind of laughing.

"See there," I said. "The minute I try to—"

The screen door opened and James Junior came out on the porch and went down the steps without a word.

"The day ain't come yet when you're grown enough to walk outta here without opening your damn mouth," I said. He stopped in the yard and looked back at me, taller than both of us, handsomer than I ever was—'cept his hair was getting long. "You hear?" I said. "You hear me talking to you, boy?"

He nodded, running the toe of his sneaker in the dirt. "Yes, sir," he said. "Can I borrow the car tonight?"

"Huh? The car?" I reached in my pocket for the keys. "You get in early, you hear? And don't go speeding around town." He nodded and reached for the keys. I had a good mind not to give them to him.

"Leave him 'lone," Rosalee said. "He's a man now."

"Don't tell me what to do," I said. "He's a man and I'm a man. But who's taking the loans out at the bank to send him to Toogaloo? To pay for this house? To keep the business going? And you listen to me," I said to him, "that car ain't but a year old. So you drive it like you got some respect for it."

"Have some more lemonade," Rosalee said. She filled up my glass. I swatted another mosquito, then pushed the button on the spray bomb and made sure it was dead. I felt terrible, but the listening part couldn't stop the other.

I gave him the keys. He took them and walked on out to the car and started it and drove off. I took a sip of lemonade and put my feet up on the banister. "You know," I said, "we gotta replant them geraniums. They need more space. And I gotta paint that garage 'fore winter."

"You gon' run that boy away from home," she said. "You and your big mouth. Don't you ever shut it?"

"Not when somebody's trying to make me do something

I know I shouldn't do," I told her. "I ain't going on that damn demonstration. And that's final."

"Who asked you?" she said. "Who the devil asked you?"

"Well, don't. 'Cause it wouldn't do you no good. I wouldn't go on it if Jesus Christ hisself was leading it."

"Then don't," she said, disgusted again.

"You telling me what to do?" I said. I couldn't stop the talking part.

Rosalee got up and started in the house.

"Where the hell you going?" I said.

"To watch the television," she said. "I'm sick of these mosquitoes." She slammed the screen door. "And I'm sick of you!" she said through it.

I pushed the button on the spray bomb and I got him. He flew on for a little bit, then faltered in the air and landed on the railing. I swatted him. Hell, nobody sympathized with me. Not even my own wife. If a man has to stand ten hours a day behind a barber's chair cutting on nappy heads, and can't come home and talk to his own family, then what the hell is there for him? Not a damn thing.

 **AURABELLE**

Here comes another one lumbering up the hill, sucking on a straw and walking like he got a load of shit in his britches. He comes to the edge of the porch, his gap mouth grinning and him looking up my dress.

"Ain't nothing up there but a pussy," I tells him. "Same as your Mammy got."

He don't say nothing but stands there slobbering and it running down his chin.

"Room's busy," I says. "Either you wait or go the hell somewhere else. Be better for me if you did. Go up on St. Catherine Street and get yourself a café whore."

"They got the VD," he says, drooling. "You sho is uppity, gal. What the hell I done to you?"

I look down the hill and see the truck parked out back of their house with the hood up, and him with his head under it. He been working on that engine most all day. Ain't been back here since Wednesday night, though. Not even passing once to speak. Not that I give two cents. But I oughtn't to have been so mean to him. He really do care for me. I can see it's for true.

"C'mon, baby," this other says. "Lemme come up on the porch and sit down."

"When Mamie Lee finish, we go in," I say. "You just wait down there. And wipe your nasty mouth."

He takes out a pocket handkerchief and wipes his mouth. "C'mon, honey," he says. "You's too purty to be so mean. C'mon now."

"Aw right," I says. "But you carry your ass down to the other end and sit. I got something on my mind."

He comes heavy-footed up the steps and goes and sits down in a chair on the other end and looks at me; grinning simple, all gums and gap teeth.

"I cain't hardly wait," he says. "You is the purtiest one. . . ."

I don't say nothing, just look off across the alley thinking my usual—how the hell I'm gon' get 'nough money together to sky outta here. Near every dime I make go to Mamie Lee for rent and food. I'm sho sick of this alley. Sick of this life. Sick of Mamie Lee and these no-'count niggahs that don't want me for nothing 'cept fucking. Gon' sky outta here one day. Chicago maybe. Or Detroit. I look over at this other again and he's still grinning at me. Then I feel a little sorry for him; ain't his fault I'm so tard.

"You want some lightnin'?" I says. "I'll fetch you a drink, but you'll have to carry it out back 'case the police ride by." He just sits there grinning simple at me.

"I wanna stay right here and look at you, baby," he says, the dumb sonofabitch. That's what I get for trying. Shit.

The screen door opens and Mamie Lee struts her fat ass out with a fella right behind her. She sees this other waiting and smiles. I get up slow, hating this minute more than all the rest, when I first have to go in with them—when we stand facing each other like dogs in the road. It's then that I want to turn and run. Run anywhere. But there just ain't nowhere.

"Aw right," I says to him. "Let's get it over with."

He gets up and I hold the screen door for him, and he goes by me smelling like a stinkweed factory. 'Fore I let the door fall to, I look again down the alley. He's laying under the truck now with just his feet sticking out. Then I think, Maybe he don't care for me. Maybe I'm wrong. Mamie Lee sees me looking and cuts her eye at me sharp, then looks herself. Then she gives me that Friday smile what ain't no deeper than her lipstick, and she say, "Don't keep your fella waiting, honey. It's bad for business."

I look down the hill again at him; then I let the screen fall to and close the inside door, and I turn to face the other, hating this minute more than all the rest.

If I drop this five-eighths through the engine compartment again, I'm gonna know something. That's three times now I dropped this wrench. My hands don't hold like they used to. S'pose Pa's dead. I never thought 'bout that. I'm gonna finish this truck if it's the last thing I do. If it takes me all night. I'll run a extension cord out when it gets too dark. When I finish, I'm going up there to see Aurabelle. And I'm packing up my things tomorrow, and come Sunday morning—if I ain't sitting in jail—I'll be on my way to Jackson. If she got good sense, she'll come. *Ditty-ditty dum. Ditty-ditty dum. Ditty-ditty dum.* We was grading leaf tobacco. "What the hell's a freedom ride bus?" he said. ". . . They's lazy, no good sonsofbitches. All of 'em. Them is niggers, boy. Niggers. You know what a nigger is. You know what they want. You know all they want is our womenfolk. I taught you that since you was little." Pa goes: *Pecka-pecka poo. Pecka-pecka poo.* Ma went: *Ah-rum-dum dee. Ah-rum-dum dee.* "I wanna be part of what's changing things," I said. *Ditty-ditty dum.* "Don't you bother," he said. "Just don't you bother. 'Cause I'd burn 'em unopened." Damn this fucking truck. Equipment's no good. Two summers is like a year. I've been three summers and three winters. Beat up bad. Blowed up. Shot at. Pissed on. Spit on. Stepped on. For what? To lay under this fucking truck looking for a five-eighths? We fought like soldiers in an army. There was momentum then. We had goals. No time to think 'bout personal differences. I saw the handwriting on the wall, but I stayed. It's hard to leave something you've loved. But if that thing's already left you. . . . "Off," I said. Heavy kerosene dark. Moonlight coming through the only window. "Here's a present," I said. "I hope you like choc'late." When it gets dark, I'm going up there to

tell her we gotta look for Josh's rhythm together. If she got good sense, she'll come to Jackson with me. I cain't offer her much, but it'll be better'n this damn hill. Here it is, the goddamn wrench. If I drop it again, I know I've lost it—lost it. These hands don't wanna hold nothing no more. And I keep forgetting things. "Anytime you want to, Pete. Just pack up and leave." *Da da dvom. Ditty-ditty dum. Ta-ta tee. La-de-da-da dah. Pecka-pecka poo. Ah-rum-dum dee.* "Off," I said. "You ever been to Jackson?"

🐾 AURABELLE

He push down hard on me with his hammer, driving his nail deep to where it hurts. But I give this fella good for his money; this big ugly motherfucker moaning over me with the slobber running down his chin. Much to endure.

He say, "Hold me tight. Please hold me tight." Then he don't say nothing and I hold him tight. In the quiet I hear a hen clucking under the house, and the crickets is loud outside. A spigot is dripping in the kitchen.

"Hold me tight," I say. "Please hold me tight, mistah."

"Is I hurting you, sugar? What that you said?"

"Nothing. Nothing. Wipe your goddamn mouth or get up. You's drooling again."

"What that you said? I'm close. C'mon now. I'm close. Honey, put down that comic book. Please, honey. Please—"

. . . And the weight of hisself pressing on me is like a ele-phant.

# PLOWERS

The two of them came into headquarters 'bout six o'clock asking a lot of questions. Calvin Drew and this big nigger, Jacks. I told them an official statement would be made in the newspaper in a day or two—soon as we finished our investigation. I said Thomas had had a fight with another prisoner and might of slammed his head against something hard. It gave him the concussion that killed him. I didn't wanna say no more 'til the department made an official statement. So I told them to clear out and let me get my work done, 'less they wanted to investigate his cell personally; and if they did, I'd be more'n glad to lock 'em in there for a few days.

"I'll be in touch with Jackson," Drew said. "They'll send a lawyer down here. You can tell him 'bout your investigation."

The other nigger just stood there, big, woolly-haired, and silent.

"Do what you please," I said. I wiped the sweat off my face. "But both of you get outta here. I got work to do." I got up and walked over to the floor fan in the corner and turned the speed up to high, then sat back down at my desk.

"What 'bout our parade permit?" Drew said, casual.

"Your *what?*"

"Our parade permit. You know what I'm talking about, Sergeant."

I reached in my pocket where I'd stuck it and pulled it out. "You mean this piece of paper?"

He looked at it. "That's it," he said and reached for it.

I pulled it back. "Hold everything. Not so fast." I held it up and tore it real slow. His eyes got like two hard-boiled eggs.

"Look," I said. "It's tore. Now it ain't valid when it's tore

like that. If you persist in having it, though—here." I handed it
to him. He took it and pushed the pieces together and read
the permit.

"Weren't no good anyway," he said. "You had the wrong
date wrote in."

He handed it back. I wouldn't take it. Then the sonofabitch
dropped it on the floor, the pieces turning like little paddle
wheels on a riverboat. I got up and came from behind my desk.

"Pick it up," I said.

He just kept looking at me with them ice-hard eyes of
his'n. But he didn't budge. I was watching both of them. I
eased my hand onto the butt of my pistol.

"I told you to pick up that paper," I said. Still the nigger
didn't budge and the other one was watching me hard. My
hand was on my pistol. "You don't pick that paper up," I said,
"I'm gon' lock your ass up." They just keep watching me. "I'll
put both you in jail," I said.

"On what charge?" he said.

"Littering."

"Who's littering? It just blew outta my hand. On account
of that fan yonder. I got a witness," he said.

The other nigger nodded and they kept watching me.
"Get the fuck outta here," I said. "Both of you. While you still
can. And lemme catch one of you niggers off the sidewalk
tomorrow. It'll be your ass. You'll go to jail so fast you won't
know what took you."

"Thank you, Sergeant," he said, the arrogant sonofabitch,
looking at me like he thought he was good as a white man.

"You arrogant sonofabitch," I said. "You got five seconds—"

They turned and walked out, stiff as Indians.

Soon as they left I called Peters in. He's the nigger on the
force. We don't 'low him to arrest whites. So he's hard as hell
on niggers.

"Listen here," I said. "I'm riding patrol with you tonight.
I'm doing a double shift."

He nodded and said, "All right," and turned to start back out. He don't have much to say to me. I b'lieve I make him nervous, the black bastard. I let him get as far as the door.

"Boy, don't you see something on my floor?" I said.

He turned and looked back at me, his eyes burning. He looked down and saw it and shrugged his shoulders.

"Pick it up," I said, watching him. He just stood there for a little, then stooped slow and picked up the pieces of paper and went on out the door, shutting it quiet behind him like he had some respect—like he knew better than to bite the hand that fed him. That's what's wrong with the rest of these niggers: they're out to destroy what's always took good care of them.

 **RICE**

Maybe I'll get up there tonight and just move my lips. Who the hell will know the difference?

There's a small clearing in the high grass at the top of the hill. You can sit and watch the sun set behind the woods. I go there a lot. I've never shared it with anyone. I'd like to share it with him. We're sitting on the freedom house porch when I ask him.

"Watch the *sunset?*" he says, and laughs.

"Sure, it's beautiful from the top of the hill. There's a clearing in the high grass, where you can watch the sun go down over the woods across the river."

"I've seen plenty sunsets. Some other time," he says.

"I want you to see it with me. Today. Please."

He looks at me and scratches his mustache and gets up.

"All right," he says. "If you're really that much into it. Let's go."

Just then Cal's car pulls in the driveway. B. Jacks is with him. Cal gets out and comes up on the porch.

"The motherfuckers ain't giving us a permit," he says. "Where the hell's Solly? I want the FBI out there tomorrow. And I want every Jackson TV station contacted. Tonight. Where the fuck is Solly?"

"In his room reading," Rice tells him.

He looks at us. "Where you two going?" Then he looks straight at me, his eyes full of question and implication. I stare right back at him.

"To watch the sunset," I say.

"To do *what?*"

"Watch the sunset. What's wrong with that?"

He goes in and slams the front door.

"What did I do wrong?" I say.

"Nothing," Rice says. "C'mon, let's go."

"What's so bad about wanting to see something beautiful and natural once in a while?"

"Forget it," Rice says. "It doesn't matter."

We go down the porch steps and follow the path around to the back of the house. As we turn to start up the alley the back door opens and Cal sticks his head out.

"Hey, boy," he calls to Rice. "Your voice in good tune? I want the folks to be proud of my house niggah."

Rice stops and looks back at him. I can almost feel his anger.

"You'll push it too far," Rice says.

Cal laughs and closes the screen.

"C'mon," I say. "Let's hurry before it's too late."

PETERS

They don't know how bad *I* feel. All they know is how *they* feel; and that I'm a niggah. So I'm their enemy. But I ain't their enemy. Just doing my duty. I'm a officer of the law. The first and onliest black policeman in the county. But 'stead of respecting me for what I am and looking up to me, niggahs give me a bad time, and white folks give me a bad time too. I get it from both. When I bust a niggah down, he say I'm Tomming. If I let him slide, the white folks say, "You ain't doing your duty. You let him go 'cause blood's thicker than water." Now here I am patrolling with Plowers. He hates niggahs. He even hates me. I won't get my usual nap in, plus I might have to whip some innocent niggah's head just to show Plowers I'm doing a job. I'm the onliest in the county; the first and onliest to be appointed. So naturally I got pressure on me. The white folks say niggahs'll run over me, but that's a lie. I got as many arrests to my credit as any on the force with equal time. And here I'm driving this white gorilla around and him smoking a great long cigar that looks like a niggah's dick. Hell, I ain't no goddamn chauffeur.

"Turn down St. Catherine Street," he says. "See what them niggers are up to."

I turn and we cruise down St. Catherine Street. Shit, I wish I could tell them how it makes *me* feel. But they wouldn't understand. All they know is how *they* feel.

RICE

We watch the sun set. It goes down.

I know Cal's had a tough life. And I know he thinks I've had all the breaks. In some ways I have. But in other ways he has more. He has clearly defined roots, a base. And he has confidence. I've had accessories, appurtenances. I've grown like a rock grows, by accretion; he by intussusception. But there is no explaining this to him. No explaining anything that doesn't fit precisely into the little pigeonholes of his contempt.

The sun is down, and the high tones of silver have begun to fade from the gray clouds, leaving them heavier-looking and more somber. Above the rose-blue horizon they drift in small thin streaks, like strings of old dull pearls. The sun has slipped huge and red into the bright green woods across the river. And the air is still hot and damp, and the tall pale grass seems to reflect the color of the fallen sun.

I don't suppose Cal would ever understand that now at last we're together.

PARNELL

Rice sees me crying and reaches out and takes my hand. When I stop, I tell him how afraid I am. "I wish tomorrow was over," I say. "I've got this horrible feeling." Above us the clouds are heavy-looking as though rain is coming soon.

"Say to yourself over and over; 'Don't be afraid. Don't be afraid,'" he says. "Then go ahead and do the thing you're afraid of. Sometimes it works for me. And if it doesn't work, it doesn't really matter anyway. We're going to Duncan Park."

I look at him. "But aren't you afraid?"

He doesn't answer at first, but looks away. "Yes," he says. "Yes, I am."

We get up and start back down the hill, walking slowly through the smell of honeysuckle riding on the wind.

 GEORGE

Most folks 'round here are sick and tired of violence and trouble. If there was a way to give in and still save face, I believe us whites would do it. But the civil righters keep folks pushed right up against the wall. Not giving space to breathe even. And this heat wave is making it worse. If the civil righters would just back off some. But they won't. I ain't never seen the likes of them. I'll be frank, I just ain't never seen niggers like these. And I was born and raised here; been thirty-one years here—but I ain't *never* seen niggers like we got now. Used to be that folks could talk to the colored, sort of be their friend. But these today— They just laugh in your face and go 'bout their business. White folks 'round here just soon kill a nigger as look at him. But I believe the television has kept them from doing it. You'd of thought they would kill niggers in droves. But the television sort of brought things out in the open. You could sit home watching what happened. Hell, it weren't but a few years back that they killed that little colored boy from Chicago for whistling at a white woman. Me for one, I wish we could live in peace and harmony and love like the Holy Bible says we oughta.

Wonder what that crazy nigger's gonna do with the dynamite?

.**W**hen we get to the freedom house, Solly meets us at the back door. "They've arrested Furman and Winston. And two others," he says.

"Peters and Ed Plowers got them," he says, his blue-green eyes huge and distorted behind the thick glasses.

"For what?" Parnell says.

"We're on our way to headquarters now to find out," he says.

"I'll go with you," I say.

"C'mon," Solly says.

"Me, too," Parnell says.

"You stay here," he says, scowling. "We got enough trouble already without having a chick around."

"Fuck you," Parnell says, and walks on in the house, slamming the screen door.

We hurry through the house and out the front door and get in the car. Cal is at the wheel. He looks at me but says nothing, and pulls the car out of the driveway and heads up Franklin Street. He cuts his eye back at me in the rearview mirror. Hell, I'm thinking, here it comes again.

"Maybe we can trade those four for one good house niggah," he says.

I say nothing, just sigh and settle back in the seat.

At headquarters he parks and we go in. Plowers stands near the wire enclosure talking to the desk sergeant who sits behind it. Plowers looks up as we enter.

"Whadda you niggers want?" he says in his slow drawl.

Cal lets out a deep sigh. After a moment he says, "I'd appreciate very much, Sergeant, you telling me why you're holding four of my people."

"Just talking to them," Plowers says. "Ain't laid a hand on them."

"What're the charges?"

"Ain't booked 'em yet."

"Then how can you hold them?"

"I already told you. We're just talking to them. We suspect they were involved in a little knifeplay at Duncan Park yesterday."

"C'mon, Sergeant. You know better."

"One of them's a Jew boy," Plowers says. "*He* could of been in there."

"Furman's never been inside Duncan Park in his life. None of my people have."

"We got a witness coming to identify him. The white boy they attacked with a knife yesterday. At Duncan Park."

Through a silence, Plowers and Cal stare at each other. Finally Cal says, "We'll sit down and wait 'til you're through."

"Suit yourself," Plowers says, and goes back to talking to the desk sergeant.

After about an hour they release Furman, Winston, and the other two local kids and we all go back out to Cal's car.

"There're seven of us," Cal says. "One too many. If we overload they'll stop us for that." He turns to Solly. "Wait here and I'll come back for you."

Solly shrugs and steps back from the car. The rest of us get in. I get in the front seat next to the window. The heat inside is terrific.

"I'll be right back," Cal says to Solly.

"Hurry," Solly says. "It's getting dark."

"Wait inside," Cal says. "Or they'll arrest you for loitering." He starts the engine and puts on the headlights. They cut into the dusk and lay two flat spots against the street.

After a few blocks Cal says, "There's a white Pontiac behind us. Maybe the Klan."

We all turn back. I feel my stomach tighten.

"Don't look back," Cal snaps, watching them in the rear-view mirror. He makes a sharp right, then a left.

"They're still behind us," he says, his voice level, cool.

"I hope they don't start shooting," Furman says, sitting in the rear in the middle, his straw hat cocked at a severe angle. He takes it off and slumps far down in the seat.

"Shit," Winston says. "If it ain't the cops, it's the Klan."

Cal turns another corner. "We're almost there," he says, still watching the rearview mirror, his lips barely moving. Then he shifts into second and steps down hard on the gas and the Plymouth bolts ahead, pushing our backs against the seats. After about a block he backs off quickly and suddenly I realize we're back on St. Catherine Street. We're cruising again like nothing happened.

"We're in niggah country now," Cal says. "They won't fuck with us here." He laughs.

I look back and see the Pontiac continue to follow us for another couple of hundred feet, then suddenly make a U-turn and head in the opposite direction. Furman puts his hat back on and lets out a long breath.

"I swear," Winston says, "if it ain't the cops, it's the Klan."

"Same thing," Cal says. He turns again and we go down-hill to Franklin Street and halt in front of the freedom house.

"Okay," he says. "One of you get out and make room for Solly."

At that instant a police car pulls up behind us, its red dome light flashing brightly.

"Shit," Cal says. "The fucking cops. Let me do the talking." He opens his door and steps out. I recognize the two police-men who get out of the patrol car—Peters and Plowers. Peters has a flashlight. He comes over to my side and shines it in. Behind the light his face is small, sharp-featured, intense.

"Furman," he says. "Paul Furman." He shines the light into each face, then stops it on Furman. "That's you. I know you. C'mon outta there, you're under arrest."

Plowers stands beside him, smoking a cigar and looking in at us. Peters yanks open the back door and reaches in for Furman. Furman pulls back. Cal starts around the car fast.

"Wait a minute. You cain't arrest that man without an affidavit," he says.

Peters just looks at him and pulls at Furman again. Plowers goes around to the other side of the car, opens the door and reaches in for Furman. Both of them are pulling him. Furman holds on to his straw hat.

"Sergeant, I'd like to see the affidavit," Cal says, leaning his head into the car and talking to Plowers. "You cain't take him without an affidavit."

Plowers and Peters stop trying to get Furman out and both stand erect, breathless, staring at Cal. Then Plowers looks at Peters.

"Show this nigger the affidavit. Hurry up."

Peters reaches in his pocket and takes out a piece of paper and unfolds it and hands it to Cal. Cal goes to the front of the car and reads it under the headlights. Then he comes back and leans down and looks in at Furman, who's sitting with his hands folded on his lap.

"They got you charged with assault," he says. "Go 'head with them for now. I'll be down to get you out soon as they set bail."

Furman looks at him but says nothing. He starts to get out. "Who did I assault?" he says.

"Go 'head," Cal says, quietly. "I'll be down for you."

Furman climbs out. Peters gets behind him and gives him a hard shove. Furman almost trips and whirls back angrily on Peters.

"Take it easy, brother," Cal says to Peters.

Peters looks hard at Cal but says nothing. Cal spits. Peters goes on. They put Furman in the patrol car and drive away, the red light still flashing.

Cal gets back in the car, not saying anything, his face tight.

I look up at the freedom house. A light burns in Parnell's room.

"See, that's the kind of shit that pisses me off," Cal says, more to himself than to us, his words hissing out into the dark. "Furman ain't no more assaulted somebody than I pissed in my coffee this morning." He slams his fist into the horn button, the horn making a short, urgent burst of sound that dies away quickly and leaves us again in silence. Finally, Cal starts the engine and we turn around and head slowly back downtown.

At headquarters the desk sergeant says, "Bail's set at two-fifty."

Cal doesn't say anything. We go back outside and he says to us, "I'll go get somebody to sign a property bond and we'll come back and get him out."

When we're all back in the car Solly says, "What the hell happened?" We tell him. Then for a while nobody says anything. We drive a few blocks and somebody says, "Oh, shit. Another police car's on our tail."

"It's been there since we left headquarters," Cal says, staring into the mirror. "They're fucking around with us. Trying to keep us from the rally."

Their red light flashes on, lighting the interior of our car. Cal pulls the car over and we stop. The police car pulls up behind us again and Plowers and Peters get out. They come over, Peters leaning his head down and looking into our car. Moonlight reflects from his polished visor. He switches on his flashlight and shines it in, this time stopping on Solly's face.

"You Solomon Greenfield?" he says. He holds a piece of paper gripped in his hand.

"Yes," Solly says. "I am he."

"Well I have an affidavit for your arrest. You're charged with malicious assault and intent to do bodily harm." He pulls open the door. "C'mon, get out. You're under arrest."

"Lemme see the affidavit," Cal says resignedly. Peters hands him the paper and Cal switches on the overhead light and reads it.

"Okay," he says to Solly. "Go with them. I'll get two bonds signed and come down and bail you guys out. Don't worry."

They put Solly in the patrol car and make a U-turn and head back toward headquarters. We sit for another long time in silence. The heat is still terrific, the air more humid now with the sun gone.

Finally, Cal says, "I need a drink."

"This is a bitch, ain't it?" I say.

He seems to draw within himself and glares over at me. "Shit, niggah," he says. "You ain't seen nothing yet." He starts the engine and races it, and we start off toward St. Catherine Street and a café; then to find some bail money for the others.

CRAYFIELD

I said to McIver, "Drew's out to steal our thunder. When you finish the regular preaching, I'll take over and get the rally going. When I finish, we'll let Drew talk. But you cut him short. Don't give him more than ten or twelve minutes. I don't want folks worked up to a frenzy. I want cool heads out there tomorrow, not a bunch of wild Indians."

"I understand you perfectly, Brother Crayfield," McIver said. "Perfectly."

"See you at the church then in 'bout half an hour, Reverend," I said, and hung up the phone.

I had Cora call headquarters to check on the parade permit and make a Monday morning appointment for me with Chief Worden. I want it from the horse's mouth what happened to Josh Thomas. It's a grave matter. I'm requesting our central office to send an investigation team down here. But for me to rush to headquarters today demanding this and that—well. . . . Relations 'tween us and the police are bad enough now. So I'll wait 'til Monday.

When Cora hung up the phone I says to her, "You got social business with Mr. Drew?" She looked surprised, then pitiful. Then she denied it. Maybe I was being too harsh, I thought. But I meant it. It was serious.

"He just took me to buy a hamburger," she says. "That was all."

"It had better be," I says. " 'Cause if I thought for a minute—" She dropped her head again. "Listen," I says. "It's not my intention to pry into your personal affairs. But it don't look good to the membership for my secretary to be taking up with one of them. After all, I'm the director. Now, mind you, I'm not accusing you. I just wanna make my position clear. We don't associate with them unless we absolutely have to, and then only on the business of civil rights. We have nothing in common socially. That's all I'm saying. I think a word to the wise—"

"Yes, sir," she says, blinking them big sweetheart eyes of hers. I couldn't help but taking a quick peep at her legs. Fine as they could be. She went back to typing and I left it at that. I'd be the last to berate her, but it's better to head off trouble before it comes in your front door; that's what I always say.

BENJIE

The light in Momma's room stopped shining and she came out on the porch—Benjie sitting since supper. Momma in a red dress, yellow hat, pink paper flowers on it. Momma with lipstick and powder. Momma smelling perfume.

"C'mon," she said. "We gon' be late for church. You ain't got dirty again, has you? I got no time to clean you again."

"No, ma'am," Benjie said. He took Momma's hand. Down the porch steps. Up the alley.

"And if you pee on yourself again, I gon' whup you good. Big ole boy like you I cain't remember the last time—You oughta be 'shamed."

Benjie's head down searching for pennies. Once a dime. Mostly pennies. Sometimes those white rubber things like balloons.

"You ain't no damn baby, you know. Now there you go. I cain't say a durn word to you that you don't go crying. Take this handkerchief and wipe your eyes."

Momma pulling hard. Up the hill to St. Catherine Street—Benjie wishing for candy.

"Where Ludy, Momma?"

"Her coming directly. Ironing her dress. C'mon here now. We gon' be so late as 'tis." Momma pulling Benjie hard again. Turning at St. Catherine Street—Benjie skipping.

"You behave in church, you hear?"

"Yes, ma'am."

"And if you feel the urge, don't bite your tongue. Speak up and tell me. You hear?"

"Yes, ma'am."

"I'll take you to the toilet. But you speak up. You 'shamed of yourself? A great big boy like you."

"Yes, ma'am," Benjie said.

The church was just a little ways down St. Catherine Street. Up the cement steps. Through the tall wood doors. Folks shouting and stomping. Singing. Benjie scared. Once with Reverend McIver preaching, Momma up sudden and shouting, crying and down on the floor kicking, eyes rolling, hollering. Then two big men. Black suits, white gloves. Carry Momma away. Carry lots of people away.

Ludy caught up and took hold of his other hand—Benjie feeling better. Ludy never falls out or shouts. Ludy's dress was yellow and nice.

"Gal, you been in my perfume again?" Momma said. "You smell like a damn whore—young as you is. What you do, pour it all over you?"

Benjie, Momma, and Ludy—down the wood path between the benches. The singing stopped.

"Momma, what's a whore?" Benjie said.

Momma squeezed his hand. It hurt.

"I told you, don't ask those many questions. You a kid. You s'pose to be seen, not heard." Momma smiling at the people looking.

"I know what it is," Ludy said.

"Hush," Momma said. "And if I catch you in my perfume again—"

Momma finding a bench up front for them. Benjie in first, then Momma. Next Ludy. Benjie sitting beside a great fat lady—Momma squeezing him in. The fat lady fanning. Cardboard—Benjie feeling the breeze. Hot and smelling. The lady smiled—her face sweat and shiny. Benjie looked up front at the stage. Reverend McIver was sitting down. What was a whore?

". . . We will all sing hymn three twenty-six," Reverend McIver said.

 # McIVER

While they sing I can get myself together. Sister Ernestine's chicken so damn good I feel like I'm gonna bust. Shouldn't of eaten that second breast, though. Can hardly keep my damn eyes open. Sure could do with a nap, too. Tried to get the sister to lay down with me after we ate, but she said it'd make her feel funny; me being her pastor and all. I know damn well she'd of felt funny, 'cause I planned to stick a dick into her. But you got to be patient with them at first, 'til they come around; so I said, "Let's rest *after* the meeting, sister, and we can pray together." Look at her over there, standing with the choir singing beautiful and her tits holding the robe straight out and all that precious ass. Wouldn't need no pillow under her. No siree. Lemme get my mind offen it 'fore I have to stand. Let's see Numbers, Ruth, Ezekiel . . . hmm. Sure wish I hadn't eaten that second breast.

 # AURABELLE

He push down hard on me with his hammer, driving his nail deep to where it hurts. . . .

I hear them singing up at the church. Hear it rolling down the hill on the wind. It comes through my window where the shade's half up; a wind full of voices, and moonlight mingling with it, and it all being together in this room standing so still in the dark—this room full of shadows and breath and singing. Poor Josh. Poor Cousin Josh.

And the weight of hisself pressing on me is like a elephant had lay his belly hard on mine and squatted down to smother out the breath from me and shut off the light from the onliest window.

"Hold me tight, mistah. Please hold me tight."

PETERS

I saw it. Plowers brought him in the interrogation room and closed the door and locked it. McClaren was in there and I was in there.

"This the nigger?" Plowers said.

"Fits the description perfect," McClaren said.

"What I done? Please, boss. Sergeant," Josh said. He was barefooted.

"Sit down, nigger, 'fore I knock you down," Plowers said.

He pushed him into the chair they had set up in the middle of the room. Plowers turned around fast and hit Josh in the face with his fist. It would've knocked him over 'cept the chair was screwed to the floor. But it busted Josh's lips open and one tooth come through.

"Sit up, nigger," McClaren said. "Take your due. You know what you done." McClaren jabbed him in the stomach with the end of a nightstick. Josh looked at me. I looked away.

"Why'd you do it?" Plowers said. "Who put you up to it? Them freedom riders?"

"Ain't done nothing," Josh said, spitting blood. "I swear.

Ain't done nothing 'cept what you 'rested me for. Driving my car."

"You lying nigger," McClaren said. "She was underage. You know that."

"I swear to you."

They beat on him until he passed out.

When he came to, Plowers went to the glass cabinet an' took out the sap glove and put it on. It was then that I commenced to getting scared. It's a leather glove that looks just like any ordinary glove 'cept it's bigger an' it got six ounces of powdered lead built into the back of it over the knuckles. Plowers showed it to him.

"Now tell us why you took that underaged white girl down to the river and molestered her," Plowers said.

He drove his bulk into the blow, and sent it pushing into Josh's ribs. I could hear them busting. Josh went sideways outta the chair. McClaren reached down and lifted him back up and held him while Plowers kept driving the sap glove into his body and into his head.

I was getting sick. I never seen anybody whipped so. The front of Josh's pants was wet with piss.

"He had enough," I said, shouting. "Y'all gon' kill him."

"Get outta here," Plowers said. "Goddamned niggers. You all stick together. Open your mouth again. . . ."

"Go 'head, Peters," McClaren said. "Talk to the desk sergeant. Take a deck of cards. He gets lonesome." They was both breathing heavy and looking at me hard.

I went on out and shut the door and I heard one of them lock it behind me. I got sick in the locker room; me, with two years on the force. I just never seen a man beat thataway.

Hell, this is a tough job I got myself into. Black folks don't know how bad I feel. All they know is how *they* feel; and that I'm a cop and I'm a niggah; so I'm their enemy. But I ain't their enemy. I'm an appointed officer of the law. The first and the onliest black policeman in the county.

Cain't see a goddamned thing with a forty-watt bulb in this drop light. There's a hundred-watter in the kitchen ceiling, Pete. Just go get it and screw it in the drop light. Screw it in and you'll see better. Screw it into this socket and you'll see the light come on bright. You get some professional help when you get to Jackson, Pete. Hands shaking in forty-watt light. Cain't see nothing past the head of the engine. All dark and silent, and that's where you keep losing your tools. Go straight to a doctor when you get to Jackson, Pete. Maybe something's stuck. Maybe a ant crawling 'round loose in your head. Or a Indian nut stuck in your ear. Chauncey Sommerwell had a Indian nut stuck in his ear once on a picnic. He was on the grass with his head laying in girl's lap; and them eating a bag of Indian nuts and she dropping every other one at his ear. One nut went in and got stuck and we had to carry Chauncey to the doctor to get it out. Go get the hundred-watter, Pete, and come back and finish the job. Not much more to do. Maybe an hour. Then go tell Aurabelle you's looking for Josh's rhythm. Damn, I can hardly see my way back to the house it's so dark. Listen, there's singing coming from the church. Damn, it's pitch black out here past the fender. Who's that there standing looking in the back door?

"What you want there? Hey, you!"

"Me, Zenola, boss. No more trouble."

"Oh, you, Zenola. Listen here, you know what he said to me, Zenola?"

"Me climb highest mountain. Bare chest to sun."

"He said, 'Anytime you want to, Pete. Just pack up and leave.' *Ditty-ditty dum.* You know what *Ditty-ditty dum* means?"

"Sweep, sweep. Me Zenola. Slop, slop. Gone forever. No more trouble. No more Judas calling."

"That's my basic rhythm, Zenola."

"Zenola, black king of the mountain. Next yellow. Then black."

"Where you going, Zenola? Come here, fella. Listen, I wanna tell you what he said. 'Anytime you want to, Pete.' And you know what I said to him? Hey . . . c'mere. Goddamn you, you crazy sonofabitch running off like that when I'm trying to tell you something. You dumb crazy sonofabitch." Shit, this hundred-watter's hot. I'll just unscrew it and take it back outside and screw it into the socket. Then I can see past the head of the engine. Maybe I can even see the fender. What did I do wrong to Zenola? There, that's better. Now I can see the whole engine. I'd give her a better life than she's got on this alley. I'll go say, "Pack your things and meet me at the Greyhound bus depot Sunday morning. I want you for my wife. I ain't a millionaire. I ain't got a house or land. But I love you. And I think you like me some." This hundred-watter is just fine. But I still cain't see past the fender. *Canvas and rope to lower us, Mother. Case us in wood and soft gray velvet, Mother. Clothe us, cushion us, then send us back forever to the unremitting Mother.* "You put a rubber on?" "You put a rubber on?" "Off," I said.

 BENJIE

The bench hard on his bottom bones—Benjie waiting for the stomping. Now clapping. Momma clapping soft. The fat lady clapping hard, singing loud. Reverend McIver sitting up on the stage looking 'round—head going up and down, foot patting; eyes big, slow. Soon the stomping. Benjie down in the seat, touching toe to floor, beating toe to singing. First soft, then hard. Heels 'round him went: Thump. Thump. Thump, against the floor. Thump. Thump. Thump. The hands clapped louder. The music went high, then low, then loud. The tambourine bells were shaking, the heels going harder. Thump. Thump. Thump. The fat lady's hands went wide apart, then crashed together. Clap. Clap. Clap. Benjie beat his toe hard: Tap. Tap. Tap. Heels went: Thump. Thump. Thump. Hands went: Clap. Clap. Clap. Then the piano went big, then long and low. Then the singing stopped. The choir ladies sat down. Reverend McIver got up. He folded his hands and looked over everybody. His eyes went 'round. Big, slow.

"That kind of singing the Lord likes to hear," he said. His hands stayed folded. "On the twenty-third of next month we will have the Jubilee Singers from Jackson visiting with us. We're also privileged to have Reverend Elton Lucas, pastor of the Holy Light Baptist Church in Red Lick, as our guest speaker on that Sunday. That's the twenty-third of next month." He put on his eyeglasses and took out a piece of paper.

"The spirit of God attends—and our hearts mourn—the passing of Saddie-Lou Tanner. Dearly beloved wife of Oscar; mother of Floyd and Estelle Jean. Services will be held at Moody's Funeral Home, at two P.M., this coming Monday afternoon." He took off the glasses and his eyes went 'round again. The fat lady wiped her eyes with a handkerchief, then blew her nose.

"Rest her soul," she said, whispering. She put the handkerchief away.

Reverend McIver walked to the high table and leaned against it and made his elbows stiff. His eyes went 'round.

"As I look out over you tonight, my brethren, I see in your faces worry and frustration. Vexation and doubt. Pain and discontentment. We live in a troubled time. A time that pits friend against friend. Father against son. Mother against daughter."

His eyes went 'round. Big, slow.

"Yes, I look out over your faces tonight and sense the mighty fear in your hearts. The danger ahead for all of us who will embark on this perilous journey tomorrow. But I don't have to remind you that we've been on a long journey already. And we have lost many along the way."

Somebody sneezed. Reverend McIver's eyes went there. Soon they came back.

"But we must keep faith in our Lord Jesus," Reverend McIver said.

"You have to pee?" Momma whispered.

"No, ma'am."

"Then stop fidgeting. And sit up straight."

". . . Yes, we must never stop believing in the Lord Jesus. He who died for our sins. Mine and yours."

"Amen," somebody said. "Amen."

"Suffered at the hands of the cruel."

"Amen," the fat lady said. She rocked back and forth.

". . . at the hands of the unjust."

"Yes, Jesus," the fat lady said. "Have mercy on us, Jesus."

"Upon that wooden cross at Calvary hung our Lord," Reverend McIver said. "Hung in that dark morning. Bleeding and suffering for our sins."

"Yes, Jesus. Yes, Jesus," the fat lady said. She rocked and hummed.

". . . And when the sponge dipped in vinegar and myrrh was fixed to a pole and offered up to his burning lips, our Lord refused it and suffered on. He suffered on."

The feet started patting.

"Yes, Jesus. Yes, Jesus," somebody said.

"Suffered on. . . ." Reverend McIver said. He spread his arms wide and looked at the ceiling. "And on the ninth hour, Jesus lifted his eyes to Almighty God and said, 'It is finished Father, into thy hands I commend my spirit.' "

"You sure you ain't gotta pee?" Momma said.

"No, ma'am," Benjie said.

Reverend McIver took out a white handkerchief and wiped his neck. The feet stopped patting. He took a drink of water.

Momma dried her eyes. "Then sit up straight like I told you," she said. "And stop fidgeting. You's in the house of the Lord."

Reverend McIver put the glass down. He leaned on the high table again and made his elbows stiff. His eyes went 'round. Big, slow.

PARNELL

"I *didn't come South for this, Tom.*" *He was kissing me, his mustache up my nose, his hand under my dress; my legs trembling, his hand understanding.*

"*Take them off,*" *he said.* "*Please.*"

"*I didn't come South for this, Tom. Tom, we oughta go. Tom, please. . . .*"

"*I can't help it. The heat. Please. Please.*"

Higher lifting Now his He to Now her She of swollen darkness comes the Yes of Them, comes his silver seeds against her She, like rain his He comes Now.

"On the twenty-third of next month we will have the Jubilee Singers from Jackson visiting with us," Reverend McIver said.

Sun runs yellow rills in the treetops. Moss roses cool against thighs.

". . . our hearts mourn—the passing of Saddie-Lou Tanner. Dearly beloved wife of Oscar; mother of Floyd and Estelle Jean," Reverend McIver said.

CLARICE

Zenola'll fuss at me tomorrow—bringing all these children here and leaving him alone to fix his supper tonight. But I want mine to see what these young people are trying to do for them. For *all* of us. *And their long hair and unshaven faces is a sign; a sign for the world to see that the true spirit of Christ lives in them—that they are truly ready to give and receive love; truly tired of words, and ready to replace them with deeds. . . .*

"We will all sing hymn six twenty-three," Reverend McIver said.

 **RICE**

Let's see, how does it go? *Oh, freedom, freedom. Oh, freedom. Ain't nobody gon' turn me 'round. Turn me 'round. Turn me 'round. Ain't nobody—* Shit, that's from two different songs. How the hell am I gonna get up there and lead if I can't even remember the fucking words?

". . . And we have lost many along the way," Reverend McIver says. "But we must keep our faith in the Lord Jesus."

What about: *Jack an' Jill ran up the hill. Jack fell down with the Civil Rights Bill.* . . . That's a good one.

"I wish this motherfucker would get through with the bullshit so we can get down to business," Cal says. He sits beside me, arms folded across his chest, looking up at Reverend McIver standing at the lectern.

"Cal," I say. "I can't sing a damn note, man. I'm not getting up there. I don't even know the words."

"Shut up," he says. "Don't you hear the man preaching? Have some respect. You're in the house of the Lord."

 **CATES**

There, finished. Close it up and go ask her. *Don't make me laugh, Pete. What would she want with a poor-assed white boy like you? She's a queen, man. She got the blood of kings in her, Pete. A fool could see that. So what would she want with a poor*

white farm trash like you? She'll never leave this alley with you. With no white man. Go see the doctor soon as you step off the bus in Jackson, you may have a Indian nut stuck in your head, Pete. You're a casualty of an undeclared war. A fucking victim of an unofficial war. Shell-shocked from too much combat, Pete. Remember how it all happened? Ever think you'd end up a victim? Unwanted? Despised by the very ones you tried to help? You poor dumb sonofabitch. Well, their goddamned truck is fixed. I can still fix things when I put my mind to it. *Listen to the singing, Pete. Black folks singing, Pete. Singing without you. How does it make you feel?* All right, goddammit. I said I'd go see a doctor. Soon as I hit Jackson. I will. Now leave me be. *Pete, you caint just march up the hill and tell her like that. Wait 'til tomorrow morning. Go wash up now. Rest. You're tired. Go up to the church and listen to the black folks singing without you.* Goddammit, stop it! I said I'd see the damn *Ditty-ditty dum,* didn't I? Their singing comes down the hill like small red bells in the dark; down the red-dust hill with no forty-watters burning in the shacks 'cause everybody's at church singing. But the singing is not at the church anymore, 'cause it's coming down the hill. We'll find Josh's rhythm together. And Pa'll see things are changing. This ain't the old South no more. Where'd Zenola go? "Sweep, sweep," he said. "Sweep, sweep." Is that his rhythm?" S'pose she won't talk to me. *Listen to them singing without you, Pete.* Dammit, when something you've loved has already left you. . . .

 AURABELL

He push down hard on me with his hammer, driving his nail deep to where it hurts. But I give this fella good for his money; this big bad motherfucker with his hair konked and his pistol shoved under the pillow where I feel its hardness against my head. Much to endure. Much to endure. And the weight of hisself pressing on me is like a elephant had lay his belly hard on mine and squatted down to smother out the breath from me and shut off the light from the onliest window.

 MAMIE LE

I seen him coming up the hill, the white boy what fixes they truck—me sitting on the porch talking to a fella and us waiting for Aurabelle to get through. He comes up the alley walking like he's drunk and it so dark I cain't see who he is 'til he passes under the one lamplight.

Wouldn't of guessed him white, his hands and face as black as mine from axle grease—like he been wallowing in it. I just knew he wasn't coming here, so I goes back to talking to whatsoever-his-name. Then I see him turn in from the road toward my porch. First I thought he had just staggered.

"You know that sonofabitch is coming *here*," I says to this other.

"What he want here?" he says.

"That's what I like to know," I says. "He must know white men ain't 'lowed in this house."

He comes to the edge of the porch and stops and looks up at us and I get up and say, "Evening, mister. You lost your way?"

"Good evening, ma'am," he says, just as polite as you'd want. "My Pa, he grows leaf tobacco," he says. "We ain't got much but we's honorable folks and I lost a brother in the Second World War."

I leaned on the banister and look straight in his eyes. "That's a shame," I says. "Sorry to hear it. Now what do you want?"

"I cain't see a durn thing with a forty-watt drop light," he says.

"Then you oughta go 'head where you was going 'fore you dropped it," I says. "The name's Mamie Lee. I got company now."

He says, "You cain't see nothing past the head of the engine with a forty-watter."

"Mister, you sho oughta be going," I says. "I don't wanna call the police on one of you fellas." I was only bluffing. I sho wouldn't of called the police here tonight the way tension is. He starts up the steps. I go and stand in front of him, my belly protruding in his face. What's-his-name don't budge— the scared motherfucker just sits there watching. "Look here," I says to this other. "You get the hell off my property. Right now. You must don't know the rules. One of you come in here, they'll close me up."

"I just want to ask her," he says, "if I ain't sitting in jail come Sunday morning, we'll be on the first Greyhound out." He takes another step up. "I'll wait for her at the depot," he says.

"If I knew what you was talking 'bout," I says, "I might could help you. But as it is you's just trespassing." He keeps on coming up the steps, his eyes glassed over like he'd been hit hard on the head. "That's far as you go, mister," I says. "Fact it's too far. This ain't no St. Catherine Street café. Ain't no damn social center neither." I had put my hands on my hips now.

"You better listen to her, kid," the other says, getting up and coming over.

"I'm just a beat somewhere, sir," the white boy says, the glassy look bright.

I'd had 'nough of his drunk talk. "You take one more step," I says, "and I'm gonna bust your head with a brickbat. Now you think I'm fooling—"

"A simple rhythm among so many," he says. "You reckon she'd like some more choc'late?"

This other gives him a hard push backward and he falls down the steps into the yard and rolls 'round in the dark grunting and trying to get to his feet. Then the other is on him, dragging him out into the alley. But he's a big one—big and strong and drunk out his mind. He gets a hold on what's-his-name and slings him out into the alley, then starts back up the steps staggering and stumbling again. I get hold to this water pitcher we'd been drinking out of and fling it in his face; pitcher, ice, and all, right in his damn face. When the pitcher busts, the ice and glass scatter ever which way. He falls backward again and I kick at him but miss it. The other gets up and runs up behind him and hits him over the head with something which I cain't see clear but which looks like a piece of wood or a pipe. But that don't stop him neither, and he stands there at the foot of the steps weaving back and forth and looking at us like he don't know where he is or what he done. The blood is streaming down the back of his neck from his head, and his face is cut bad, and blood there too. Then he starts up the steps again, wiping it outen his eyes with them greasy hands and coming steadily at me. I see the other run out the front yard and up the hill, maybe gone to get help or maybe just scared 'cause you'd have to kill this sonofabitch to stop him. He keeps coming up the steps, making grunting sounds deep in his throat and wiping the blood

and stumbling ahead. I move quick 'cause I finally know he is crazy 'stead of drunk.

"I come to see her," he says. "Aurabelle. I gotta see her. I gotta see her tonight. Right now."

I run and stand at the other end of the porch. He is crazy. He comes up and sways back and forth and I says, "You cain't go in there now. Somebody's in there. Business. You cain't—"

He looks at the closed door. Then he looks at me and says, "She'll hear me. I know she will. We gon' find Josh's rhythm together. *Ditty-ditty dum. Ditty-ditty dum.*"

And then the crazy sonofabitch throws hisself at the door. Just throws hisself. Trying to bust it down. And then I see the lock starting to give and I says, "Oh, Lord. Oh, Lordy! Lordy!"

AURABELLE

He push down hard on me with his hammer, driving his nail deep to where it hurts. *"You know that sonofabitch is coming here. He must know white men ain't 'lowed in this house."* It's maybe the Lord's way of making me suffer, of giving me my burden. *"My Pa, he grows leaf tobacco. We ain't got much but we's honorable folks and I lost a brother in the Second World War."* But I give this fella good for his money. *"You caint see nothing past the head of the engine with a forty-watter."* *"You get the hell off my property. You must don't know the rules."* This big bad mother-fucker with his hair konked and his pistol shoved under the pillow—and him with his hand resting on it. Much to endure. Much to endure.

"What's that noise?" he says.

"You asking me?" I says. "I wish you wouldn't hold that pistol so close to my head."

And the weight of hisself pressing on me *"You take one more step and I'm gonna bust your head with a brickbat"* is like a elephant. *"You reckon she'd like some more choc'late?"* had lay his belly hard on mine. . . .

"Listen. Shhh. Who is that out there?"

"I don't know. Take the pistol away. It ain't the police. Honest."

"Who the hell is it, then?"

"Some fella from down the hill. Momma's throwing him out. Ain't you finished?"

"My mind's off it. That racket."

"Please take your hand off the pistol."

"I come to see her. Aurabelle. I gotta see her. I gotta see her tonight. Right now. . . ." to smother out the breath from me *"You caint go in there right now. Somebody's in there. Business. You caint—"*

"Mister, please. Please don't."

"Listen! Listen! That motherfucker's coming in here."

"Please. He'll go away. Listen—"

"Goddammit, he's coming in here!"

"You don't need the pistol. I know him good. He don't mean nobody no harm."

"She'll hear me. I know she will. We gon' find Josh's rhythm together. Ditty-ditty dum. Ditty-ditty dum."

"Bitch, you get the fuck up and go to the door. Stop him. You hear him at the door, don't you? You don't wanna see the niggah shot, do you?"

"I hear him, mister. Please put the gun away. He don't mean no harm."

"Oh, Lord. Oh, Lordy! Lordy!"

. . . and shut off the light from the onliest window. The onliest window. The onliest window.

# GEORGE

Wonder what else's on the television tonight other than this John Wayne picture. You seen one, you seen 'em all.

# AURABELLE

He's looking right at me. Right at me, his eyes burning and me laying naked under this sheet listening to the other click the hammer back.

"You got the wrong house, fella," the other says. "You musta made a mistake. Just pull the door to and go 'head where you was going." He's got the pistol pointing right at Pete.

"I'm through with the Movement," he says. "Anytime you want to, Aurabelle. Just pack up and we'll leave. I want you for my wife."

Just like that he says it, standing there with his face a mess. Bleeding.

"Get him outta here," the other says.

Bleeding. He comes to the edge of the bed and gets down on his knees, crying like a baby and laying his head on me. I hold him tight.

The other jumps up and grabs Pete 'round the neck from behind and pulls him down on the floor and sticks the pistol up against his temple with the hammer still cocked. I'm crying too; the first time in so long. Ain't nobody ever said that to me. I put my head in the pillow and that's when I feel the lump from his switchblade. I reach under and come out with it and hit the button and the blade whips open and I get out of the bed fast and lay it against his windpipe. "You pull that trigger and I'll open you," I says. "I'll slit you from ear to ear."

The other lets out a deep breath and says quiet, "You didn't think I was gon' shoot him? I'm just trying to quiet him."

"Then move the gun while you's trying," I says.

"Little sister, you put that knife away," he says. " 'Fore somebody gets hurt for real."

"Listen to him, honey," Mamie Lee says, standing in the door. "We don't want no more trouble."

"You take that pistol away first," I says.

He moves the pistol and I move the knife. Pete gets up slow. I close the knife and throw it on the bed. "Go home," I says. "You're tired and need some sleep. Come and talk to me tomorrow 'bout that other if you've still a mind to."

He nods slow with his eyes glassy.

"Pack your things," he says. "We'll be on the first Greyhound out the depot Sunday morning."

"Go 'head home," I says. "You know we don't 'low no white men." He wipes his face and goes out the door saying something 'bout Cousin Josh that I cain't hear. Then he slams the door hard behind him. We hear him stomp across the porch and down the steps. Then all you can hear in the quiet is the crickets and the singing from the church.

"After all I done for you," Mamie Lee says, taking a handkerchief from her bosom and wiping nothing from her eyes. "After I worked my po' hands to the bones raising you. Putting bread and 'tatoes on the table to feed you. Now here you 'bout to run off and leave me all this burden. And with a *white man!*"

"Listen," the other says, shaking his finger in my face, "You ever pull a knife on me again, bitch—"

I cain't stand nobody shaking their damn finger in my face. "Kiss my ass, motherfucker," I says. "Take your pistol and your knife and your black ass and get the fuck outta here."

"You fresh hussy," Mamie Lee says. "Shut your damn mouth."

I look at him and laugh; him standing there buck naked with his pistol still in his hand. Shit, least I had on stockings. Then I look at her. She's still trying to work up some tears. I laugh. "How much you think a ticket to Jackson is?" I says.

ZENOLA

Zenola into ghost shack. Cobwebs. Boomsticks hiding. *Plowers say: "Light long fuse and run for your life, black king. Good luck."* Zenola into inner ears of goats, knowing secret powers—suns, continents, piss, jail cells, eyes, teeth, soap bubbles, soup. Zenola into freedom house. No sounds coming. Boomsticks into fireplace. *"Don't forget long fuse, you simple sonofabitch," Plowers say. "And run for your life. Good luck, black king. Good luck."* Time happens anyway. Plowers going away with Josh. Slap. Slap. *"What I ever done to you? You Judas. You no-good motherfucker."* Boomsticks into fireplace. Fuse lighting. *"Good luck, black king."* Time happens anyway. Don't forget circles: soap bubbles flying. White, yellow, black. Yellow circles rising. Black circles floating. Sweep, sweep. Slop, slop. Finished. *"Run for your life, black king."* Run. Run. What's that? Who coming? *"Run for your life, black king."* Who coming?

Ditty-ditty dum. Ditty-ditty dum. Da-da doom. Pecka-pecka poo. Ah-rum-dum dee. La-de-da-de dah. Ta-ta tee. For blacks only. We want you out. We hereby proclaim this a black Movement. "Anytime you want to, Pete. Just pack up and leave." Da-da doom. Da-da doom. Da-da doom. "Anytime, Pete. Anytime. . . ." Who's that in there?

"Hey, Zenola? Wait. Don't go. I gotta talk to somebody. I gotta tell you about my basic rhythm. 'Anytime, Pete,' he said. Can you believe that, Zenola? To me he says, 'Anytime Pete. Anytime you want to.' After all we been through. Zenola, come on back inside with me a minute. I gotta tell you what's on my mind. Gotta tell somebody. Stop trying to get away now. C'mere you crazy sonofabitch. You ever had a Indian nut stuck in your head? You know what it is to love something what's already left you? Sit down. Stop trying to get away. You want a cup of coffee? I ain't letting you go nowhere 'til I've talked. Stop shoving me. You ain't strong as me. Don't care if you did climb trees. I useta crap tobacco. You gonna listen if it's the last—"

"Boss. Please. Black King run for life. No more trouble."

"You been hanging 'round here all summer, dammit. Why you wanna run off now, just when I need to talk to you? Sit still. Listen. You see this blood? You think some redneck got me? Hell, no. Something I loved got me. You listening? Zenola, I'm quitting. I'm through. Don't cry, Zenola. My blood is your blood. Brothers under the skin. You and me, brothers in blood. I ever tell you 'bout my Pa? He grows leaf tobacco up near George, North Carolina. That's where I come from. We ain't never before sat down and had a real talk, Zenola. This is the freedom house. A place where all people can meet and talk. Man to man and woman to woman, regardless of race. Like now, you and me—a black man and a white man. Together. You know, I done a lot for this Movement. Suffered so's your people and mine would all have it better."

"Lemme go! Lemme go! No more trouble. Run for your life, black king."

"And you know, Zenola, I'll tell you something else. If she'll leave here with me, I'll make her a happy woman some-day. There's the chance. She said to talk to her tomorrow 'bout it. Times are changing, Zenola. Mark my word."

"Boss! Boss!"

"Zenola, goddammit, you ain't listening to me. Get your damn fingers out of your ears. What the hell—"

AURABELLE

It was louder than all the loud I ever heard; me standing alone in the hot damp, in the kerosene light, seeing the blood from him still on the sheet, and holding my ears against the next loud that never came—but me knowing they'd done it, and knowing that he was in there.

I run out the door and down the hill. The sky over the freedom house is bright with burning, and Mrs. Pritchard's house is on fire too, and the sparks blow up the hill on the wind where the singing was. But all I hear over the crackling flames is the remembering of that loud. *"I want you for my wife,"* he said. *"I want you for my wife."*

 **RICE**

Winston and I lead—me just moving my lips, not knowing all the words but singing loud and happy when it comes to the chorus: *Freedom. Freedom. Ain't I gonna find you here one day? And if I to go to heaven without you, freedom, ain't you still gon' pass my way?* Then I hear it come shattering through the singing like the breaking edge of thunder, the sound merging with the voices, with the stomping of feet and the clapping. Then smaller sounds come; the implosive bang of collapse. Then Cal says, "The freedom house!" And as one, it seems, we rush the great wooden doors and pour out of that heaviness into the lamplit dust of St. Catherine Street; running through the hot gloom, running toward the oscillating sky above Long George Alley.

 **BENJIE**

There was a big noise and everybody started running. Momma jumped up and grabbed his hand and they started running—Ludy right behind, her mouth open wide.

"Jesus help us," Momma said. "C'mon, boy! C'mon!"

On the sidewalk, Momma said, "Look at the sky. Jesus help us. Everything we got in this world."

Benjie looked. It was bright and smoke went through the bright.

"Momma! Momma!" he cried.

"Hush," Ludy said. She took his other hand. "Hush up and run! Run!"

They passed Mrs. Pritchard. She went slow. Mr. Peavine ran by, then a lot of kids. He saw Puddin' Head and Lollypop running in the street. "Momma! Momma!" he cried.

"Hush," Momma said. "Run, boy! Run!"

Then he saw the sky blinking over the trees, the smoke still in it—the sky yellow through the trees.

"C'mon, boy," Momma said. "Run, boy! Run!"

"Run, Benjie," Ludy said. "Run! Run!"

B. JACKS

Those cats sho can run. Here I'm right behind them, and them neck and neck like they's racing each other, Cal and Rice. Goddamn, but those cats can run. I can smell rags burning. Shit, maybe that white bitch brought this bad luck on us. I oughtn't made that date. It don't make sense. Goddamn, those cats can run.

 **GEORGE**

. . . They had sicked the dogs on him and when he first came in sight he was running ahead of them, running 'long the bluff by the river where they'd chased him; running in the bright clear moonlight with his shirt tore and it streaming behind him like confetti; and him breaking through the weeds and thorn bushes 'til he was in the open, then running fast again with his fists beating the air and his head throwed back. He moved swift and easy ahead of them 'til they broke free of the bushes; then the lead hound moved swiftly too, yelping loud and closing fast—and all of them locked together in a furious motion of speed and light and form and darkness. . . .

 **RICE**

We run down St. Catherine Street, along the sidewalk and across the scorched patches of ground that pass for yards. Out of McIver's church we spew like stampeding cattle, running side by side—Cal and I—running beneath the bright fire-scarred sky, beneath moth-littered lamplights; on through the red dust, running toward the flickering explosions of light above Long George Alley. Out of the corner of my eye I see Cal running, head thrown back, neck taut, eyes leaning down his nose, arms pumping the hot dense air—and across the dark asphalt the soundless blur of sneakers streaks white and secret. We turn into the lot at the head of the alley; turn as one, in tandem, our feet pounding along the dusty path through the high grass, our faces nervous and tight as the shadows ahead on the uphill shacks. I see the freedom house and the first two shacks behind it burning. The wind, gentle, sulphurous, blows smoke into our faces. We stop and stare down the hill, both of us winded. Cal is saying something but I can't make him out.

"What?" I say. "I can't hear you."

"Stay here," he says, shouting. "Tell 'em to get their belongings out 'fore the kerosene stoves go. Get every bucket you can find into the road and start a line. Don't wait for the goddamned fire engines. Water the shacks that ain't burning. Move!"

He starts away, running down the hill alone, running toward the burning freedom house.

 **GEORGE**

I heard it clear out here. I was just 'bout to turn off my television set and go to sleep. First I thought it was one of them jets from the airbase practicing again, but then when I got up and went out on the porch to listen, I saw the sky over the quarter lit up. It looked like a bad fire. I went back and got in the bed but couldn't sleep. Outta pure curiosity I called up Linwood Potter down at the No. 1 Pump Station to see what the hell was going on.

"That noise?" he says. "Just a explosion over in nigger town. Nothing to worry 'bout. Go on back to sleep."

"The way the sky's lit up it looks like one hell of a fire," I says.

"That's what I hear," he says.

"You're the Chief," I says. "Ain't you gonna do nothing?"

"We're getting the equipment ready now," he says. "Go on back to sleep, George. Stop worrying. You worry too much. We know what we're doing. It's the civil righters," he says. "It's their place. Somebody blowed it sky high. 'Bout ten minutes ago. We got the call and we'll get over there soon. You just go on back to sleep."

When I hung up the phone, I went back out on the porch and smoked a cigarette and watched the sky. It kept getting brighter, then darker; brighter, then darker. That nigger wasn't crazy as I thought if he could plant the stuff like that. From my porch it looked like the whole damn south end was burning. I went back in the house and switched off the television and put my pants and shoes back on and got the keys to my car. I had to see for myself. Hell, I wouldn't of been able to sleep nohow.

PEAVINE

A crowd of us stood on the hill, watching. Somebody had called for the hook and ladder.

"Maybe Zenola's still at the jail," Clarice said. "I don't see him anywhere." Then she went to crying again 'bout those devilish books of hers. You'd of thought one of her kin was burned to death, her standing there with her children and them watching their house go up. I noticed she had a Bible in her hands. I felt real sorry for her. "My books," she was saying. Then somebody came running over and said Calvin

Drew had gone in the fire looking for somebody they thought was still in there. Well, that hushed Clarice up and we all stood staring at the back door where Drew went in.

Then Tom Rice came running over, hollering at us to join the bucket line. We did. But I was thinking: What the hell good can we do with these little piddly buckets? Damned if the fire department wasn't taking its sweet time.

CAL

He found Cates in the meeting room, half-buried under a pile of bricks, and pulled him through the smoke, through the burning and noise, and laid him on the sloping ground near the truck. He kneeled above him, coughing, his lungs burning. *And I started running, running through the dust and dark, through the high thin sound of glass. And outside, the wind knocking us down. Cates unconscious. The ambulance came and took him away. He still favors it if you notice him close.*

Cal felt her presence even before he saw her, and when he turned and looked, Aurabelle stood behind him, staring over his shoulder at Cates. She stood silent, rigid as concrete, not even her eyes moving.

"Catlett!" he shouted. "Where the hell's Catlett?"

Still she did not move her eyes, but stood fixed like some hard angry tree growing deeper, its roots into the firm, resolute, motionless earth. Out of the crowd emerged the old doctor, his camel's hair spats coated with red dust, his frail seersucker sports jacket patched at the elbows, his hair wound on his head like white steel springs. He bent down, grunting, and felt Cates for signs of life. He looked at Cal, their eyes meeting across the prone figure and speaking in that language that outraces talk. Then his mouth moved. "He's dead," he said. "Sorry."

Cal heard the rush of breath, the sibilant ejaculation of sound as the inrushing air passed her lips, and he saw her turn and start slowly up the hill, her feet barely lifting—and on her back the light from the fires flickering and dancing. Cal looked again at Catlett.

"I'll get something to cover him up," he said. He stood up and reached in the bed of the truck and got a tarpaulin and folded it twice and draped it over Cates. Then he heard the sound, a steady, flat, insistent blast that came suddenly out of the voices and fire. He whirled around looking for it, angry, defiant, heavy in himself; tired and edgeless now with it all collapsing around him. Then he located it.

"Get off that goddamn horn!" he yelled into the cab of the truck where someone now sat cranking the engine. "You stupid fuck!" he said. He ran over and jerked open the cab door.

"It's stuck," the other shouted back, his voice struggling to rise above the noise of the horn. "I was gonna move it out the way when this damn horn—"

Cal smashed his hand against the horn button again and again, but the sound persisted, flat, sustained, peremptory, louder now than the ambient sounds. "Get it the fuck outta here!" Cal shouted. "Get it up the hill and disconnect that goddamned thing. Move!" He watched as the other started the motor and drove the truck away, leaving him standing alone beside Cates. He watched the truck move slowly up the hill, up through the smoking doomed trees, up through the spreading desolation. He looked down at the tarpaulin once more and shook his head slowly. "Poor bastard," he muttered beneath his breath. "Poor sonofabitch." Then he looked at the freedom house and the flames leaping in columns above it, brilliant and angry against the dark sky. He saw the uphill shacks catching fire now. The whole fucking thing's going, he thought. The whole goddamned hill. He snatched up a water bucket and ran to join the line.

▦ AURABELLE

Burn, you sorry sonofabitch. You tard old no-good mother-fucker. Burn. Burn. I'll get me a job at the laundry. Save my money. Sky outta here. Chicago maybe. Or Detroit. *"You ever been to Jackson?" "You ever been to Jackson?" "You ever been to Jackson?"*

"There goes everything we got in this world," Mamie Lee says, standing right next to me—us watching it burn. "What I ever done to deserve this? Why the Lord is so hard on us that's down and out?"

"I want you for my wife. My Pa, he grows leaf tobacco. We ain't got much but we's honorable folks and I lost a brother in the Second World War." I know he's gone now. For ever and ever he's gone.

"What we gon' do now?" she says, staring hard at me. "You don't care, do you? You little ungrateful bitch. How you can be so damn honery at a time like this—"

"Anytime you want to, Aurabelle. Just pack up and we'll leave. Ditty-ditty dum. Ditty-ditty dum. I want you for my wife." Gone forever and ever.

"I could of least been blessed with a youngun who cares something 'bout me," she says. " 'Stead of a burden like you that's drove me to sin. To hating your own flesh and blood. I oughta—" She raises her hand to hit me and I just look at her. Then the kerosene stove goes off, flames and smoke shooting out the windows. I hear her scream and she slaps me across the mouth and grabs hold of my hair and starts pulling it— her eyes big, crazy-looking and red with fire in them.

"You damned little ungrateful hussy," she says, hollering, pushing me backward toward the fire. "You don't 'preciate all the years—"

I kick her in the stomach hard and she lets me go. Then I wrassle her to the ground and get hold of her throat and start choking her. Some man comes running over and pulls me off. We get to our feet and stand looking at each other hating and knowing that now it's over. Then she starts in again. "I worked my hands to the bones for you. After all the pain—"

I turn and start walking down the hill so's I don't have to hear it. I done heard it plenty. Don't aim to ever listen to it again. I walk slow down through the smoke to where they laid him, to where Catlett had said it. But there ain't a trace of him or the truck. Both gone, like I been dreaming it all and just wake up. I sit down on the ground in the shadows and burning. I sit there and curse them who have caused it to be—this alley, this misery. And I curse them for all they've done to us, to me and my mother . . . to my cousin. And now to him. Then I hear the sirens coming down Franklin Street. *"Hold me tight. Please hold me tight." "I want you for my wife." "On or off?" I says. "You ever been to Jackson?"*

 **GEORGE**

I watched it long as I could from Franklin Street, then got back in my car and drove home. I still couldn't sleep. Potter and them could of done better. They took their good time coming and backing it into position and connecting up the hoses. Ain't I seen 'em practicing enough times in the pump station yard to know they could of done better? Seen 'em run up and down them ladders like trained monkeys. You'd think when it came to human life they could forget this race stuff and do a job.

The way I heard it, they found that crazy nigger dead in the freedom house. Probably blowed his own self up. I wonder if Percy sold him a short fuse on purpose.

But I still couldn't sleep when I got home. Just laid there tossing and turning and hearing that explosion again and seeing that whole hill burning; burning up everything them folks had. I laid there thinking 'bout what I could do to help. I couldn't think of one thing. What good would it do for me to speak my mind? Who'd listen to me? Finally I dropped off to sleep thinking that tomorrow'd be rough at the store 'cause I'd be by myself all afternoon while Percy went to the demonstration. I'd sure like to do something to help, but what can one person do by hisself?

By the time the hook and ladder came, and the firemen connected up their hoses, it no longer mattered. Even the shacks highest on the hill were burning out of control. And the roof of the freedom house had collapsed, leaving the upright beams of the main room standing charred and somber against the sky. They protruded into the night like blackened fingers—burned and rigid and outraged.

They found Zenola later, after the fire was all but out. They covered him with a bedspread and laid him beside Pete. We all stood around in silence, staring at the tarpaulin covering Pete. Then an ambulance came and took them both away. Some ladies took Mrs. Pritchard by the arms and led her up the hill.

Nothing seems real now. I guess it's too soon for us to believe Pete is dead; that it has come to this. Solly has gone to the Western Union office to send off a wire to Pete's father. As the minutes pass, the anger begins to replace frustration. Slowly but surely it rolls through all of us, melting through our dazed confusion like morning sun through fog. The people stand in tight restless groups, talking and watching the last of the fires burn out. The men watch vacant-eyed, standing with their hands shoved deep in their pockets; the women with their arms folded across their breasts. Some of the men poke at the ground with sticks, marking letters in the red clay.

"Sonsofbitches," somebody says. "What we ever done to them?"

"Devils," another says. "It's the Ku Klux that done it. They said they would and they done it. The devils!"

"What the hell y'all gon' do 'bout it?" Cal says, his face and eyes quiet; his stance defiant, angry. "Run your mouths or *act?* Fuck them shacks. It weren't your property they burned, but some white man's. Another shack ain't hard to find. A niggah can always find a broke-down shack to live in. And them little piddly belongings you lost weren't nothing to begin with—just enough to keep you thinking you had something.

"So they ain't touched you where you live. In your souls. In your hearts. And you can do something to show them you ain't scared no more. You can join us tomorrow. We assemble at two o'clock. Right here. So let's show those motherfuckers they cain't turn us 'round now. No way!"

He looks at me and the others. "C'mon," he says. "We gotta help find these folks places to stay tonight." He starts on up the hill and we follow behind him, walking wearily through the smoke and heat, looking again at the smoldering shacks, and smelling now the sullen and sulphurous aftermath of fire.

BOOK TWO

SATURDAY

No sign of rain. An incandescent broil of sun—Cal bracing the clipboard against his chest, pencil poised.

"How old are you, boy?" he said.

" 'Leven," the other said.

"You ain't no damn 'leven. Who you with? Your Daddy? Your Momma?"

"Naw. Nobody." The boy stuffed his hands deep in the pockets of his overalls. A toothpick angled petulantly from his lips. "I'm 'leven," he said. "I went on the first march this summer. I'm bigger now." He stuck out his lips in a pout.

Cal wrote the name down hurriedly. "All right, goddammit. I ain't got time to waste on you. Get in line 'side a grown-up."

The kid bolted for the line that now stretched all the way down the alley. Cal moved on through the crowd.

Benjie waited next to Momma—wool bathing suit itching under overalls. Over underalls. Momma with his hand and Ludy standing behind near Puddin' Head. Puddin' Head with a yo-yo—Benjie watching him do it. Momma said the swimming pool was like a big square washtub with blue water. Over under. Under over. The scared came back again.

Clarice waited near the front of the line. In her hands she clutched the Bible she'd had at prayer meeting the previous night. Her knees and feet pained. The heat seemed unbearable, and the borrowed black dress made it worse. She looked down the alley at the ruins of her house, then looked along the line at her children. Finally she turned to Aurabelle, who stood beside her—head high, eyes straight ahead.

"This is the glory day," she whispered. "It's the glory day, honey."

Aurabelle sucked her teeth loud and grunted. "Glory day my ass! We been standing here damn near a hour. I shoulda known when niggahs said two o'clock they meant *three!*"

Peavine stood looking out the window of his shop. It was empty now and soundless except for the whir of the overhead fan. But half an hour ago it had been full. Then the exodus began. They filed past him and out the screen door that banged repeatedly behind them; banged behind their swift foolish eyes, banged and banged with peremptory indifference, with an insufferable loudness that even now rang in his ears. Across St. Catherine Street he saw them among the milling crowd at the head of Long George Alley. Fools, he thought. Grinning, singing fools. What the hell did they think they were going to—a carnival? He turned angrily and went to the cash register and opened it. He shook his head. Hard to believe it was Saturday afternoon. He swore bitterly into the heavy stale air that not even the fan helped, and reached for the push broom and began sweeping up.

The demonstration marshals trotted up and down the line of marchers that now moved out of the alley and slowly along St. Catherine Street. The line stretched for almost four blocks. Occasionally the marshals shouted instructions, encouragement. "When do you want your freedom?" they'd shout. The marchers replied as one, chanting: "Now! Now! Now!" At Main Street they turned and started through the business district. From inside each store whites stared out through the sun-glazed windows, their faces taut, furious, silent—full of constrained outrage; and their eyes shone with old, sad, permanent passions. The marchers went on.

They passed by groups of whites gathered along the curb. Some cursed the marchers. Others spat at them. Someone heaved an empty beer bottle into their midst. It broke harmlessly on the sidewalk. The marchers went on.

The heat was terrific—the sun standing almost directly overhead, seemingly fixed at a single point in the blazing sky; locked in phase with the marchers, so that it seemed to move only when they moved, halt when they halted. The marchers went on.

When the first horse appeared, Parnell watched it with apprehension. Once, in Atlanta—on her very first demonstration—she had seen an old Negro man trampled to death beneath a police horse. Now she stared at the policemen astride these horses. Beneath the polished blue helmets their sunned faces shared a common expression—anxious watchfulness. And the horses themselves pranced nervously, their eyes huge, dark-rimmed, excited. Ahead she saw more police positioned along the curbs and at each intersection. She glanced back along the line and saw Benjie and Bertha McCloud. Parnell waved. Benjie waved back. Parnell turned to the horses again.

. Cal halted them at the first traffic light on Main Street. "Cross when it turns green," he said, standing at the head of the line. "And remember—move! Ten at a time. And goddammit, I mean move!"

It changed. "Move! Move! Move!" he shouted.

George saw them coming. They were still a block away. He stood in the doorway of Percy's Hardware, his white jacket unbuttoned and the necktie pulled down from his collar. They came along Main Street on his side and were soon close enough for him to see their faces. More women and children than I expected, he thought. Then he noticed the horses keeping pace with the marchers—big handsome sorrels, their dark brown saddles immaculate and gleaming, their tails groomed and swishing and diaphanous in the sun. As the marchers passed the store, George looked at each. He had never seen so many niggers at once on Main Street. It frightened him. And their faces seemed to lack the customary gentleness he was used to. These blacks were somber, determined, and aggressive-looking. The last of them passed and George stepped onto the sidewalk and watched the end of the line trail off down Main Street. Finally he turned and went back inside and checked the register again. Only five sales in the last hour and a half. He sighed. What the hell. Percy would understand. No business. Hurriedly he took off the white jacket and put on his street coat. He went to the mirror above the feed barrel and hitched up his tie and smoothed down his hair. He put on his stiff-brimmed straw hat and went to the front door, where he turned the OUT TO LUNCH sign forward. He locked the door and joined the crowd of whites hurrying down Main Street behind the marchers.

Peavine locked the door to his shop and stood for a time on the sidewalk looking across at the vacant lot before Long George Alley. Nobody in sight. He looked up and down the sidewalks along St. Catherine Street. Barely a soul stirred. He sighed and got in his car and started it and drove off toward Duncan Park.

B. Jacks felt in his pocket for the gun. Touching it, he experienced a sudden flush of confidence. It had saved him before. It would again today if needed. But just for insurance he'd tied a red mojo around his neck. He removed his hand from his pocket and wiped the sweat from his forehead, and marched proudly and resolutely on through the violent and terrific heat.

They turned at the end of Main Street and marched another block down a small residential street which dead-ended at Duncan Park. Now the curbs and lawns were thick with whites. And police cars and motorcycles cruised back and forth, their radios at full volume. The mounted policemen still followed the marchers, still sat stiffly erect in their polished saddles, their eyes swift and alert. The marchers went on.

Peavine parked his car and hurried to find a place where he could watch them pass into Duncan Park. He found a spot not far from the entrance and stood beneath a shade tree, waiting, inhaling deeply to slow down his fast-beating heart.

From this place on the fringes of a small crowd of whites (some of whom he recognized) he watched the marchers come into sight. He looked among them for his son but didn't see him—too many marchers. Fools, he thought again, irritated and somewhat shamed by the spectacle.

They had almost reached the gates when Cal suddenly halted the line. "Goddammit," he swore, staring toward the entrance. There he saw a small group of white men standing near two parked cars—brand-new Fords positioned bumper to bumper with their hoods raised. Together, they blocked the narrow access road leading into the park. The men had axe handles and baseball bats. Cal swore again.

"What'll we do now?" someone behind him asked, the voice tight and high in the speaker's throat.

Cal said nothing, his eyes scanning the grounds immediately beyond the entrance. A large contingent of police was positioned just inside the gate. And beyond them—on a grassy knoll—he saw another group of white men, civilians, about twenty of them. They stood in a long straight line, framed against the horizon like Indians in an old Western— the baseball bats angling upward from their shoulders. Cal sighed and turned toward the marchers.

"I don't know," he said to the other. "I don't know what we're going to do." He looked around again. "Anybody seen the Chief?" he asked.

"Over yonder," the other said. "Parked on the grass under that shade tree."

"I see him," Cal said. Alone, he started over toward Worden's car.

They sat with both doors flung open against the heat— McClaren at the wheel. On the seat between them were two riot helmets and two batons. A rack over the dashboard held a 12-gauge shotgun. Worden saw him coming. He nudged McClaren. McClaren snickered. Cal came over and bent his head down to their level.

"What's the problem?" Worden said. He kept his eyes flat, his face straight and noncommittal.

"Those two vehicles yonder are in our way," Cal said. "I'd appreciate it if you'd ask those fellows to move 'em."

"Nothing we can do," Worden told him. "I've already talked to those boys. They say they're stalled and cain't do nothing 'til the wrecker comes. You just have to wait," he said, suppressing a grin. Cal stood up and stepped back from the car.

"Then we'll push them out the way," he said.

"Suit yourself," Worden said. He grinned. "They'll be beholden to you coons for any help you can give." Cal turned and started away. McClaren snickered again. Cal went on away. Worden lit up a cigar and looked around for Plowers and the nigger.

Cal walked back to the marchers. "We're going in," he told those at the head of the line. "I need ten men. We'll push those cars out the way." He waited. B. Jacks came forward first, immense, swagging, the undershirt barely covering his chest and leaving his powerful arms and shoulders completely bare. A small piece of red cloth was tied to a string that went around his neck. Rice came forward too, his eyes fixed on Cal, his lips set firmly but his face looking somewhat frightened. Finally there were ten. Cal turned back to the marchers: "There won't be much time 'fore the police jump in," he told them. "So c'mon through soon as you see us make room." They nodded solemnly.

From somewhere back in the line Crayfield came striding up. "This has gone far enough," he shouted at Cal. "You must be crazy, fella. Don't you have any regard for these people? You damn lunatic!" He grasped Cal by the arm. "I won't let you jeopardize—"

Cal shoved him hard and he fell back a step. "They ain't complaining," Cal said. "Freedom comes high, brother. Now get the fuck outta my way." He turned to the others. "C'mon," he said. "Let's move those goddamned cars."

George watched from across the street. The leader—a tall young Negro with broad shoulders, long hair, and sunglasses. He watched him go over to the Chief's car. Then he came back and talked to the marchers. Then another colored man—light-skinned, older—walked up and started arguing with the leader. The leader pushed the other aside roughly and, with a small band of blacks, started toward the entrance where the whites waited. George looked nervously at the marchers again. So many children, he thought. Christ, what if— Suddenly the crowd in which he stood edged off the curb and surged forward, drawing him with them.

They had almost reached the two cars at the entrance when the whites rushed them. Cal saw one of his men go down almost immediately, then he himself was narrowly missed by a blow from an axe handle aimed at his head. He ducked beneath it and drove his fist into the other's groin, and saw the man go down and double up on the ground. He pivoted quickly, looking in every direction. Another one came at him from behind with a baseball bat, and suddenly Cal saw B. Jack's huge bulk descend on the other, flailing him with his fists until the man fell back and went down. B. Jacks snatched the bat and drew it back to deliver a blow.

"Forget him," Cal shouted. "The cars! The cars!"

They ran to the cars and someone released the hand brake on one. B. Jacks planted his feet wide and stood swinging the bat in a vicious and furious half-circle, holding them off until Cal and the others had leaned their weight against the Ford. It began to inch backward. B. Jacks cursed at the top of his lungs and swung the bat faster and harder.

"Push," Cal shouted. "Push, man. Push!" He felt the Ford roll backward for almost a car's length before it stopped. But it was far enough, and Cal turned in time to see the marchers flooding through the breach and into Duncan Park. Then he heard the dull, fleshy thud of the blow, and the brief contracted pain at the back of his head. He fell unconscious beside the car.

When the fighting broke out at the entrance, Peavine started back toward his parked car. He forced himself not to run, but hurried along the sidewalk, walking as fast as he could without looking conspicuous. As he neared his car, he saw a group of white youths approaching from the opposite direction. Peavine picked up his pace, head lowered but eyes watching them. Suddenly they saw him and one of them yelled, "There's one. Look. He's trying to get away."

Peavine stopped dead still, his heart beating swiftly. They were coming toward him, walking faster now.

"Git that nigger," another shouted. "Don't let him git away. The black bastard." They broke out in a run.

Peavine turned and started running in the opposite direction, the only direction left now—back toward Duncan Park.

George saw the police converge on the marchers as they passed through the entrance and into the park.

"Never thought I'd see this day come," an old old man standing beside him said. "Niggers inside Duncan Park."

George said nothing. He watched the police horses galloping through the crowd of marchers, whose ranks had now been broken, scattering them into turbulent little groups that scrambled to get out of the path of the horses. The riders leaned low over the backs of their mounts and pounded their batons like hammers against the marchers' heads. The horses turned and curvetted, pranced and galloped, and filled the hot air with thickening dust. Suddenly George saw a small boy go down beneath one of the charging horses. The child reached for its mother, but she had already fallen from a blow. The boy lay motionless as the horse went over him again. George broke free of the crowd and ran into the street, running toward the place where the child had fallen.

"Jesus! Jesus!" Momma said—Momma laying in the street, her face bleeding. The horse went over him.

"Momma! Momma!" *Where Momma in the cold ground?* The horse came back.

George ran to where the boy lay and bent over him, and saw the blood pumping from his mouth when he breathed. George looked for the mother. She was out cold. He lifted the child in his arms and started running with him toward the nearest police car. Then he heard the horse coming behind him fast, and George turned once to look. They bore down on him, the horse and its rider; the man's arm raised, poised high above his head, the baton already descending toward George. George ran faster.

"You put that nigger down," the other shouted at George.

George kept running, no longer knowing where, but sensing that the boy had stopped breathing. Still he kept running, no longer with a destination. *He moved swift and easy ahead of them 'til they broke free of the bushes; then the lead hound moved swiftly too, yelping loud and closing fast—and all of them locked together in a furious motion of light and form and darkness. . . .*

They swept past him, the horse and rider as one, a swift blur of motion and noise and pain, and George fell forward through it; holding on to the child for as long as he could concentrate—until he saw the hot asphalt rush toward his face, and the sweet black night come gliding over.

B. Jacks swung the bat viciously, holding them off. But finally there were too many, and he went down, bloodied and furious. The police came running over and dragged him away to a waiting van. When they reached down to lift him into it he said to himself, Now! Now! And he relaxed every muscle and went limp; and listened to them grunt and strain to lift him.

The youths caught Peavine and he fought back as best he could. But there were four against one and soon he fell. He lay fully conscious at first, his body in a tuck position: his hands covering his head, his arms and elbows tucked against his chest and stomach, and his knees pulled up to protect his groin. He had learned that from the civil righters, while he'd watched them dragged off picket lines and beaten by the police. Now it was he who was getting kicked and beaten. Before he passed out he felt no pain, only the cool wet of the grass against his bare arms. When he came to, he was riding in a police van on his way to jail. He did not believe it was happening to him.

Peters had already loaded three vans with demonstrators. Now he stood guard over a dozen or so more as they lay on their stomachs on the grass, their hands cuffed behind them. Peters felt terrible. He wished it was over. He wished they knew how he felt. But it was the thought of the boy that bothered him most—the kid the horse had trampled. Hadn't he warned Worden about those damn horses? He felt terrible about the kid.

"I think my arm's broke, you sonofabitch," one of the demonstrators said.

Peters looked down at her. It was the prostitute girl from Long George Alley. "Aw, shut up, bitch," Peters said. "You lucky it ain't your head."

The girl spit up at him. Peters raised his club threateningly, but she only stared back at him defiantly. Peters thought about the kid again and lowered the club.

The police van moved steadily through the streets toward the jail. Clarice felt her head. The bleeding had stopped. She listened to the sounds around her—the steady, almost sonorous moans of those more seriously hurt.

"We got in there, though. Didn't we?" a familiar voice nearby said.

Clarice peered through the semidark and saw Aurabelle. Her right eye was swollen almost closed, and she held her right arm with her other hand.

"Some sonofabitch stepped on it," she said. "Feels like it's broke. But we got in there, didn't we?"

"Yes, sugar," Clarice said. She reached out for Aurabelle and touched her gently on the face. "I told you it was the glory day, didn't I?"

Rice saw them shove Parnell into one of the police vans along with another group of demonstrators. The group with whom he now waited lay on their stomachs with their hands cuffed behind their backs, waiting for an empty van to shuttle back from the jail. Rice wondered what had happened to B. Jacks. He had seen Cal fall beside the Ford and the police drag him away. When the marchers rushed the gates, Rice had joined them. But they only got a short distance inside the park before the police descended on them. Rice laid his head on the cool grass now and waited, thinking about the kid. He didn't want to believe it, though he knew it could well be true. Now that so much seemed absurd, he was prepared to believe anything. Still, he hoped it wasn't true. Then he wondered how jail would be. This was the first time he'd been busted. His mind quickly recollected stories he'd heard from others about jail. Horror stories, he called them then. Now he wondered. He also began to wonder what he'd do when and if he got back to New York. It would be hard to get into the swing of things again—perhaps even impossible. He felt too angry. Almost bitter. He felt he had lost the motivation so basic to success in his old life. He felt now it was a lot of crap, that *gray* existence he'd led. Somehow he felt reborn; as though at last—in Mississippi—he had found his way, and gained at least a tenuous grasp of his roots, and had accepted the burden of his antecedents. He thought of Mr. Simons again. Then he thought of Cal. What would he do when the war was over? What happened to people like him? Then he thought of the kid again and wondered if Parnell knew. After a while a policeman came over and ordered them to get up, and herded them into a waiting van.

Cal had a splitting headache and a great lump on the back of his head. He sat on the floor in the rear of the van, listening to the tires sing on the road. Silently he watched the two men sitting across from him. One was white, of about medium height, nondescript features, red hair. Cal regarded him stonily. He had seen him somewhere, though exactly where he couldn't remember now. Certainly he wasn't one of

the marchers. The stranger was speaking to an old Negro
man sitting beside him.

"I tried to save him," he said. "I swear I did. When the
horse—"

"Which kid?" the other asked. "There were a lot of kids."

"Just tell me," the stranger said. "Is he all right? Does anybody here know if he's all right?"

"Yeah," someone said out of the gloom—the voice face-
less, weary. "Yeah, I know. He's dead."

"Oh, my God," the stranger said. "Good Lord. I sure
tried. Honest, I tried."

"Maybe he's better off," the other said. "Shit, to have to
live in this motherfucking stinking—"

Parnell sat in a dark corner of another van, her hand to
her mouth, stifling the sounds. But she couldn't control the
shaking, so she kept her shoulders pressed against the wall,
her body away from the others. It all came out of her now,
the whole summer of frustrations and disappointments. A
sense of hopelessness slowly overcame her. For the first
time she had witnessed reality deal a terrible blow to her
idealism. She felt overwhelmed by events, helpless in the
face of the enormous forces beyond her control. And
beneath the crush of events during the past two days, her
once spotless idealism now seemed like nothing more than
a higher set of fallacies. She wept on in silence, thinking
again of the rabbit's foot she had given him at the beginning of the summer.

In still another van McIver and Crayfield sat together.
Crayfield hadn't uttered a word since the van started toward
the jail. And McIver had also turned inward to his own
thoughts, to his announcements for tomorrow's service. He
saw himself standing at the lectern addressing the congregation: "A week from this coming Sunday we'll be privileged to
have visiting us the Clara Morgan singers. And the Reverend
Louis A. Page, Senior, will be the guest speaker." McIver saw

himself pause and look out over his congregation, then intone, "The spirit of God attends—and our hearts mourn— the passing of Benjamin Ronald McCloud. Dearly beloved son of Bertha; brother of Ludy Mae. . . ."

With a jerk the truck stopped at the rear of the jail and a policeman opened the rear door.

"May his soul rest in peace," McIver said aloud.

"What?" Crayfield said, his reverie broken. "Released? Sure we'll be released. We'll be bailed out soon as I can get to a phone. But just *our* people," he added.

Filing out through the double doors of the van into the jail yard, McIver returned to his service. "We will all stand and sing hymn three twenty-six," he told them, watching Sister Ernestine as she got up. It was his favorite hymn.

"I swear to y'all I tried to save him," the white stranger said again. "I swear I did. I couldn't get to y'all—to him—no sooner. You believe me, don't you?" He wiped the sweat. "Listen," he said, "When the horse—"

"Shut the fuck up," Cal said. "You talk too goddamned much."

The stranger fell silent for a time as Cal regarded him stonily again. Then suddenly, as though unable to bear prolonged silence, the other blurted, "Now wait a minute. Y'all don't think it was me who sold that fella the—"

Before he could stop himself, Cal had hit him in the face. The stranger fell back and looked at Cal in bewilderment.

"I told you to shut the fuck up," Cal said.

The other wiped the blood from his nose and continued to stare at Cal, but said nothing.

Cal looked away, listening again to the tires singing over the roadway. He completely forgot about the white man, his thoughts elsewhere now. The demonstration had failed. There was no denying that. But what of it? They would try again, that's all. Maybe in a month or two. At least we showed the white folks we mean business, Cal thought. Showed 'em we weren't scared to go up against them with our bare hands. So we'll try again, that's all. Maybe in a couple of months. Surely before Christmas. Better fucking believe it. He sighed deeply and listened to the truck tires against the macadam again. What the hell, he thought. This'll be my last winter in the Movement.

 **ACKNOWLEDGMENTS**

I am deeply indebted to Ekwueme Michael Thelwell—scholar, civil rights activist and author of the classic novel *The Harder They Come*. His friendship and steadfast belief in my work helped sustain me during the many years when *Long George Alley* was "off the radar screen." So I thank him for that and also for recommending my novel to Atria Books Senior Editor Malaika Adero, whose efforts in my behalf at Simon and Schuster made this new edition possible. My sincerest thanks to Malaika, in whom I hope I've found not only a wonderful editor but also a friend. And thanks to John Paul Jones, Editorial Production Supervisor at Simon and Schuster; during production he sent me a beautiful note— he'd read *Long George Alley* in college and now, twenty years later, still found it as moving. That made me feel really good.

Thanks also to Esther Terry, Chair of the W.E.B. Du Bois Department of Afro-American Studies at the University of Massachusetts, Amherst; and to Professors William Strickland and John Bracey of that department—all three of whom have been true colleagues and friends, and have given me so much support and encouragement. Also thanks to my friends Harlan Sturm (who a few years ago was so eager to see *Long George Alley* republished he started making Xerox copies to handout!); Robert Abel (who amazingly located an original edition of my novel and gave it to me for a Christmas present because I didn't own a decent copy); Christopher Howell, who believed in *Long George Alley* and tried very hard to get it republished in small press edition; and Emery Austin

Smith, the remarkable jazz pianist who reads everything and made me feel like an artist.

Finally, with much love and gratitude, thanks to my soul mate, Deborah DuBock, who has given me spiritual nourishment of a magnitude I cannot define.

Richard Hall
February 2004

LONG
GEORGE
ALLEY

RICHARD HALL

A READERS CLUB GUIDE

ABOUT THIS GUIDE

The suggested questions are intended to help your reading group find new and interesting angles and topics for discussion for Richard Hall's *Long George Alley*. We hope that these ideas will enrich your conversation and increase your enjoyment of the book.

Many fine books from Washington Square Press feature Readers Club Guides. For a complete listing, or to read the Guides online, visit http://www.BookClubReader.com

A CONVERSATION WITH RICHARD HALL

Q: As a native of East Orange, New Jersey, how did you come to write the novel Long George Alley, *which is set in Natchez, Mississippi? Did you spend a considerable amount of time in the South?*

A: I grew up in East Orange, New Jersey, but our family had strong southern ties. Most of my family had migrated from the South to New Jersey and New York City. Working-class people struggling to make ends meet. Some of my warmest childhood memories center around family gatherings. My southern aunts, uncles, and older cousins traveling from Brooklyn, New York, to East Orange, New Jersey, on weekends for our big family dinners. So growing up around them I would hear the "southern talk." Hear them remembering the old South. The *Jim Crow* south. Lynchings and beatings. And the strict codes of behavior they'd had to endure under the evil system of racial segregation. (Some of which I also experienced as a child during summers visiting my grandmother in Goldsboro, North Carolina.) So growing up I had a strong connection to the South, though I was a Northerner. When the Civil Rights Movement swept the country in the early 1960s, I was living in New York City working for a major corporation. I had a nice apartment in the West Village, an expense account, a closet full of expensive Brooks Brothers suits. I had an enviable life. But I'd go home after work, turn on the TV evening news, and watch southern policemen beating civil rights demonstrators to the ground. Fire hoses being turned on them, police dogs attacking. Finally, I couldn't take it anymore, had to do something. I left my job, joined SNCC (Student Non-Violent Coordinating Committee—the most militant civil rights organization at that time), and went to Mississippi—Natchez. I spent the summer of 1965 living in a SNNC freedom house located in a Natchez black ghetto—working as a SNCC volunteer registering black voters.

Q: Oftentimes when an author sets out to write a fictional work, autobiographical bits make their way into the story. Is there a character with whom you identify? Do you feel allied to any one group represented in the novel?

A: This is true, and bits of autobiographical material certainly found their way into *Long George Alley*. The character I most identify with is the summer volunteer, Tom Rice. He's a middle class, college-educated young black man who's left a lucrative corporate job in New York to join the southern Civil Rights Movement. Also, just as I once did, Rice struggles with racial ambivalence—that *gray* area between the black world and white world. And like Rice, I traveled through the South with my mother until I was five; she danced in a vaudeville tent show.

Q: When Long George Alley *was originally published in 1972, Americans were still in the midst of the Civil Rights Movement such that the book's impact was immediate and profound. Thirty years later, how do you think audiences, particularly college-aged readers, will respond?*

A: I'm confident that *Long George Alley* will have as profound an impact on today's readers (especially college-aged readers) as it had following its original publication in 1972. I say this from personal experience. I teach a junior-year writing course at the University of Massachusetts at Amherst. The class is racially diverse. Over the years and almost every semester, one or two students (who've heard I was a civil rights worker during the 1960s and wrote a novel about it) ask me to read sections of *Long George Alley* to the class. Which I've done. Their responses are always moving; humbling, I suppose, would be a better word. But beyond their praise for the book are the probing questions they ask. They seem to have an insatiable curiosity about that period in our history. So yes, I think *Long George Alley* will be well received by today's readers, and particularly college-aged readers.

Q: What was your motivation/inspiration for writing the novel? Did you have an agenda when you set out to write the book? What did you want readers to take away from the book in 1972? Has your motivation/agenda changed for today's reader?

A: My motivation and purpose for writing *Long George Alley* was to share with a broad audience an experience that had moved me deeply. In the summer of 1965, I was basically a Northerner who had never set foot in the *deep* South. I'd seen urban black poverty in the North but not its southern rural counterpart. Working as a SNNC volunteer that summer in Natchez and the outlying farm areas, I met some amazing black people whose stories I wanted to tell. Amazing because they displayed great depth of spirit and an almost inexplicable fortitude. Though they lived in abject poverty and under the constant threat of Ku Klux Klan violence, they had an abiding dignity that impressed me. Made me respect them and want to tell the world about them. Also, I wanted to tell the story of a few idealistic young civil rights workers like myself, people who had gone south to help southern blacks stand up to racism and demand their constitutional rights— including the right to vote. So that's why I wrote the book, and my motivation hasn't changed for today's reader.

Q: Why did you choose to tell the stories of Long George Alley *in numerous and varying narratives as opposed to a singular, more objective, narrative voice?*

A: I chose the multiple point-of-view technique because I felt it would immerse the reader deeper inside the story. The singular narrative would have been a shade more objective, which I didn't want. I wanted the story told through voices of the people involved in the action/situation. Told in first person, present tense. That's the kind of immediacy I wanted. That way, the reader would suddenly be *inside* each character's mind—would know their every thought and feeling. That's what I wanted for the reader; to have her/him *feel* what it was like to be in those characters' shoes. However, I decided to write the Cal sections (he's the twenty-two-year-old embittered SNNC freedom house leader) in third-person narrative to provide a degree of objectivity, reader distance. Cal opens the novel and the reader is asked to meet a veteran southern freedom fighter soaked with hate and bitterness. A large pill to swallow!

Q: How were you able to illustrate, in such detail, the factions and hierarchies within the Civil Rights Movement? Did the knowledge come from personal experience?
A: That was the easy part. It's like "on-the-job training"; you pick it up fast. In meetings, on demonstrations, etc. Soon you know all the civil rights factions involved in a particular area, their position on various issues, inter-organizational disputes and so on. I happened to work for SNCC, then composed mostly of young people considered by more moderate civil rights groups (the NAACP for instance) as somewhat radical.

Q: What is your opinion on the state of race in America today?
A: That's a hard one. In legal terms, the country has made good progress on the race issue in the early 1960s, when most southern blacks couldn't vote. And there's been some movement in areas such as Affirmative Action and corporate hiring practices. Also, many universities are striving to racially diversify their campuses. But that said, I do not think the *attitude* of American white adults has changed significantly. Most still do not accept blacks as equals. In other words, you can legislate people's actions, but you can't legis-

late their attitudes. A great divide still exists between blacks and whites in America, and I don't expect that'll disappear any time soon. On the brighter side, however, I think this current generation of young people—white and black—show lots of promise regarding the race issue. From what I can observe in my classes, which are interracial, the divide still exists but doesn't seem as absolute—as clear cut—as in past generations (excepting, of course, the "Flower Children" generation, the '60s!). So I think there's hope, but the immediate future of race relations looks pretty bleak to me.

Q: Several of the characters in Long George Alley *are women with distinct voices and perspectives. How hard was it to render the female voice and sensibility?*
A: With the women characters I tried to limit myself to their essential humanity (thoughts and feelings they might have had being caught in such trying circumstances); and not pretend I had some profound understandings of what it was to be a woman. To attempt that would've been a disaster because only a woman writer can truly handle that sort of complexity and make it real. In short, I knew my place! So I rendered my women as *people*, expressing the same verities we all understand.

Q: How much was left to the imagination when deriving the diverse characters of the novel? Were many of the characters based on actual acquaintances? Were the incidents portrayed inspired by true events?
A: Since the narrative format was voice driven, I'd ask myself at the start of each writing day, "Who will advance the story?" Sometimes the answer would be an actual acquaintance. Other times I had to make up characters, people who didn't actually exist but certainly could have given the novel's setting (like Benjie, the eight year old, who was a composite of many boys on Long George Alley; also Aurabelle and her

mother, and Peavine the barber, and a few others). Regarding the incidents in the novel, the march on the segregated town park was based on a real civil rights demonstration, though for dramatic purposes I heightened the level of violence. None of the marchers were killed, nor did the freedom house or Long George Alley burn down.

QUESTIONS AND TOPICS FOR DISCUSSION

1. *Long George Alley* is told in twenty-two viewpoints. Why do you think the author chooses multiple narratives? Do you think the story is effectively told in this way? Which character's story do you find most intriguing? Who do you feel you know the most about?

2. Calvin Drew, known as "Cal," is the leader of the Freedom Fighters. Before this time he was a lost soul on the verge of succumbing to the despairing times, "but the Movement saved him, came rushing like a tidal wave across those fallow acres of his spirit . . . rescuing him from the very edge of those unrelenting woods" (page 18). Discuss "The Movement" as a religious experience.

3. The Movement is likened to war in many ways. At one point, the freedom fighter Rice states, "We aren't allowed weapons. A strange war" (page 11). What, then, must the people use to fight the good fight against their oppressors? Besides the obvious war that exists between whites and "the civil righters," discuss the many battles that take place on a smaller scale.

4. Cates, one of the few white men in the Movement, is possessed by a rhythmic chant: "Ditty-ditty dum." He refers to it as his "life rhythm, my self—my basic beat" (page 81). He also hears the basic rhythms of others. Is Cates just going crazy or is this "life rhythm" a valid notion? What do you think it represents?

5. There is a contingent of residents of Long George Alley who don't agree with the Movement and are quite content with the status quo. Among the outspoken is Mamie Lee who claims that the freedom fighters "ain't brought nothing but tribulation, and if you ask me that's all they'll ever bring" (page 51). What does Mamie Lee, and others like her, fear? What fuels this shared complacency?

6. Cal considers Rice a "house niggah." Rice, himself, claims that "Inside I'm neither white nor black but *gray;* drifting in a sub-twilight between two worlds (page 57). Cates also struggles in this limbo of sorts. Discuss how Cates and Rice have similar plights.

7. From the moment it is announced at the barbershop that there were plans to march through Duncan Park, Peavine declines to have any part of it. He explains that a "cold, low-down feeling came over me; like something heavy that had nudged itself against my navel and settled here for good" (page 69). How do you explain this feeling? Is it guilt? Cowardice? Fear?

8. When the marchers finally reach Duncan Park, they find a large group of local white residents and two trucks barricading the entrance. When Cal is criticized by Crayfield for deciding to continue with the march, Cal responds: "Freedom comes high, brother" (page 208). Did Cal make the right decision to proceed considering the inevitable confrontation that lay ahead? What would you have done as a leader in that position?

9. Discuss the voices of the women and children in the novel. How are they portrayed? What role do they play in the Movement? Discuss Parnell, one of the only women actually in the movement, who is also white.

CLASSIC TOYOTA
3751 RTE 42 SOUTH
TURNERSVILLE NJ 08012
(856) 728-5000

10:31 AM 07/12/04

VS 4482750104173355 0507
SALE TERM# 0003

AMOUNT $ 22.02

REF #015 AP 036640
BATCH #056
RO #301337

I AGREE TO COMPLY WITH
THE CARDHOLDER AGREEMENT
SIGNATURE

X

WHITE-MERCHANT   YELLOW-COSTOMER

10. The character Zenola is introduced in Peavine's first narrative section. One of the barbershop patrons says, "Zenola ain't got the sense he was born with. Crazy as he can be (page 7)". Seeing Zenola from his perspective allows the reader to witness his cryptic language and his reasoning (or lack thereof). Discuss Zenola as a character. Why do you think he bombs the freedom house? Does he have a mind and will of his own or is he just the white police officers' pawn?

11. While conversing with Paul Furman, Solly makes the following statement: "Every man is free. As free as he is willing to accept the consequences of his acts. But we're controlled by fear—fear of the consequences" (page 127). Do you agree? Discuss the theme of fear in the novel. What other major themes appear throughout the novel?

12. Peters, the first and only black police officer in the county, laments that no one knows how *he* feels—he gets grief from both whites and blacks. Do you sympathize with Peters as a character? Do you feel he's on the wrong side of justice? Is his paycheck really worth what he has to endure psychologically and emotionally? Is his presence on the force a political statement in and of itself?